SPELL CHASED!

The messenger was running, chased by pursuers much faster than she. Looking back, she saw a half dozen animals with narrow heads and glowing eyes. After them rode a red-cloaked man on a pale horse—Lord Death! But she wasn't dead! Why did Death hunt her?

The messenger ran on for her very survival. And then, over the pounding of her life in her ears, she heard a different sound and risked another glance over her shoulder.

Gaining quickly, came a white unicorn. Her concentration broken, the messenger stumbled and fell. As she got to her feet, the unicorn reached her side.

"Get on!" it commanded, even as its flashing hoof neatly crushed the skull of the foremost hound.

The messenger grabbed a handful of silky mane and dragged herself awkwardly up on the broad back, and the unicorn leaped forward, galloping like the wind until suddenly, terrifyingly, they were at the edge of a cliff. The unicorn reared and managed to halt, then backed away from the edge. "Hang on," it warned. Powerful muscles bunched and it launched itself forward.

And screamed shrilly as razor sharp teeth tore into its hind leg. . . .

CHILD OF
THE GROVE

TANYA HUFF

DAW BOOKS, INC.
DONALD A. WOLLHEIM, PUBLISHER

1633 Broadway, New York, NY 10019

For my grandmother,
who wouldn't have understood
but would have been proud of
me anyway.

Genesis

In the Beginning there was Darkness and out of the Darkness came the Mother. From her flesh She formed the Earth. With her tears She filled the seas and lakes and rivers. She walked upon her creation and where She passed grew grasses, trees, and flowers. Her breath became the winds. With her right hand She created all animals that run and swim and fly. With her left hand She created all animals that slither and sting. Her laughter became the song of birds.

When She had walked all the Earth, She sat to rest in a circle of silver birch. As She was lonely, She gave form to the spirit of one of the trees that it might keep her company. And the form was that of a beautiful woman. Her name was Milthra and she was the Eldest of the Elder Races.

When the Mother left the Grove, She gave form also to the other birches that Milthra would never be lonely as She had been. It is said there is form in all trees if the Power is there to call the spirit out.

And as the Mother walked the Earth, She bled four times. From her blood came the other Elder Races, the Centaurs, the Giants, the Dwarves, and the Merfolk. And so She could see what She created, each time She bled She hung a silver light in the night sky.

Then another came out of the Darkness. His name was Chaos and He lay with the Mother and She bore him a son. And the name of the Mother's son was Death. He was very terrible and very beautiful.

As the Elder races were of the Mother's body and blood, they could see Death's beauty but not his terror. Though they could be killed, they did not die; and so they had no fear of him.

Death went to the Mother and begged her to create a people he could rule.

Because She loved him, She did.

But because She loved her newest creations as well, She gave them a gift so they could keep Death in his place. She gave them the power to create. And She gave them a promise that once Death had come to them, they would return to her once more. She called them Humans, but Death called them Mortals which means "to die."

Humans used the Mother's gift to create Gods. They worshiped and made sacrifices in the hope that their Gods could keep Death away. But the powers of the Gods, being Human given, were of no use against the Mother's true son. Soon Humankind abandoned the Gods and learned to face Death. Some even came to see his beauty.

But a God once created cannot be uncreated and so, no longer worshiped, the Gods grew bored. Those given the aspect of men by their creators took to walking the Earth in human form. Eventually, they all lay with mortal women and from those unions the race of Wizards was born.

The Wizards used the powers of the Gods to pervert the Mother's gift and their first act was to turn on their fathers and destroy them. There would be no new Wizards. They formed a great council and for many centuries ruled the creatures of the Earth. Even the Elder Races feared them, for it appeared the Wizards had conquered Death.

Over the years, as their powers grew, so did their corruption. By forcing the breeding of man and animal, they created the Werfolk in a mockery of the Mother's work.

And then the Wizards dared to create something using the very Earth itself. They formed mighty Dragons, giant beasts with command of fire and frost, rulers of the air or seas. But the Earth was the Body of the Mother and the Wizards could not control it. They had created their own destruction.

The Dragons turned on the Wizards and in a battle that changed the shape of the land, slew and devoured their would-be masters. The Dragons that survived returned to the Earth from which they were made.

It is said that, at the end of the Age of Wizards, Death smiled.

One

"Mother?"

There was no answer, so the tall young man reached out a slender hand and placed it gently on the bark of the silver birch before him.

"Mother?" he said again.

The tree stirred under his hand, as if, newly awakened, it sighed and stretched. He stepped back and waited. Slowly, very slowly, his mother drew herself out of her tree.

She was tall, with ivory skin, silver hair, and eyes the green of new spring leaves. Her name was Milthra and she was the eldest of the Sisters of the Sacred Grove. She looked barely older than her son.

She opened her arms and he came into them, then she held him at arm's length and smiled.

"You have grown, Rael. You look more like your father every time I see you." He looked so much like his father that her heart ached with the memories. Not for many years had Raen, King of Ardhan, come to the Sacred Grove, and Milthra had to be content with seeing the man she loved in the face of their son. Raen would not come to her for reasons of his own. She could not go to him for a hamadryad dies away from her tree.

She hid a sigh from her too perceptive child and brushed a lock of blue-black hair off his face. "Are you well? Are you happy?"

"I'm both well and happy, Mother." Rael returned

her smile, his eyes lit from within by green fires. Immortal eyes in the face of mortal man.

Rael could no longer be content spending whole summers with only his mother, her sisters, and the forest for company—the king's court held more attractions for a young man of seventeen—but when he had time to spare, he spent it at the Grove. It was peaceful there and, unlike his father, his mother had time to listen. No courtiers or supplicants made demands on her, for no one found the circle of birches without her help.

Until Rael's birth the Grove had been legend only. But when the king of Ardhan showed his son to the people in the Great Square outside the palace gates, he named Milthra as the child's mother and placed the Grove firmly in the real world. It was fortunate the king was popular and well-liked, for many disbelieved and not a few muttered of insanity. It was also fortunate that the king was no fool and would not allow the acceptance of his son to rest on his own popularity. He called the six dukes and their households together and had them meet the infant's eyes.

Milthra had walked with the Mother-creator as She rested after birthing the world. A fraction of that glory she passed on to her child.

It was enough.

"My aunts still won't wake to greet me?" Rael asked, sprawled on the velvet grass at the foot of his mother's tree. He dug into his pack for the food he'd cadged from a sympathetic kitchen maid.

Milthra shook her head and accepted a piece of honey cake. She had no need to eat—she drew nourishment from her tree—but did it to please her son as once she had done it to please his father. "It has been a long time since the Mother walked in the forest and we wakened. My sisters are tired and want only to sleep."

Rael looked around at the trees he knew as beautiful women, women who had coddled him, fussed over him, and been as much a part of his childhood as his mother and father. He hadn't seen them since . . . his forehead creased as he tried to remember. Had it really been three years? He stretched out a long arm and tugged on a low-hanging branch from a neighboring tree. Leaves rustled but no hamadryad appeared.

"You're the oldest, can't you wake them."

"Perhaps. But I will not try."

"Why not? Aren't you lonely?" As much as Rael loved the Grove, he'd hate to be the only creature awake in its circle.

"No, for when you are not here I also sleep. My sisters have no ties to the world of men to wake them, that is the only difference between us." If she ever regretted the ties that bound her, or acknowledged that they had brought her more sorrow than joy, it could not be heard in the music of her voice.

Rael scooped up his mother's hands and kissed them. "The only difference?" he teased. "I refuse to listen to such foolishness. What of your beauty? Your grace? Your wisdom? I could continue for hours . . ."

Milthra laughed and Rael laughed with her. He'd always felt his mother laughed too seldom. In later years, Rael would recall that afternoon and her laughter when his spirit needed soothing and the shadows needed lifting from his life. He lay with his head in her lap and told her of the things he'd done since he'd been with her last—well most of the things; she was, after all, his mother—and he even told her of his feelings for the Duke of Belkar's blue-eyed daughter, something he had confided to no one else . . . particularly not the Duke of Belkar's blue-eyed daughter.

But he did not speak of why he had come to the Grove.

All too soon the thick, golden sunlight bathing the Grove began to pale. The shadows grew longer and the breezes grew chill. Rael rose lithely to his feet and extended a hand to the hamadryad. When she stood beside him, he kept her hand clasped tightly in his and stared at the ground, unsure of how to begin.

"I . . . I won't be back for some time."

"There is to be war."

He looked up and saw she gazed sadly at him.

"How did you know?"

"The breezes tell me. Even in sleep I hear them; they say men gather on the western border clutching steel in angry hands."

Rael spread his own hands helplessly. "The King of Melac has a new and powerful counselor and the man plays the king's weaknesses and desires like, like a shepherd plays his pipes. He's driving the king to create an empire. Father says they begin with us because Melac hates my father for something that happened when they were young.

"And my son will go to see they conquer no empire."

"I have to do what I can." He tried to keep the anticipation out of his voice and wasn't entirely successful. This war would be his chance to prove himself. His skill with weapons was his father's heritage, but he moved with a strength and grace no man born of mere mortal could match. In his mind's eye he saw himself a hero, returning from battle not only accepted but adulated by the people he was destined to rule. In his heart, he only hoped he would not disgrace his training.

"And your father?"

His voice was gentle. "The king must ride at the head of his armies."

"Yes." War had brought the young king to her so many years before. He had staggered, lost and wounded, into the Grove, stinking of steel and violence, Lord Death close by his side. Against the advice of her sisters, for the Elder Races did not involve themselves with mortals, she had saved him. Saved him and loved him, and Rael had come of it.

Full dusk was upon them now.

"I must go, Mother."

"Yes." War took her son from her, replaced her loving child with this stern young man, so ready to do violence. If he survived he would be further changed, and who knew if he would return to the Grove where nothing changed at all. She held him. Held him tightly. And then she let him go because it was all she could do.

"Rael?"

He turned; half in, half out of the Grove.

"Tell your father, I am always here."

"He knows, Mother." He waited but she said nothing more. "Mother?"

She shook her head, the brilliant immortal color of her eyes dimmed by a very mortal sorrow. She was the Eldest. She could not beg for the return of her love.

Accustomed to thinking of the hamadryad as his mother, and mothers as always strong, Rael had never noticed before how young Milthra looked, or how frail. He suddenly wanted to protect her, to take her in his arms and tell her everything would be all right, but as he watched she faded and dissolved back into her tree. Only the breezes remained and he had never learned to hear what they said.

Although dark had fallen over Melac, the building of the counselor's tower continued. In the flickering light of torches, long lines of naked and sweating men struggled with block and tackle to lift massive slabs of marble into position. As each slab reached its zenith, a slave was removed from the coffle staked at the work site and placed beneath it. Some screamed, some sobbed, some lay limp and resigned, pushed beyond terror. The slab dropped, then the whole process was repeated for the next. The tower was to be the tallest in the city.

If the men who built it felt anything at all, it was, for the most part, relief that they were not beneath the stones themselves.

This night, as most nights, the king's counselor watched the construction from the wooden dais that gave him an unobstructed view of the work. This night, the king stood beside him, leaning into each death, his tongue protruding slightly, his breathing ragged and quick.

A new slave was unchained; a young man, well formed, who, in spite of lash marks striping his back from neck to knees, fought so viciously that four men were needed to escort him to the stone. He screamed, not in terror but in defiance.

The king started at the sound and actually saw the slave. His eyes widened and he clutched at the blue velvet of his counselor's sleeve.

"That looks to be Lord Elan's son."

"It is."

"But you can't . . ."

"He spoke against me, Majesty, and so spoke against you. To speak against the lawful king is treason. The penalty for treason is death." The golden-haired man smiled and removed the king's hand from his arm. "At least this way his death serves a purpose. Life makes the strongest mortar."

On the stone, Lord Elan's son strained against invisible bonds, muscles standing out in sharp relief. He threw back his head and howled as the slab above him fell.

On the dais, the king swayed and he moaned deep in his throat.

Rael stretched the two-hour ride home from the Grove to nearly four, dismounting to sit for a time in the moonlight. To his left, waited the shadow that was the forest. To his right, a ribbon of brown led to the distant lights of the town that spread like a skirt outside the palace walls. The Lady's Wood. King's Road, King's Town.

His horse nickered and lipped at his hair, more interested in returning to the comfort of stable and stall than in philosophy.

Grasping the gelding's mane, Rael pulled himself to his feet, mounted, and kicked the horse into a trot. He had always known that someday he would be king. He enjoyed the power and privilege, and even the responsibilities, of being prince and heir. But sometimes, in the moonlight, he wished he had a choice.

Hoofs thudded onto packed earth, and Rael turned up the King's Road.

The watch had just called midnight when Rael reached town. Because the King's City was so close to the center of Ardhan, miles from any invading army and surrounded on all sides by loyal subjects of the king, it had no wall. The scattered farms and cottages of the countryside merely moved closer together along the road until they gave way to the houses, shops and inns of the city. At the Market Square—well lit even at this hour, for when business in booths and stalls shut down, business in taverns and wineshops began—Rael turned, avoiding the light, preferring to remain unseen in the residential neighborhoods where the inhabitants had long since sought their beds. He told himself he avoided the trouble that would arise if anyone recognized the young man tucked deep in the worn cloak as the prince and heir, riding alone, unescorted. He told himself he didn't need his pocket picked, an unprovoked fight, or an escort back to his father.

He had just passed silently through the merchants' quarters and crossed the invisible but nonetheless real line that separated their homes from the only slightly larger ones of the nobles, when the dark and quiet were snatched from around him.

"Bertram, aren't we home yet?"

"Very nearly, sir."

"I'm sure it wasn't this far before."

The whiny, self-indulgent voice belonged to a minor official of the court, one Diven of House Tannic. Rael had endured too many hours of petitions to mistake it, even distorted as it was by drink.

The torchbearer rounded the corner first, followed by an overdressed man leaning heavily on the arm of his body servant. A City Guard, hired as evening's escort, brought up the rear.

Rael kept his horse walking. With luck they would

be too interested in gaining their beds to pay any attention to him.

Luck was busy elsewhere.

"Awk, Bertram! Brigands!"

Bertram looked to the heavens, exasperation visible even to Rael, and patted his master comfortingly on the shoulder. "It's only a single rider, sir."

"Oh. So it is." Any other would have been content to leave it at that. Diven stepped forward, past the torchbearer and directly into Rael's path. Drink made him determined to erase the embarrassment of his fright. "You there, state your business in this neighborhood. Speak up, or I'll call the patrol."

Rael reined in. The torchbearer grinned, obviously looking forward to telling his cronies of how the drunken noble had accosted one of his equally noble neighbors and threatened him with the patrol. Bertram, now up behind his master, was thinking much the same thing, but not with amusement. The guard looked bored.

"Well, boy, do you tell me your business or do I call the patrol. I will, you know, don't think I won't."

Rael wondered how a voice could whine and be shrill at the same time. He had no doubt the idiot would do exactly as he said, and wake the neighborhood doing it. And that would be the end of the dark and quiet, no mere interruption. He sighed, made his smile as friendly as he was able, and pulled back his hood.

"Highness!"

For a moment the smile held them—they began to return it—then the torchlight flared in his eyes.

The guard saluted and all four men began to back away.

Respectfully, and nervously, they backed away.

From the torchbearer and the guard, it was almost understandable for they met the prince and heir for the first time. Bertram also; for all he served in a noble house he was not accustomed to facing royalty so closely and so informally. But Diven of Tannic saw the prince almost daily. And still he backed away.

Rael held the smile until his horse carried him out of the circle of torchlight. Once he would have said something, tried to find the camaraderie his father seemed to share with every man, woman, and child in the kingdom. Once. But all the words had been said and still the people moved away. Not rejecting, not exactly, but not accepting either.

Let them move if they will, he told himself wearily, replacing his hood. *I have enough who stand by me.* Then he moved back into the dark and quiet.

At the smaller of the palace gates, he allowed the guard to get a good look at him, and passed unchallenged through the outer wall. Except for a sleepy groom waiting to take his horse, and the men on watch, it appeared the palace slept. It didn't, of course, for within its walls the palace was almost a city in itself and the work needed to keep it running smoothly continued day and night.

He walked quickly across the outer courtyard, slipped in a side door, and began to make his way silently through the maze of stone to the tower where he had his chambers. Once, he froze in shadow and an arguing pair of courtiers passed him by.

At the cross-corridor leading to the king's rooms, Rael noticed the royal standard still posted, the six swords on a field of green hanging limp and still against the wall. His father had not retired for the night. Wide awake himself, Rael turned toward the royal bedchamber, hoping the king would not be too busy to speak with him.

The guards saluted as he approached and moved aside to give him access to the door.

"Is he alone?" asked the prince.

"Aye, sir, he is," replied the senior of the two.

Rael nodded his thanks and pushed the door open. "Father?"

The king sat at his desk studying a large map, one

hand holding down a curling edge, the other buried in his beard.

Rael was thinner than his father, his eyes an unworldly green, but aside from that the resemblance was astounding. Both were handsome men, although neither believed it. They shared the same high forehead over black slashes of brow, the same angular cheeks and proud arch of nose, even the determined set to their jaws and slightly mocking smiles matched. Those who had known the king as a young man said to look at the prince was to look at a piece of the past. The people of Ardhan might wonder at the identity of his mother, and they did, but none could doubt that Rael was the king's son.

Raen looked up as the door opened and his face brightened when he saw who it was.

"Come in, lad," he called. "And shut the damn door before it blows out my lamp."

Rael did as he was bid and approached the desk, collapsing with a boneless, adolescent grace into the sturdy chair across from his father.

"The Western Border?"

The king nodded. "And you'd best get familiar with it yourself. We march as soon as the armies are assembled."

Rael leaned forward to study the map. "You're surely not assembling all six provinces here?" He wondered where they'd put everyone. The six dukes and their households jammed the palace to the rafters during seventh year festivals. The six dukes and their armies. . . !

"No, only Cei and Aliston will come here to Belkar. We'll join with Hale on the march." He traced their route with a callused finger. "Lorn and Riven meet us on the battlefield." His mouth twisted. "And it's to be hoped those two hotheads will concentrate on fighting the enemy instead of each other. I'm thankful you've no rival for your lady's hand."

Rael felt his ears redden.

"You can keep no secrets in this rabbit warren, lad.

It's a good match; her father and I both approve. You're lucky I've no need to join you to some foreign princess to tie a treaty.''

"Join?'' Rael repeated weakly. He'd barely gotten beyond worshiping from a distance and his father spoke of joinings?

The older man laughed. "You're right,'' he mocked, but kindly, "it's bad luck to talk of joining on the eve of war.'' He turned again to the map. "And on the eve of war we are; I want the armies on the road in two weeks.''

"In two weeks? Father, it can't be done.'' The Elite, the Palace Guard and the Ducal Guards that made up the standing army, yes, and, he supposed, most City Guards could adapt fast enough, but when Rael thought of the chaos involved in turning farmers and craftsmen into soldiers his head ached.

"It's going to have to be done,'' the king said shortly. "We have no choice. Melac's moving very fast; he wants those iron mines in Riven badly and has had plans to invade us for years. Though he's a fool if he thinks he's in charge, not that madman he has for a counselor.'' He looked down at the map and shook his head. "Still, madman or not, he's a brilliant leader. I've never heard of anyone getting an army into the field so quickly.'' Teeth gleamed for an instant in the lamplight. "If I didn't know all the wizards were dead. . . .''

The wizards had destroyed themselves before there was an Ardhan or a king to rule it. Their dying convulsions had reshaped the face of the world.

"Father! You don't think. . . ?''

"Don't be ridiculous, boy. I was joking.'' Raen leaned back in his chair and looked fondly at his son. His expression hardened. "You're not wearing your sword.''

Rael's hand jerked to his belt and he flushed.

"I saw Mother today, to tell her I wouldn't be back to the Grove for some time. You know how steel upsets her.''

"Well, your guards were armed, I hope?"

Rael looked at the cold hearth, the hunting tapestry on the wall, the great canopied bed, everywhere but at his father.

"You took no guards." The king's voice was sharper than Rael's missing sword.

"The guards won't go into the Grove."

"The guards will go where I tell them." And then he thought of Milthra's reaction to heavily armed men tearing up her peace and reconsidered. Gods, he missed her. "Well, they can wait with your horse at the edge of the forest, then. They needn't go into the Grove."

An uncomfortable silence fell as both considered another who would not go into the Grove.

"You'll take them with you next time," Raen said finally. "I don't want a dead son."

Rael turned the brilliant green of his eyes on the king. "Who would want to kill me, Father?"

"Balls of Chaos, boy, how should I know?" Raen looked away from the Lady's eyes. "Melac's men. Madmen. You're prince and heir, my only son. When you ride from now on, you ride with guards." King's command, not father's. "I don't care where you're going. I will not lose you."

"Yes, sir." Suddenly, Rael made a decision. He was tired, he decided, of bouncing from the pain of one parent to the pain of the other and tired too of pretending he didn't see that pain because they both so obviously tried to keep it from him. He took his courage in both hands and asked what he'd never dared ask before. "Father? Why don't you go to the Grove?"

Raen stared at the map without seeing it. He remembered ivory and silver and green, green eyes and strong smooth limbs wrapped around him. He remembered a love so deep he could drown in it.

"How did your mother look when you left her this afternoon?" he asked hoarsely.

Rael thought about his last sight of the hamadryad as she merged back into her tree.

"As always, beautiful; but worried and sad."

"And her age?"

"Her age?" He remembered how he'd wanted to protect her. "She seemed very young."

"Now look at me."

"Sir?"

"LOOK AT ME!" Raen stood so suddenly that his chair overturned. His hands clenched to fists and his voice rose to a roar. "Once my hair was as thick and black as yours. You'll notice that what I have left, and there isn't much, is gray. There was a day I could defeat any man in Ardhan with my bare hands, but no longer. I used to be able to follow the flight of a hawk in the sun. Now I'm lucky if I can see the damned bird at all! I grew this beard to hide the lines of age!" He paused, drew a shuddering breath and his voice fell until it was almost a whisper. "Your mother hasn't changed, but I am growing old. She must not see me like this."

Rael was on his feet as well, staring at his father in astonishment. "You're not old!"

The king's smile was not reflected in his eyes. "Fifty-two years weigh heavily on a man, and your mother is ageless." He raised a hand to stop the next protest. "I appreciate your denials, lad, but I know what I see."

Unfortunately, there was nothing to deny. His father was a mortal man and his mother stood outside of time.

"Mother loves you. It wouldn't matter to her."

"It would matter to me. Let her love me as I was."

Rael ached with the pain in his father's voice that was a twin to the pain in his mother's.

"Father . . ."

"No, Rael." Raen put his hands on his son's shoulders but avoided the leaf-green glow of his eyes. "There is nothing you can do. Go to bed. We have a busy time ahead of us."

"Yes, sir."

Is he too old for me to hold? Raen wondered, looking for his child and seeing only a young man.

Am I too old to be held? Rael asked the dignity of his seventeen years.

No.

It comforted them both greatly.

If I can only get him to the Grove, Rael thought as he left his father's room. *If I can only get him to the Grove, everything will be all right.*

Two

"Out of bed, milord. The Duke of Belkar and some of his men rode in last night and your father wants to see you in the small petition room."

Rael buried his head under the pillow as the middle-aged man who had been his servant/companion since before he could remember, pulled back the heavy curtains and let in the weak early morning light. "Oh, go away, Ivan, it's barely dawn."

"It's an hour past." Strong hands dragged the blankets away with the familiarity of long service. "Get up or you won't have time for a wash and bite before you see the king."

There was time for the wash but not the bite and Rael's stomach complained bitterly as he slipped into the room where the daily business of the kingdom was most often conducted. Raen looked up at the sound, pushed the remnants of his own breakfast across the table, and turned his attention back to the document he studied. More than a little embarrassed, Rael took a chunk of bread and slid into the only vacant chair. The Duke of Belkar smiled at him and the other man, who by his armor could only be one of Belkar's two captains, raised an edge of his lip in what have been either a greeting or a grimace.

Finally the king scrawled his signature at the bottom of the document, set his seal in wax, and gave the paper to the Messenger standing patiently at his elbow. Then he looked up at his son.

"Belkar and I have talked it over and it's been decided that you'll command the Elite."

Rael choked on the bread. The men of the Elite were the best fighters in Ardhan. Every young man who could use a sword dreamed of joining their company. And he was to command them. He suddenly thought of something. "But, sir, the king commands the Elite."

"The king also makes the rules, and I've changed this one. As prince and heir, you must have a command. I thought of creating a company for you out of the Palace Guard. You've trained with them and most of them know you, but the Elite is already a self-contained unit, used to serving under a royal commander." Black brows rose. "Or don't you want to command the Elite?"

"Yes, sir!" *The Elite*, Rael thought.

"As prince and heir," the king continued, a smile twitching at the corners of his mouth, "you'll be obeyed, but I hasten to point out that, training aside, you know little of actual warfare, so defer to the captain."

"Yes, sir." Rael had every intention of deferring to the captain. He'd been terrified of the thickset little man for as long as he could remember.

"Before you head down to the barracks, stop off at the armorers and get fitted for a new helmet, breastplate, and greaves. Your sword's fine."

"Yes, sir."

"Well, get going."

"Yes, sir!"

"He'll be in the thick of the fighting with the Elite," Belkar pointed out as the prince dashed out of the room.

"Aye," agreed the king grimly. "But they'll have to go through the Elite to get to him. It's the safest place I can think of."

"You could order him to remain here," suggested the duke, not at all pleased to have both the king and his only heir in such danger.

"I could, but I'll be damned if I'll chain my son to the walls." Raen smiled ruefully. "And that's what I'd have to do to keep him here."

By the time Rael arrived at the Elite's training yard, the euphoria was beginning to fade. Though the news of his appointment had obviously preceded him, the Elite weren't yet ready to change their allegiance from captain and king/commander to captain, king, and prince/commander. Every one of them, soldier and servant, politely ignored him as he made his way to the practice ring.

Doan, the captain, perched on the top rail of the fence surrounding the ring, looking like a well armed gargoyle. He welcomed the prince with a grunt and slapped the rail in invitation, never once taking his eyes off the men training.

Rael climbed up and sat down, a little farther from Doan than was strictly polite. He couldn't help himself; something about the captain put him on edge. It wasn't the man's appearance—although the barrel chest, bandy legs, and habitual scowl made him far from appealing—it was more the feeling of tremendous power just barely under control that he seemed to project. Palace rumor whispered Doan had dwarf blood and Rael believed it. When he looked at the captain through his mother's eyes, he felt the same strong belonging to the land that he felt in the Grove but none of the peace or serenity.

Wood cracked on wood and then wood on bone and then one of the men in the ring was down, blood streaming from a cut on his forehead, his quarterstaff lying useless on the sand beside him.

"Get him out of there," grunted Doan. He turned to the prince and pointed at his sword with a gnarled finger. "The swordmaster says you know how to use that thing."

Rael's back stiffened. He'd never trained with the Elite, for theirs was a very close fraternity, but Doan had seen him work with the Palace Guard often enough to know he could use his sword. And his strength and speed were common knowledge.

"Show me."

As regally as he was able, Rael shrugged and slid off the fence. He drew his sword and tossed his scabbard to one side.

Suddenly, every Elite not on duty surrounded the ring.

Rael looked around at the grinning faces, swallowed nervously, and met the eyes of the captain. They reflected the early morning light in such a way they appeared to glow deeply red. Rael swallowed again and his chin went up. So the new commander had to prove he was worthy, did he? Well he'd show them.

"Who do I fight?"

A slow smile spread over the guard captain's face. "Me," he said. "Your Highness." And he dropped into the ring.

Doan's attack came so quickly, the fight almost ended before it truly began. To Rael's astonishment, his strength and speed alone were not enough and he was forced to use every bit of skill the swordmaster had drilled into him over the years. The prince was a slender flame tipped with steel. Doan stood solid, each movement deliberate and so slow next to the Lady's son that it seemed he must be cut to shreds. But Rael could not get past his guard, and when their swords met he had to use all of his unworldly strength to block the blow.

Less than three minutes later it was finished.

Doan bent and retrieved Rael's sword. "You'll do," he said as he handed it over. "Commander."

A cheer went up from the surrounding Elite and Rael became aware that a great deal of coin was changing hands. Snatches of conversation drifted back from the dispersing men.

". . . told you he'd get his own in . . ."

". . . expected the captain to beat him to his knees . . ."

". . . four coppers, you jackass, but then I've seen him fight before . . ."

And echoed from more than one direction: "He'll do."

"They'd follow the prince because they had to," Doan grunted as Rael sheathed his sword. "Better you make them want to."

Rael straightened his shoulders. "And how do I make them want to?"

"You've started already." Doan hacked and spit in the sand. "You've proven you can fight."

"But you beat me."

"I know. I beat them too. But you showed them you could've made the company on your own."

Rael flushed with pleasure. "I could've?"

"Just said so, didn't I?" Doan hooked his thumbs behind his broad leather belt and headed out of the practice ring. "Now if you'll come with me . . ." The pause was barely audible. ". . . Commander, I'll fill you in on your command."

". . . but the strength of the Elite lies in flexibility. We fight on any terrain, on any terms. It all depends on the lay of the land, the enemy, and the Duke of Hale who runs mostly cavalry. We've fought beside his horsemen before though, and it . . . am I going too fast for you, Commander?"

"Huh?" Rael flushed and dragged himself out of a pleasant daydream where the enemy had been falling back in terrified disorder before his charge. "I'm sorry, captain. I, I didn't hear."

"Obviously." Doan smiled, an expression that lessened neither his ugliness nor his ferocity. "Drink your ale."

The mug was at his lips before Rael realized he'd followed the order without thinking. As it was there, he drank. *The chain of command definitely needs work*, he thought, putting the empty mug down amid the ruins of lunch. When he looked up, he saw by Doan's expression that the thought had clearly shown on his face. He reddened, then raised his chin and met the captain's eyes squarely. To his surprise, Doan merely nodded in what seemed to be satisfaction.

"Excuse me, Captain, Commander." The Elite First sketched a salute intended to take in both his superior officers. Rael had observed his father with the Elite often enough to realize that the First's apparent disregard for royal rank was, in fact, a form of acceptance and his heart swelled with pride. "The lad's been found. He's waiting in the guardroom."

"Send him in."

"Did you lose someone?" Rael asked as the First left the room.

"Did I lose someone?" Doan's brow furrowed as he turned to stare at the prince. "Did I lose someone?" And then he chuckled, a friendly sound so at odds with his appearance that it was Rael's turn to stare. He was still chuckling when the lad in question entered the room.

The young man, in the full uniform of the Palace Guard, was the prince's age or possibly a year or two older. He carried his helmet on his hip but, as his pale hair was damp, he'd probably just removed it. He had a strong face with high cheekbones, a thin-lipped mouth, and deepset, light blue eyes. The glint on his upper lip may or may not have been the beginning of a mustache. He stood self-consciously at parade rest, his eyes regulation front and center, his gaze locked on a spot some three feet above Doan's head. Every achingly correct inch of him fairly trembled to know why he'd been called into such exalted presence—the exalted presence obviously being the captain of the Elite and not the prince and heir.

Rael wondered what the guardsman had done to bring him to the notice of the Elite Captain. There were no openings in the company. And besides, he was too young.

"Rutgar, Hovan's son, from Cei." Doan had stopped chuckling.

"Yes, sir." It wasn't a question but it seemed to need a response.

"Joined your Duke's Guard at fifteen and moved to the Palace Guard last year."

"Yes, sir."

"You're moving again." He pointed with his chin across the table. "The commander needs an armsman. You're it."

"Sir?" This from both young men. It was enough to drag the young guard's eyes off the wall. They studied one another for a heartbeat and then Rutgar went back to looking at nothing and the prince turned to Doan.

"But I've already got a servant."

"I didn't say he was to be your servant. He's your armsman. The men fight in pairs, live in pairs, the officers can't. He'll take care of your armor and your horse—trust me, you won't have time—and guard your back if it needs guarding." Red-brown eyes raked over the newly appointed armsman. "He's young but," he added pointedly, "so are you. You can learn together. Anyway, he'd have made the company himself before this war's over."

A small explosion of air escaped from the pressed line of Rutgar's mouth.

"Did you say something, Armsman?"

"No, Captain."

"Good. Get outfitted. Meet us on the reviewing square in half an hour."

"Yes, sir." Only the gleam in his eye showed the young man's emotion as he wheeled and exited the room.

Rael shook his head and his brow furrowed.

"Problems, Commander?"

"It just happened so fast . . ." Rael squared his shoulders. "What if I wanted someone else as my armsman?"

Earth-colored eyebrows rose. "Do you?"

"Well, no, it's's just . . ."

"A good commander should have faith in his officers." The tone was not quite sarcastic. "Now, if you're ready, Commander, we'll review the troops."

* * *

The men of Belkar, farmers and herdsmen for the most part, began to gather outside the city. Soon they were joined by the fishermen of Cei and the shepherds of Aliston. Most of these men were skilled with a quarterstaff or spear and some were fine archers, but very few of them could use a sword. In less than two weeks, they had to be an army. It would have been impossible had they not wanted to be an army so badly. Raen was a good king, more importantly he was a popular king, but they wouldn't be fighting for him. They'd be fighting for their land.

"Riven and Lorn know the mountains and they take care of border raids every winter," Raen said, jabbing at the map with a dagger. "They'll do. We can count on Hale to supply cavalry out of those crazy horsemen of his." He sucked his teeth and looked grim. "They say Melac can field tens of thousands of trained soldiers."

"Impossible," scoffed Cei. "Mere rumor."

But none of the men in the room looked very happy.

The palace bulged with the three dukes and their retinues, officers and couriers, clerks and servants, until it resembled an anthill more than a royal residence.

Rael was up at dawn and in bed long past dark but still there weren't enough hours in the day.

He had training.

"You just removed the ears from your horse, Commander. Try it again and swing wider."

He had fittings for new armor in the plain, cold steel of the Elite.

"Stop squirming, Highness."

"You're tickling."

"I assure you, Highness, it's unintentional."

He had Royal Obligations.

"But I don't want to have dinner with the dukes, Ivan. Why can't I eat with my men?"

"You eat with the dukes, milord," Ivan finished fastening the red velvet jacket and stepped back to view his handiwork, "because your father commands your

presence.'' He picked the gold belt off the bed and
slung it artfully around the prince's hips. ''And because, milord,'' he continued, firmly removing Rael's
hands when he tried to hitch the belt higher, ''it is
good policy for you to get to know the dukes.''

''I know the dukes.'' Rael held out a foot so Ivan
could force it into a tight red leather boot. ''Aliston
will pay attention only to his food and perhaps grunt
once or twice if father addresses him directly. Cei will
worry out loud and continuously. And Belkar . . .'' A
violent shove almost tore the second boot from Ivan's
hands. ''I haven't anything to say to Belkar.'' Belkar's
daughter had been left at home.

''Then the dukes must get to know you, milord.''

''They know me, Ivan.'' His voice was suddenly
bleak and his eyes flared. ''And only Belkar looks at
me.''

The older man met the brilliance of the prince's gaze
without fear. ''Someday they will see you, milord.
And when they do, they will stop looking away.''

Rael let the green burn brighter. ''And what will
they see,'' he asked softly.

Ivan smiled. ''All that you are. All that you can be.
All that you are not.''

The unearthly fires were abruptly banked.

''You're talking in riddles again, Ivan.'' Grumbling,
Rael went to have his dinner with the dukes.

He had new people to know.

''What I don't understand,'' he asked as Rutgar un-
buckled his practice breastplate, ''is why it's such an
honor to be an armsman.'' The armor came free and
he took a deep breath, the morning's maneuvers had
been particularly strenuous as the Elite honed itself
for the battles to come. ''I mean, you were moving up
in the Palace Guard and now,'' he shrugged himself
free of the padded undertunic, ''now, you're just a
well-armed servant.'' He winced. ''Uh, no offense,
Rutgar.''

''None taken. Commander.'' The armsman bent so
Rael could reach his buckles in turn. ''Perhaps you

haven't noticed, but all the officers of the Elite were armsmen once. It is, after all, the best position to observe and learn in. Only the best are chosen to be armsmen.''

Rael's jaw dropped and the corners of Rutgar's mouth twitched.

''If you'll sit down, Commander, I'll get those greaves.''

And still the day to day governing of the land must go on.

''Your Highness, please inform your father that unless something is done soon, the water situation in the camps will become desperate.''

''Prince Rael, I must have more men if I am to make all the arrows ordered by the king.''

''Young sir, a moment of your time. The men of the camps have been tearing the town apart and I can't get near the king.''

''Rael! Haven't you got something to do?''

''Yes, Father, but . . .''

''Then do it, lad!''

''Yes, sir.''

There could be no letting up of the pressure, no thought of taking more time to prepare. Not only was there an invasion to meet, but so many men in so little space would become a serious problem if the army lingered too long.

Although it seemed as if he'd done enough work for two years, only two short weeks later Rael heard his father tell the dukes and the captains that they would march with the dawn.

''And tonight, milord?'' inquired a captain, one of Aliston's by his badge.

''Tonight,'' replied the king, hitching up his broad leather belt to get at an elusive itch, ''I will ride amongst the men.''

''They'll be glad to see you, Sire.''

''I certainly hope so. Would you like to ride with me, son?'' he asked, turning to Rael.

"Me, sir?" Rael felt as if he hadn't been out of the palace in months.

"Yes, you. If I have another son in this room I haven't been told."

One of the captains snickered and Rael felt himself turning pink. "Yes, sir, I'd like to go with you."

When the king and the heir rode out that evening, they wore plain armor and took only two of the Palace Guard, but everyone in the camp knew the iron-haired warrior and the young man with the fire-green eyes.

Rael drank in the sights and sounds and smells: the kraken pennant of Cei, blood red against the gray of evening; two men cursing genially as they diced; sweat and leather and steel. Here was a different world from those he had known—the forest and the court—cruder, less disciplined, more rawly sensual.

Raen watched the tall young man riding beside him with pride, and some amusement, as his son tried to take in everything without appearing to notice anything at all. He submerged the thought that in war young men die and he buried the fear that this one he loved so dearly could be taken from him.

The men were in good spirits and some called out to the riders as they passed. They had a long march ahead with Lord Death waiting at the end of it and a soldier, even a temporary soldier, makes merry when he can. Many of the sentiments were not those normally heard in the presence of the king and the heir to the throne. A grizzled archer bellowed out a riddle so coarse that the prince blushed, but the King roared with laughter and gave back the answer.

"Aye, the king knows his women," slurred a loud voice from the crowd. "Pity he can't find a real one to get a son on."

Raen stopped laughing. Silence fell. So complete a silence it was possible to hear the soft whistle of the horses' breath. He held up a hand to stop the Guard from riding forward, and watched his son. He remembered how Milthra had handed him the squalling, naked babe, the love in her eyes lighting up the whole Grove. When Rael looked up, he nodded.

A pulse beat in Rael's throat like a wild thing held prisoner, but it was the only movement visible. His eyes flamed and one by one, not even aware they did it, men stepped aside until a massive soldier stood alone.

Silently, Rael swung off his horse. Slowly and deliberately, as if afraid a sudden movement would release the emotions held rigidly in check, he moved to stand before the man. He felt his mother's heritage well up within him. The strength of the tree. The strength to withstand wind and storm. The strength to root into bedrock and hold on. His blood sang and his eyes blazed. And his fists clenched, for he was also his father's son.

"You have no right to speak of my mother."

His voice was so soft it might have been the passing breeze that spoke.

Swaying unsteadily on tree-trunk legs, either too foolish or too befuddled by wine to see the threat in the slim young man who faced him, the soldier narrowed his eyes belligerently. "Your mother," he slurred, "was likely a common street whore who spread . . ."

In the stillness, the sound of Rael's fist striking the other's jaw rang out like a thunderclap. The soldier's head snapped back, he hung for a moment on the night, and then crumpled to the ground.

Still outwardly emotionless, Rael remounted. He ignored the blood running down his fingers from where the skin had split over a knuckle. Only the trembling of his hand as he took up the reins betrayed that he felt anything at all.

"His neck's broken," said the old archer looking up from the body. "He's dead."

"Then bury him," said the king. And they rode in silence back to the Palace where they went to their separate rooms and spent the rest of the night staring sleeplessly in the direction of the forest.

* * *

The Grove was silver and shadow in the moonlight. Clothed in night, its beauty became sharp edges and satin blackness, drawing away from the world of mortals to that of an older time. Within the circle of birches, no nightbirds called, no animals, large or small, stalked prey or were stalked in turn, no breeze wandered to disturb the listening quiet of the trees.

One moment the Grove waited empty and still, the next Doan, the Captain of the Elite, stood before the eldest of the trees and said: "All right, you called. I'm here."

The tree murmured in protest as Milthra pulled herself from its heart.

At the sight of her face, Doan winced. "You know."

"The breezes told me when it was done," Milthra admitted, the clear chimes of her voice flattened with worry. "But they have not returned again and I must know what is said of my son."

Doan shoved his thumbs behind his belt and paced about the Grove, breaking the moonlight into Doan-sized patterns. He had done little since he'd heard the news but listen for reaction to the deed. He knew this summons would come. "Those who saw," his rough burr broke the silence of the Grove at last, "say the man deserved it. Not death perhaps, but the blow at least. Fortunately, the man was not well liked. Most admire the prince for standing up for you himself when he could've hidden behind the Guard. Many are impressed by his strength and are anxious to see it on the battlefield. But," his fingers drummed on the leather around his waist, "there are those for whom it only marks his difference, and difference is always distrusted. And in everyone's mind, although for the most part it remains unasked, is the question, 'If he kills so easily now, when he is king, how can any of us be safe?'" He met Milthra's eyes and smiled grimly. "It would've been simpler for all concerned, Lady, had you loved a woodcutter or a farmer and not a king."

"So you have said before, old friend, but I could no

more have refused that love than I could refuse to breathe; I am sorry for the burden it places on my son.'' She sighed and, behind her, her tree swayed in sympathy. "Even you, who are fully of the Elder Races, are accepted in the mortal world more easily than Rael.''

Doan shrugged. "I play a part. And even if I convinced them of what I truly am . . .'' He spread his hands. "Dwarves brought mortals fire and taught them to build; helped them to rebuild after the destruction of the wizards. We showed them a number of ways to cheat Lord Death. We've never been either revered or feared.''

"And I am both?''

"They don't know you, Lady.''

Milthra shook her hair over her face and wept behind its silver curtain.

Anger and pity rose in the dwarf's breast. Anger that she who was Eldest and most beautiful should be reduced to weeping over mortal man. Pity for much the same reason. He reached out a hand and Milthra pressed her cheek into it. Then she stepped back to the safety of her tree and he held only a tear that ran down his palm. It slowed, stopped, flared suddenly, then darkened to an emerald that held all the greens of the Grove in its depths. He slipped it in his belt pouch and bowed to the silver birch before him.

"I will continue to watch him, Eldest,'' and his eyes glowed deeply red, "both for your sake and his. But remember, not all the Dwarves from the Mother's blood could keep Lord Death away if he comes to claim his own and, your life mingled within or no, your son is as mortal as his father. Perhaps you should save some tears for that.''

And then the Grove was empty, save for the silver of moonlight, the blackness of night, and the sound of the Eldest weeping for her child.

Three

Rael swore as sweat rolled into his eyes and he blinked furiously to ease the burning. He used his shield to smash aside the vicious hooked blade of a Melac spearman and in the same move swung his sword around, over, and down onto the man's arms. The meaty thunk of metal through flesh and bone was absorbed by the sounds of battle. Beneath him, his horse struck out with steel-edged hoofs, giving Rael time to yank free his blade, turn, and open the face of the man who threatened on his right. He tightened his legs and the warhorse leaped forward. Another Melacian went down, gurgling blood, his ribs a mass of splintered bone.

Then there was nothing in front of them but a rock-strewn slope, and the stallion stretched into a canter. They thundered up the hill, wheeled at the crest, and looked down over the valley. The warhorse stopped so suddenly at Rael's command that the prince rocked in the saddle. After four passes across the valley, cutting their way through the enemy position, the animal knew that this was his chance to rest and he stood, sides heaving, while Rael, no less winded, lifted his visor to better suck in great lungfuls of air. Beside and behind him, other members of the Elite did the same.

The valley held a seething mass of men and weapons and dead and dying. Hale's horsemen, more lightly armored than the Elite, darted in and out of the melee, sabers red and dripping. The space was too enclosed for their speed and maneuverability to be totally effective, but they stung the flanks of the enemy like gadflies. The ducal guards of Belkar, Cei, and Aliston fought in clumps, lending their strength and skill when they could to the farmers, fishermen, and herdsmen who fought beside them but too used to fighting as units to do more than slow the slaughter of the common folk. Over it all, crows and other carrion birds rode the updrafts, waiting for nightfall and their time in the valley.

Safely out of it for the moment, Rael was conscious of the noise in a way he hadn't had time to be while he fought. It filled the bowl of the valley, the deep-voiced defiance of thousands of men and the slam and clatter of thousands of weapons, with eddies of greater noise where the fighting was fiercest, and every now and then a scream piercing through the din like torch-light through smoke.

From here, Rael mused, the Ardhan and Melacian dying sounded very much alike.

From a distance, as though he wandered through someone else's mind, he considered the absence of terror and disgust and shame—at what he'd seen and what he'd done. His ability to feel had gone as numb as his nose; he'd long since stopped noticing the omni-present stench of blood and guts and sweat. His brain had apparently decided to concentrate on the essentials, survival and command, and let all else wait until later. *"Much later,"* he prayed, remembering how he'd felt during the butchery of the first charge. *"Please, much later."*

"Over there, look!"

Down the line, one of the Elite called and pointed and the men raised a ragged cheer as a flight from Belkar's archers collapsed an advancing enemy line. Although the rest of the Elite saw the arrows as smudges against the sky and could tell only by their direction which side fired and which died, with his mother's eyes, Rael watched each double-barbed arrow land, diving deep to burrow through armor and into the soft meat beneath. He tried not to flinch. It wouldn't look good.

"Cristof lost his horse, Commander, but he got out on his Half's stirrup. And we've got two cut reins from those damned hooked blades."

Rael started as the First broke through his thoughts and, glad for an excuse to stop watching the carnage, he turned to face the officer.

"Keep the Halves together." That much, at least, he knew he had to do. The Elite fought in pairs; each man a Half and each man's Half closer to him than mere comrade or friend. It was not a commitment all chosen for the Elite were willing to make and those men who weren't stayed in the Guard, but it was a part of why the Elite fought so fiercely; each Half *knew* another's life depended on his skill. "Have Cristof's Half give his reins to repair the two reins cut. Then the Pair can head back, get outfitted again and rejoin us on the far side of the valley after the next pass."

"Very good, sir." The standard response sounded like praise. An unorthodox solution, perhaps, but it kept together three Pairs who would have otherwise been split. The First moved away and began barking orders. The company's respite was nearly over.

"Yes, Commander, very good." It seemed Doan's surly chestnut could move as silently as its rider. One moment the space to Rael's left stood empty, the next the captain filled it, perched—given the length of Doan's legs, there could be no other word for it—on his horse beside him. "These cross valley charges of yours seem to be working as well. You were right, the enemy does find it demoralizing to have us thunder down and through the middle of their position."

Rael searched the captain's words for sarcasm and found, not praise, exactly, but acknowledgment of success. He was almost too tired to be pleased.

"You hurt?" Rutgar moved his horse closer to Rael's right and nodded at the blood that clotted and congealed down the prince's leg.

Rael looked down and shrugged. "Not mine." He turned and studied his armsman. "How about you?"

Rutgar touched a dent in the side of his helmet with his shield hand and grinned. "My ears'll ring for a while, but I'm all right. Who'd have thought they'd throw rocks?"

A quick glance around showed the Elite to be ready. Rael, prince and commander, slammed his visor down with the edge of his sword, touched his heels to his horse, and led the Elite on another slash of destruction through the foe.

The command tent was hot, smoky and entirely too full of sweaty, tired men; three dukes and Aliston's heir, for the Duke of Aliston was too old to travel so far and far too old to fight, eleven captains, the king, and the prince, all with the smell of battle clinging to them. Sweet candles had been lit, but the odor of blood and death refused to be defeated by jasmine and spice. Rael gritted his teeth and hoped his nose would go numb to this as well.

"We have to keep him in the valley where his position works against the number of men he's throwing against us." The king jabbed at the map with his dagger. "If he forces us out to the Tage Plateau, he'll be able to expand his front beyond our ability to contain him. He's got the manpower to flank us easily."

"I hardly think easily, Sire." Hale played with one beaded end of his mustache. "More room to maneuver could work to our advantage as well."

"Well, I don't think every horse in your province could stop the number of men Melac is putting into the field." Cei dabbed at his dripping nose with a square of cotton. "You can't herd men like cattle, you know."

Hale raised both brows in a barely polite expression. "Oh? Can't I?"

"Gentlemen." Raen's voice developed an edge. "It's a moot point what Hale's horsemen can or cannot do because I have no intention of allowing Melac out of the valley even if he dumps every able body in his kingdom on us.''

"Which he seems to be doing," Belkar added dryly.

"Yes . . . well . . ." Raen directed their attention back to the map. "I think we can all see why he chose this pass. The Melac side may be difficult to maneuver through, but it opens so smoothly into Ardhan that once the valley's gained it's damned difficult for us to defend against him.''

Belkar scratched at a bandage wrapped around his knuckles and shook his head. "And unfortunately this madman cares little how many men he wastes getting to our side of the mountains.''

"Fortunately for us," Hale corrected smoothly. "The enemy arrives to fight us exhausted from fighting the mountains. It gives us a small edge against his superior numbers.''

Cei sniffed and rubbed at his nose. His already lachrymose disposition had not been improved by a reaction to the plant life of the area. "What I don't understand is how a whole army got so close before we knew where it was going. What I want to know is, why weren't Riven and Lorn watching their borders?''

"They were. Only by their vigilance did we manage to arrive in time to contain Melac where we have. It would've gone a lot worse with us if the Dukes Riven and Lorn had not been watching their borders. And it would go a lot worse for us now if they and their men were not out in the mountains making sure that this is the only breach Melac makes.''

Cei hunched his bony shoulders under the lash of the king's voice.

"What amazes me," Hale, cool and slightly amused, defused the rising tension, "is how they ever managed to agree that the attack would come here. They can't even agree whose province this valley is in." He stretched out long legs, still in stained riding leathers. "I suppose if we win, they'll both claim it.''

Belkar nodded. "And if we lose, neither will want it.''

Many of the men chuckled and even Cei managed a smile. The young Dukes of Riven and Lorn were cousins, born less than two days apart. They had ascended their Seats within a year of each other and were alike right down to their taste in women and tinder-dry tempers. Tempers that had flared lately over a woman they both had a taste for.

Rael breathed a quiet prayer of thanks that neither duke was present. In reminding the company of their constant, albeit generally affectionate, bickering, Hale had averted a potentially bad situation. For all his wildman posturings—and the barbaric affectation of his beaded mustache—Hale was a born diplomat. The prince hoped that someday he'd be half that smooth.

"I don't think we've any more to discuss." Raen leaned forward. "We've had a long day, gentlemen, and we all need some sleep. It'll be more of the same tomorrow."

The dukes and captains bowed and left, breaking into smaller groups outside the command tent as they headed back to their men. Finally, only Rael remained.

The king stood and put his arm around his son's shoulders as they walked to the open flap.

"I was proud of you today, son. You fought well."

Rael flushed. "I did no more than any man, sir."

Raen smiled. "Yes, well, I was proud of them all."

They ducked out of the tent together and stood breathing deeply, clearing their lungs of candle smoke and their minds momentarily of battle plans. Two of the Palace Guard stepped forward to escort the king to his tent. Raen turned and cupped his son's face between his hands.

"And what did you think of your first day's battle?" he asked quietly.

Rael looked past the numbness that had mercifully continued even after the fighting had finished. "I hated it."

"Good." Raen kissed his child on the forehead—

yes, still his child in spite of size and age and armor—
and allowed the Guard to lead him away.

In the tent he shared with his armsman, Rael stood
while Ivan stripped him and sponged off the worst of
the battle.

The old servant muttered to himself as he sponged,
for purple and green bruises began to show against the
clean skin. He wanted to scold but couldn't for fear of
waking Rutgar who already slept, one arm flung up
against the light. He turned down the blanket, trimmed
the lamp, and would have suggested he pour wine had
the prince not dismissed him. Still muttering, he gathered up the day's clothes and left.

Rael threw himself on his pallet and stared up at the
canvas above his head.

"Hey." Rutgar had risen up on one elbow. "You
okay?"

Rael turned so he could see his armsman. "I thought
you were asleep."

Rutgar shrugged and grinned. "Nah, who could
sleep with all that serving going on."

Both young men turned their gaze on the outer
chamber where Ivan still puttered about, then Rael
leaned back and sighed. "Rutgar, you've fought before, haven't you?"

"Yes, Commander, at the Tantac raids two summers
ago."

"How did you feel?"

Rutgar studied the prince's profile. There was a
tightness to it that had not been there before. "How
do you feel now?" he asked instead of answering.

"Numb. I don't feel anything."

The armsman nodded. "That's how I felt," he said
and chewed his lip at the memories. "Numb."

Rael sighed again. "I don't think I like it, this not
feeling."

"Don't worry," Rutgar's voice was caught in the
battles of two summers past, "it wears off." He
reached up and pinched out the lamp. "Good night,
Highness."

* * *

The man should have been dead. With every beat of his heart more of his life pumped out the gaping hole in his chest, but still he advanced. His lips drew back in a rictus grin, blackened, rotted and fell away. The flesh of his face writhed with maggots, whole chunks dropping off to expose the yellow skull beneath.

Rael gagged on the stench and tried to back away, but his feet seemed rooted to the ground. He struggled to lift his leg, looked down, and saw that skeletal hands rising out of the earth held him firmly in place. Blackened nails dug into his ankles and anchored themselves by driving deep into his bones.

Still the Melacian spearman advanced, a shambling corpse hardly more than an arm's reach away.

The smell clotted into solid matter in Rael's nose and throat and he gasped for air.

He waved his sword at the monstrosity before him and found to his horror that the blade had become a strip of birch bark torn from the living surface of his mother's tree. The bark bled and called his name.

He forced enough air into his lungs to scream.

"Highness! Commander! Rael!"

Rutgar's face hung above him and Rutgar's hands were on his shoulders and nothing was coming at him out of the darkness.

Rutgar's mouth twisted in sympathy. "I told you, it wears off," he said gently.

"I was dreaming . . ."

The armsman nodded. "I know. I had nightmares for months after the Tantac raids." He sat back on his heels. "Still do occasionally."

Rael released his grip on his blankets and lightly touched the back of Rutgar's hand. Warm. Living. "Thank you for waking me."

Rutgar smiled, a warmer expression than his usual one-sided grin. "I'm here to guard your back, Commander. It's just a part of the service."

His commander managed a weak smile in return.

"It won't always be this awful," Rutgar reassured him, returning to his own pallet. "Too bad in a way. If the horror of wars stayed with us, maybe we'd stop having them."

"Maybe," Rael agreed. And lay for a long time listening to the quiet breathing from across the tent.

So ended the Ardhan army's first day in the valley.

He had flung himself off his horse when his Half went down, not knowing he was already too late to help, and now he was trapped. The Elite were the best and he had no doubt that one man at a time he could cut his way back to the Ardhan lines. But the enemy didn't face him one man at a time, or even two or three, there were a dozen at least. And he was surrounded. Through the bars of his visor he saw the last of his comrades break free of the battle and ride up the slope of the valley. He raised his sword in a fast salute and prepared to die.

"Commander! Nicoli is . . ."

"I see him." The muscles in Rael's legs trembled as he forced them away from his horse's sides, forced them away from giving the order that would send the Elite charging down to rescue their fallen comrade.

"Commander, we can . . ."

"No." And although he didn't have to explain, he continued. "We couldn't reach him in time. And I will not risk more lives to save a corpse. They'd know where we're heading and be waiting for us." A murmur ran down the line as his words were passed and a mutter ran back. Rael felt their eyes on him, but he sat straight in his saddle, clenched his jaw, and kept his gaze on Nicoli as he fell.

That night, after the day's slaughter had ended, Rael sat in the dark on his pallet seeing again the two broken suits of armor that had been retrieved from the battlefield with the other bodies. Nicoli's lips had been drawn back in a snarl. His Half had merely looked surprised.

He froze when Rutgar entered the tent and protested

weakly when the armsman lit the lantern hanging from the center pole.

Rutgar made no mention of the tear tracks that marked the prince's face or of what had happened that afternoon. He merely folded long legs, sat down beside his commander, and wordlessly held out the wineskin he carried.

Rael looked at it for a moment, as if unsure of what it was or what he was to do with it, then he took it, tilted back his head and filled his mouth.

His tongue curled up, his throat spasmed, and he barely prevented himself from spraying the mouthful of wine across the tent.

"What is this stuff?" he demanded, coughing and choking.

Rutgar rescued the wineskin and took a long pull. "It's what the men drink. A little rough for the royal palate perhaps, but . . ." He offered it again.

Rael took it, shrugged, and drank; this time managing to relax his throat enough to swallow. He drank again, then returned it. "You may end up protecting my back from my own men," he said at last, staring into the flickering lamplight and rubbing his palms across his cheeks.

"They're soldiers. Any one of them would've made the same decision."

The wineskin made another pass.

"But they didn't make it. I did."

"You're the commander. It was your decision to make."

Rael reached for the wineskin. "Yes."

"They understand that."

"But they would've preferred a rescue."

"Yes."

Rael drank again. "Mother-creator, but this stuff is awful."

"It is," Rutgar agreed. "But it does what it has to."

And they drank in silence until it was gone.

So ended the Ardhan army's second day in the valley.

"Commander, over there!"

"I see them."

The Elite had gained the valley's edge but had left a Pair behind in the battle. As one man, they turned their gaze on Rael. The day before, a Pair had died.

This day Rael looked and smiled. "One squad," he called to the First beside him, pulled his stallion's head around and charged back down the path he'd just cut. This Pair was close enough and one was still mounted; this Pair, he could save. At the edge of his vision he saw the armored head of Rutgar's bay and close behind he heard the thunder of a dozen heavy horses.

The Melacian position, barely recovered from the last pass, crumbled before them.

Rael rammed the point of his lance through an enemy visor, rode it free and reached the lost Pair. The downed man, Payter, was pinned beneath his horse. There was only one way to get him out. Rael kicked his feet clear of the stirrups and dropped to the ground.

Rutgar and Payter's Half stayed close while the squad began to circle their position, forming a living barricade against the Melacians.

The pike that had killed Payter's horse still stuck from its chest. It had reared and come down on the point, driving it deep into its own heart, then it had dropped like a stone, giving its rider no time to get free. His legs were trapped beneath the double weight of horse and armor.

"Leave me, Commander," he gasped, "and take my idiot Half with you. You can't free me."

Rael's brows rose and Hale would've recognized the tone as he said, "Oh? Can't I?" He squatted, shoved his hands beneath the horse, and lifted. His gauntlets slid free. The weight he'd intended to throw under the horse shifted, and he sat suddenly, nearly doing more damage to Payter in the process. Cursing under his breath, he yanked off the offending gloves and shoved them under Payter's unresisting hands. This couldn't take too long or the Melacian archers would begin to make their presence felt. He squatted again and gripped the still warm body under shoulder and haunch. Then he stiffened his back and straightened his legs.

Slowly the horse lifted a foot, then two feet off the ground.

"Can you get out?" Rael grunted, his knees braced under the saddle.

"Uh . . . yes, Commander . . ."

"Then do it, damnit!"

"Yes, Commander!" The man crabbed backward on hands and elbows.

When Payter's feet came clear, Rael stepped back and the horse crashed to the ground. He grabbed his gauntlets, grabbed the man by the shoulders, and flung him up and over the pommel of his Half's saddle, hoping his armor would cushion the blow. Using the dead horse as a mounting block, and completely disregarding the weight of his own armor—although something in his muscles said he'd pay for all this later, mythic parentage or not—Rael launched himself into his own saddle, set his lance, and screamed: "Back!"

The circling Elite formed a wedge, pointed their heads toward the rest of the company, and began the fight back. Rael and Rutgar bracketed the rescued Pair and readied to move out.

I've done it! Rael crowed. He beat away a spear that came a bit too close. *Nothing can stop us now!*

Suddenly Rutgar threw up his shield and an arrow ricocheted off the rim. "Cover!"

One of the Melacian longbowmen had found a bit of unoccupied high ground. He stood, safely out of range of return fire, but close enough to Rael and his men to be able to choose his targets with care.

From a standing start it would take a moment or two to fight their way clear and get moving. During that moment they might as well have targets painted over their hearts.

"Why, you . . ." Rael's jaw went out and his eyes blazed behind his visor. In a single fluid motion, he stood in his stirrups, twisted, and flung his lance at the bowman.

It seemed that both armies watched it fly, and watched it land, point buried a foot in the earth and the Melacian bowman hanging off the end.

The squad was virtually unopposed as they rode back to join their company.

Doan met Rael at the top of the hill. "You seem to have taken the heart out of them, Commmander."

Rael turned to look and, sure enough, the Melacians were leaving the field, forming shield lines and retreating with the Ardhan army harrowing them every foot of the way.

"A bit showy." Although Doan's tone was dry, he couldn't stop his lips from twitching back into a smirk. "But definitely effective."

So ended the Ardhan army's third day in the valley.

"It took them a while," Doan nudged the prince and pointed, "but they've finally learned. They've moved their pikemen out of squares and down both sides of the valley. We try to charge into that and we'll skewer ourselves."

Rael raised a hand to shade his eyes and Rutgar, who was forcing a new strap through a buckle, growled low in his throat. "If you don't mind, Commander . . ."

"Sorry." Rael lowered his arm and squinted instead. "I guess we'll just have to try something else."

Doan and the armsman exchanged questioning glances.

"It looks as though we've made them nervous," the prince continued. "They seem to be placing a barricade of pikemen between their bowmen and the Ardhan lancers."

"They are." Doan's eyes were as good as Rael's and he could shade them against the early morning sun.

"The trouble is, the Melacians aren't in possession

of a rather important piece of information." Rael turned to face his companions.

"And that is?" Rutgar sighed, pulling Rael back into position by the recalcitrant strap.

"The Ardhan lancers are bowmen as well." The commander of the Elite looked down at his captain. "The strength of the Elite lies in flexibility."

Doan's jaw dropped. He recognized his own words to Rael on the day the prince took command. He stared at the Melacian lines, then said: "We ride at them in ranks of three, fire, wheel, and repeat. Between the dust and the ranks of pikemen blocking their sight, they'll never hit a moving target."

"And they'll never expect it," Rutgar added. "As far as they know . . ."

". . . we have no mounted archers," Doan finished. "And when we break the line, Hale's horsemen can lead the foot soldiers through. It just might work."

"Might?" Rael grinned in a way that made him look very much like his father. "Of course it'll work. Captain, inform the Firsts. Have the Elite form up in three ranks. Today, we're archers."

Doan's salute was faultless. "Very good, Commander." He spun on his heel and marched off to pass the commander's orders to the officers of the Elite.

Rael turned back to stare at the distant line of the enemy. "Well?" he asked Rutgar. "What do you think?"

"I think," muttered his armsman, finally cinching tight the buckle. "That you're getting a bit cocky." He looked up and smiled. "Commander."

The commander grinned and slammed an elbow into his armsman's side with a sound of clashing kettle drums. "You're just jealous. I tell you, it'll work."

It worked.

At the end of the fourth day, the Ardhan army still held the valley.

The fifth day, by throwing lives in a seemingly endless parade onto the Ardhan weapons, by making a path on their dead and dying, by washing away the Ardhan barricades with a river of blood, the Melacian army left the valley and moved the war onto the Tage Plateau.

Four

Deep in the shadow of the mountains, the armies of Ardhan and Melac slept, but eastward, in the camp that attended Melac's king, it was dawn.

"Still four bloody hours from the front!" The cavalry officer dropped the hoof she'd picked up and straightened with a groan. "Shopkeepers and peasants are moving up into battle and here we stick, guarding the rear."

"Guarding the king," her companion reminded her with a jut of his chin toward the starburst pennant hanging limply from the center pole of the largest pavilion. His raised eyebrow reminded her that although the nearest of the King's Guard appeared to be out of earshot, things didn't necessarily work that way anymore.

She grimaced but dropped her voice. "We could serve the king better by fighting."

"We serve the king best by doing as we're told."

"Right." She peered over her horse's withers and added: "They're moving out the troops."

Across the camp, a double line of foot soldiers began the march that would take them to the battlefield.

"You know, I've never seen conscripts so willing to meet Lord Death."

"Lord Death is preferable to what they'll meet if they stay behind."

And both pairs of eyes turned again to the largest pavilion.

"Still, they're only peasants."

He grunted in agreement and raised a hand to block the sun. "Isn't that Lord Elan?"

Even at that distance the lord's stocky figure was unmistakable as he entered the tent.

"Maybe he's going to plead our cause with the king."

"Right."

The looks exchanged said very clearly that both knew it was not, nor had it been for some time, the king who was in charge.

"Still," she bent to lift another hoof, "after losing three wars in as many years, I'd follow Chaos himself if it meant we could win one."

"We have taken the valley, Sire, and the battle has moved to the open area beyond."

"Good." The reply came not from the king, but from the man who sat by his side. Red-gold curls fell in silken coils about his face as he inclined his head and repeated the words to the wasted body that slumped on the throne.

Slowly, his movements a series of tiny jerks, the King of Melac raised his head. Eyes, sunk deep over axe-blade cheekbones, opened. "Good," he echoed, then fell silent once again.

The king's counselor looked regally down at the kneeling lord. "Was that all?"

"Sire," the elderly man came as close to turning his back on the counselor as was safe, "you must send the cavalry on ahead."

The king ignored him. The king's counselor did not.

"Must send the cavalry? Do you dictate to your sovereign? Would you leave him unprotected?"

"Sire, you are still on the Melacian side of the border. Still four hours' hard ride from the battle. Your Guard can protect you. Without the cavalry, every foot the army advances is piled high with the bodies of the dead."

"If the cavalry consists of such doughty fighters,

able to turn the battle by their mere presence, should they not remain here to guard against assassination?'' Slender hands spread, the tracery of gold hair on their backs glittering in the torchlight. ''Or do you mean to deny His Majesty protection by the best?''

''Sire, I don't . . .''

''Or perhaps you don't feel His Majesty is worth protecting?''

''Sire, of course I . . .''

''Then why do you deny him the cavalry?''

''Sire, I can only repeat that without the cavalry on the field, we cannot win.''

''But we are winning, are we not?''

''Are we?'' the lord snapped, turning at last to glare at the man beside his king. ''We gain the ground, but is it winning when three out of every five men we send into the field die?''

Red-gold brows rose. ''But what better death is there, than to die for your king? There will always be more men and they go willingly to fight.''

''Willingly? They're driven!''

''Really? By what?''

''You know very well by what, you . . .''

''Are you about to criticize me, Lord Elan?'' His voice was as soft as the velvet that fell in sapphire folds from his shoulders, and rather more deadly than the dagger that hung at his waist.

For an instant, for just an instant, Lord Elan's jaw went out and the hatred that bubbled and seethed below the surface showed on his face. For an instant. Then the flesh sagged, the gray returned, and his eyes dropped. ''No,'' he whispered.

''No, what?''

The hand that rested on Lord Elan's knee quivered. ''No, milord.''

The counselor smiled. Lord Elan could always be counted on for a few moments of amusing bravado. That was why he still lived. The cavalry *was* needed at the front, but there was no need to rush, not when the delay kept the old lord so frustrated and entertaining. In the meantime, what difference did it make if a few more peasants died. "The cavalry stays here . . ." He paused and his smile grew mocking. ". . . to protect the king."

As though animated by the sound of his title, the king suddenly pulled himself erect, satin robes rustling like dead leaves. He leaned forward, pinning Lord Elan with his fevered gaze. "How many?"

"Sire?"

Bony fingers crabbed along the broad wooden arms of the throne. "How many have died?"

Hope flared in the old lord's face and he leaned forward as well. If the king could be made to care . . . "Hundreds, Sire, thousands even."

"Thousands . . ." He sank back into the cushions, his expression almost beatific. "Thousands. And they all died for me."

"All for you," the king's counselor agreed, and only Lord Elan heard the laughter in his voice.

"There are just too damned many of them!" Rutgar pulled off his helm and slicked back his dripping hair. "They've no need to kill us, we'll die of exhaustion killing them."

Rael snorted and dropped down beside his armsman on the felled tree that served as bench, table, and occasionally surgery. "At least it's over for today." He dropped his own helm and began to worry at the straps of his greaves. After a moment, Rutgar slapped away his hands and began to work at them himself.

"They'll jam if you twist them like that," he muttered, "and I'll be the one who replaces the straps if we have to cut you free."

"Highness."

Rael looked up and managed a weary smile. "My Lord Belkar."

"I thought I should warn you that as prince and heir, you'll be taking the council tonight."

"I'll what?" Rael pulled his leg from Rutgar's grasp and stood. "Has something happened to Father?"

"Your father," Belkar paused, and his voice became decidedly acerbic, "the king, has ridden out with a patrol to prevent us being flanked by the enemy."

"Father has?"

"Yes."

"But that's crazy."

"So I told him, Highness."

"The king can't just go riding off with patrols in the dead of night! Did he take his Guard?"

"I believe some members of his Guard rode with the patrol, yes."

"What if he gets killed out there, miles from anywhere?"

"I asked him that question myself."

"And he said?"

"He was tired of strategy and tactics."

"That's it?"

Belkar's lips twitched. "Except for some personal and unsavory comments about nursemaiding directed at myself, yes, that was it."

"Oh, that's just great." Rael stepped past Belkar. Stopped. Returned. And threw himself back down on the tree. He had a sudden vision of what his father's reaction would be if he took the Elite out after him. "Just great," he repeated and thrust his leg back into Rutgar's reach.

Now this is more like it, Raen thought, lips pulled back from his teeth, his eyes shining beneath his plain iron helm. He lifted his sword and flicked the point left. The nearest member of the patrol, a shadow against the broken shadows of the forest, nodded and passed it on, then the line moved forward.

They could hear the Melacians coming toward them—had been able to hear them for some time.

Ten, maybe twenty yards and we'll be right on top of them. Raen ducked under a low branch and hoped his men were not advancing with the same amount of noise as the Melacians.

The Ardhan line advanced, three feet, four, then a

bellow of astonishment filled the night, closely followed by the clash of steel on steel. While the Melacians dealt with the idea of an enemy patrol where no patrol should be, the Ardhans overcame their own surprise and attacked.

How in Chaos did they get so close! Raen blocked a spear with his shield, slashed low to take another man in the knees and dodged a blow that would have removed his head had it connected. He slid around a tree, taking an instant to ram his shield edge into the downed man's throat, and bellowed the Ardhan warcry. The rest of the Ardhan patrol picked it up and the woods rang. Dark adapted eyes could tell friend from foe, armor differed enough that the silhouettes were unmistakable, but there was no sense taking chances. Besides, the King of Ardhan preferred a noisy fight.

So I'm old. Raen grinned as a Melacian fell, screaming at his feet. *But I haven't lost it yet.*

The flash of blue light at his gut attracted his attention seconds before the pain hit. He glanced down to see a spear point, glowing eerily sapphire, pressed up against his breastplate just under his navel. Time slowed as the point, and the light, poked through the steel plate and into his belly. He grunted, the pain so intense it closed his throat, preventing a scream, and his sword dropped from spasming fingers.

The head of the spearman hit the ground beside his sword, still wearing the astonished expression with which it had greeted the blue light.

"Sire!"

As the spear was snatched away the pain lessened, becoming more a normal agony. His back braced against a tree, Raen managed to stay standing and find his voice. He tried to sound reassuring, but the words came out a powerless husking whisper. "Not as bad as it looks." His probing fingers discovered this was the truth. His breastplate was holed but the wound beneath it was through skin and muscle only, nothing vital. He dragged his cloak forward, ripped off a strip a handspan wide and shoved the ball of fabric up under his armor.

"Sire, your breastplate . . ."

"Was obviously badly forged." He bent and retrieved his sword, teeth gritted against the wave of dizziness. "Well, come on." He forced his treacherous voice closer to normality. "There're more of them out here."

"But Sire . . ."

Raen's eyes did not glow with the power of other worlds, as did his son's, but the worldly power they held was quite sufficient.

"Yes, Sire. I'll re-form the patrol."

The surgeon stepped from the king's tent, wiping her hands on a towel.

"His Majesty," she said to Rael and the Duke of Belkar, "is not a young man."

Rael winced.

"He is also," she continued, "an idiot. Had he returned directly to camp when this happened, he would have been up and bashing heads this morning. As it is, he's going to spend a good long time in bed."

"He's not going to like that," Rael pointed out.

The surgeon glared at the prince. "Too bad," she said, and pushed past him back to the infirmary.

Belkar and Rael watched her go, her back ramrod straight and uncompromising.

The duke shook his head, managing to be both admiring and irritated at the same time. "She'll fight Lord Death every foot of the way and if he wins, she'll spit in his face. I almost pity him." He draped his arm around Rael's shoulders and pushed him toward the tent. "Don't worry, lad, Glinna's the best surgeon with the army. If your father was in any immediate danger, she never would've left him."

"But his breastplate . . ."

"Flawed. And it still absorbed most of the blow. You might be able to pop a spear through unflawed steel like it was paper, but that's beyond the rest of us poor mortals.'' His tone was light and reassuring, but he carefully kept Rael from seeing his face. There had been nothing wrong with the breastplate except for the hole punched through it . . . as though the steel had been paper.

Rain during the first three days on the Tage Plateau kept fighting intermittent and casualties light. The fourth day the sun shone and the killing began again. The strength of the Elite fell from fifty-five to forty men. The Duke of Cei lost half his Guard but the remainder held. The Duke of Belkar lost twenty archers when their position was overrun. The Duke of Hale lost his life.

''Then who is Hale now?'' Rutgar asked, his fingers digging the tension out of the prince's shoulders.

Rael rolled a blue glass bead between his thumb and forefinger. He'd found it near where Hale had fallen. He couldn't imagine the duke with an unbeaded mustache. He couldn't imagine the duke dead. ''The eldest son, just ten this summer. I think his name was Etgar.''

''Was Etgar?''

''It's Hale now.''

The Melacians died by the hundreds, but more continued to come through the pass.

''Father, are you sure you should be out of bed?''

Raen glared at his son. ''I'll not lie in bed, while my people die.''

''It won't help them if you die as well.''

The king put his foot in the stirrup and pulled himself up into the saddle. ''I have no intention of dying,'' he growled and turned his warhorse toward the battle.

At the end of the day, the edge of the king's surcoat was stained with blood and he had to be lifted down from his horse.

''I'm fine,'' he protested as two of the Palace Guard placed him gently on a litter. ''I'm just a little stiff.''

"Father!" Rael pushed through the gathered crowd and flung himself to his knees, desperately catching up his father's hand in his.

"I'm fine," the king insisted. He managed a weak smile, but his face was gray and slick with sweat.

Rael looked up at Belkar, his whole body begging the duke to say it would be all right. Belkar shrugged.

"The king is down," ran the whisper through the ranks. "The king is dying." Weapons, tools, meals, lay forgotten as the army fell silent and waited for news.

"Get out of my way." Glinna's voice, impatient and commanding, pushed apart the silence and split the circle surrounding the litter. The surgeon strode through the break and glared down at the king. Her mouth pursed and her eyebrows lowered. "I told you so," was all she said, but there were several lectures worth of meaning in the words.

A wave of near hysterical giggles rippled outward. The king would live. No one used that tone on a dying man.

Glinna looked up at the sound. "Don't you lot have something to do?" The crowd melted away and she shifted her gaze to stare pointedly at the prince. He stared back, the green of his eyes growing both deeper and brighter. She raised one eyebrow. "Very pretty, Highness. Now get up off your knees so we can move your father inside."

Rael sighed as he scrambled out of the way. *It's not fair,* he thought. *When I want people to be impressed, they never are.*

As the litter moved away, Glinna slipped her hand under the bloody surcoat.

"Madam!" Raen gasped, his eyes wide, pain mixed equally with surprise. "Try to remember, I am your king."

"And if you want to remain my king," the surgeon told him dryly, lifting the tent flap and standing aside to allow the litter to pass, "or anyone else's king, for that matter, you'll do as I say.'' The flap fell behind them.

"She's got a terrific way with her patients," Rael muttered and started back to where he'd left Rutgar holding his horse.

The Duke of Belkar fell into step beside him. "Think of it as an incentive to stay in one piece, Highness."

"What do you mean?"

Belkar's voice quivered on the edge of laughter. "If you're injured, she'll be taking care of you as well."

Rael shuddered.

The sun rose high over the mountains, turning arms and armor to a burnished gold, but the Melacians remained in their camp at the valley's edge. Rael, Doan, and the remaining dukes gathered on the highest bit of ground they held; little more than a hillock but enough to give them a clear line of sight. Not that it did them much good.

"Even I can see they're still in camp, Prince Rael." Cei blew his nose vigorously. "What we need to know is why."

Rael squinted, trying to bring the tiny figures of the enemy closer by force of will. Finally he shook his head and gave up. "Something's upset them, they're scurrying around like headless chickens. The only thing I can say for certain is that, for now, they show no interest in us."

"Then we attack. Ride in and grind the scum into the mountain."

With the Duke of Hale's death, and the heir only a child, command of his forces had gone to Allonger, the senior of his two captains, a vicious fighter, a man of quick and explosive temper, who was also the dead duke's uncle. Most of his conversation since he took command had centered on revenge.

"Too risky," Doan grunted. "They hold the high ground. It's got to be a trap."

"Then we wait?" Aliston's heir suggested.

"We wait," Rael agreed. Allonger opened his mouth to speak but snapped it shut again as the prince continued. "It's a pity we can't get scouts close enough to nose out what's going on, but there's no cover and I'd never order a man to commit that kind of suicide."

Belkar hid a snicker behind a cough. Doan became very interested in the space between his horse's ears. Cei and Aliston's heir, safely out of line of sight, exchanged amused glances. Rael looked steadily at Hale's captain.

Allonger glared at the prince, well aware he'd been neatly outmaneuvered. A very long moment passed in silence. "Oh, all right," he said at last. His voice was gruff, but the edges of his mustache trembled as he tried not to smile. "We wait." He inclined his head, adding respectfully and without a trace of sarcasm, "Your Highness."

They waited all that day, thanking the Mother-creator for the rest, and wondering what kept the Melacian army in camp. Not until the sun began to set did they find out.

"Highness!" The Messenger darted into Rael's tent, glanced quickly around and headed for the inner room.

Ivan snagged her sleeve and dragged her to a stop. "And just where do you think you're going, young woman? You can't just run in here like you owned the place, this is . . ."

"Let her go, Ivan." Rael ducked through the inner flap and smiled down at the Messenger, who twitched her sleeve free and ducked her head in a shallow bow.

"It's the Dukes Riven and Lorn, Highness. They're in the command tent. Milord Belkar asks you to attend them at once."

Lorn was not in the command tent when Rael reached it moments later, but Riven sat, head buried in his hands, at the center of a milling crowd of the dukes and their captains. Voices were hushed and shoulders tense and every eye on Riven.

"They blocked the pass, Commander; Riven, Lorn, and their men." Doan fell in at the prince's side as he crossed the tent. "They drove wooden wedges into cracks in the rock then poured water over them until they swelled and slid a couple of tons of rock into a canyon just the other side of the border." His voice was frankly admiring. "Couldn't have done it better if they'd had a company of dwarves."

"Most of the men in these parts are miners, they know what they're doing. Where's Lorn?"

Doan paused before answering, weighing the words to use. "They took him to the infirmary," he said at last, his tone carefully neutral.

Just then Riven looked up. His dark hair hung in a tangled mass down his back, his face was pale and streaked with dirt, his nails were broken and his fingers were scraped raw. Blood stained his hands and clothes; much more blood than his own wounds could account for.

"He wanted to die, but I brought him back. I couldn't leave him out there." His throat convulsed and the sound that emerged quavered halfway between a choke and a sob.

Belkar, who stood close by Riven's side, looked up and shook his head at Rael's silent question. "I don't know, lad, that's all he'll say."

Rael dropped to the bench, took a goblet of wine from a hovering servant, and shoved it into the Duke of Riven's hands. "Drink," he commanded.

Riven sipped, coughed, then drained the goblet.

"Now, tell me," Rael prodded gently. "What happened?"

Once, twice, Riven opened his mouth but no sound came out. The third time the words spilled free. "I, I was on the other side of the canyon. They said, his men said, one of his captains was standing too close to the edge when the rock began to fall. He tried to save him. They both went over." Riven's eyes went dark with memories and tears began to cut new channels through the dirt. "I got to him as fast as I could. He wanted me to kill him."

Startled, Rael looked up at Belkar.

"His legs were crushed," the duke said softly.

"I couldn't kill him." Riven turned to Rael for support. "I couldn't. I dug him out. I brought him back."

Rael had no idea of what to say or what to do. He reached out a tentative hand and touched the grieving man lightly on the shoulder.

Riven drew a shuddering breath. "I couldn't kill him." Then he threw himself to the floor and began to smash his fists into the canvas leaving scarlet smears, his blood and Lorn's mixed together.

"He carried Lorn every step of the way himself," Doan said later as he stood with Rael looking toward the enemy camp. "The men with them say that he wouldn't let anyone help. And during every lucid moment, Lorn begged Riven to kill him. When begging didn't work, he tried curses."

"Will he live?"

"Probably. But he'll never walk again. Myself, I'm more worried about young Riven."

Rael remembered Seven Day Festivals, when the boys who'd grown up to be Riven and Lorn had come to the palace with their families. They were only five years older than the prince. He'd watched them running and playing and fighting as a single unit. He'd envied them their closeness.

Doan shoved his hands deep behind his belt. "It won't mean much to them now, but the two of them have ended the war. With supply lines cut, no cavalry, no new troops, and no line to their king, the Melacians will have to surrender. It's the only logical thing to do."

Rael pushed away visions of falling rock and two boys who would never run together again, and brought himself back to the present. "How did the King of Melac think he could command from four hours behind the lines?"

"He may have sent up the occasional order," Doan grunted, "but the real commanders are out there on the field."

Over the Melacian camp a cold blue light suddenly flickered and then darkness claimed the night again.

"Sheet-lightning?" Rael wondered aloud.

"Maybe."

Just for a moment the captain's eyes flared brilliantly red. Rael blinked and the moment was gone. He had the feeling Doan knew more than he was willing to tell, but after one glance at the rigid set of his jaw, Rael decided not to ask. Now that the war was over, there would be plenty of time for questions.

In the morning, the Melacian's expected surrender turned into an all-out attack.

"This is crazy!" Rutgar yelled, tossing aside the splintered remains of his lance and drawing his sword. "They can't possibly hope to win."

"Don't tell me!" Rael bellowed back, in the breathing space they'd cut for themselves. "Tell them!"

Rutgar stood in his stirrups. "You guys are crazy! You can't possibly hope to win!"

Rael laughed and bashed his armsman lightly on the shield. "Feel better?"

Behind his visor, Rutgar's teeth gleamed and he laughed as well. "Yeah, I do!"

When the Elite charged, crashing through the screaming chaos the enemy pikeline had become, the Melacians swarmed about them, rats turning on the terrier. The horses' legs were soon red to the hocks. Weapons dripped and armor ran with gore.

"I don't believe this," Rael muttered as the press of bodies, the dead, the dying, and the living behind them, slowed the charge and forced the Pairs apart. He roared the retreat, ripping his throat raw with the sound. All around, he heard the call repeated. And then he heard the scream. Behind him.

He twisted in his saddle.

Rutgar.

His shield arm hung limp and blood ran down the armor, pouring from his fingers in a ruby stream. His sword wove dizzying patterns of steel, trying to protect his wounded side, but he was tiring, and there were too many attacking.

"No!" Practically lifting the animal onto its hindquarters, Rael yanked his horse around, cutting and chopping like a madman the entire time. The Melacians surrounding him began to fall back. If they were crazy, he was crazier. If they welcomed Lord Death, he'd happily send them Death's way. But Rutgar was not going to die.

Three horse lengths apart.

Rutgar faltered. A sword drove through the seam between breast and back.

Two.

Hands stretched up to pull the swaying armsman down from the saddle.

Too far away to help, Rael saw the terror on Rutgar's face; saw Rutgar's hand reach and close on nothing; heard, as though there wasn't another sound on the battlefield, Rutgar call his name.

It was Doan who kept him from vaulting out of his saddle, Doan who steered him back to the Ardhan lines when he would have ridden into the heart of the Melacian army and tried to cut it out, and it was Doan who held him while he wept.

Later, in the command tent, he glared out at the assembled men and said, "Enough."

"Granted," Cei agreed. "But what can we do?"

"We take out their commanders, tonight."

"Tonight?"

The raw emotion on Rael's face choked off the babble of questions before it truly began. "Doan."

The captain of the Elite stepped forward.

"The Elite will follow where you lead, commander."

"Will you follow him into Lord Death's embrace?" Cei sniffed. "Because without a moon, that's right where you'll be going."

Although Cei stood almost two feet taller, Doan managed to look down on him as he repeated, "The Elite will follow where he leads."

"Cei's right," Belkar said gently. "Without a moon, that valley will be pitch black."

"Then they won't expect an attack. The lack of a moon can work to our advantage as well, giving us cover and a better chance of success." Rael ground out the words, the lack of expression in stark contrast to the pain that twisted his face.

Belkar sighed. He wished, not for the first time, Glinna had allowed Raen to attend. A king and father could command where others could only advise. "I want to end this as much as you do, Highness, believe me, but men cannot see in darkness."

"If the Elite will follow," Rael lifted his head and green fires blazed in his eyes, "then darkness will not stop us."

Five

It was raining the next morning when Rael came to his father's tent. He stood for a moment and stared blindly at the wet canvas, letting the water cut channels into the red-brown mud that caked his armor. The lines etched into the pale skin about his mouth and the purple bruises beneath his eyes, eyes in which the green fires had all but died, bore eloquent testimony to the night's work. He had never looked less like his mother.

The Guard before the entrance saluted and stood aside but Glinna, standing guard within the canvas walls, could not be so easily passed. She folded her arms on her chest and blocked the way.

"The king finally sleeps. Anything you have to say can wait."

"I have news of the war."

"No doubt," she said dryly. "But I don't care if the war is over, you may not wake him."

"The war is over."

Her eyes widened. She looked down at the dried blood that stained his sword hilt, so thick in places that it filled the hollows in the ornate scrollwork, then she stepped aside.

"Don't allow him to become excited," she cautioned as Rael passed. "If he opens the wound again. . ." Her words trailed off, but the meaning was clear.

When Raen had left his bed and reopened the

wound, it had infected, swelling and putrefying. From a serious, although hardly fatal injury, it had grown to be dangerously life threatening. Glinna, however, refused to admit defeat, draining, cleaning, cauterizing, and pouring potion after potion down the king's throat. Three times she forced Lord Death away, and in the end she won; the king lived. But under the scented smoke that eddied around the inner room, the smell of rot remained.

"Less than a week," thought Rael, looking down at his father, "how could he change so much in less than a week?"

As the war had aged Rael, the wound had aged Raen. Flesh hung from his bones as if it belonged to another man, and the lines of his face were now furrows. Not even the most loving son could deny that the king had grown old.

Rael dashed a tear away with an impatient hand. *You will not mourn him while he still lives,* he told himself fiercely. *He needs you to be strong.* He dragged a chair over to the bed and perched on its edge. "Father?" Reaching out a slender hand, he placed it gently on the sleeping man's chest. The steady rise and fall seemed to reassure him. He sat quietly for a moment then called again.

With a sound that was half question, half moan, the king woke, blinked, and focused slowly on Rael's face.

"Father, the war is over."

"You have the battle commanders." It wasn't a question. Late in the night, Belkar had told him what Rael planned to do, indeed, was doing, for the prince had ordered the duke not to speak until he and the Elite were well on their way. "You did the right thing. The only thing. I wouldn't have stopped you." The boy had needed an outlet for his grief. The war had needed to be ended. That both had been accomplished at once, and with a plan only the prince commander himself could carry out would further consolidate said commander's position with the army. That said commander was his son, and the plan placed him in mortal danger had given Raen a sleepless night. "Did they surrender?"

"Not quite." Rael leaned forward and propped a pillow behind his father's head. "We torched their camp, destroyed half their army, and still had to knock a tent down on the commanders to get them to quit."

"Prisoners."

"Besides the seven commanders, about eight hundred; at least half of them wounded."

Raen brought up a skeletal hand to stroke his beard. "Hmmm, not many." His eyes unfocused as he considered the best course of action. "The men are rabble without the leaders. Strip them of their arms and have them taken back across the border."

"But, Father, the pass is blocked."

"Oh," Raen looked momentarily confused. Had he known that? Memories of the last few days were soft edged and smoke-filled; he remembered pain clearly but not much else.

"And they don't want to go back."

"Are you sure."

"Very sure." Rael shrugged wearily. "But I don't know why."

"Well, I've a pretty good idea," Raen snorted, suddenly more energetic as he came across something he thought he understood. "They lost. Melac and that idiot who advises him aren't likely to be very welcoming."

"Father, about that counselor. . ."

"An ambitious upstart," the king dismissed their unknown enemy with a choppy wave of his hand. "I'm not surprised someone like him showed up to grab power. Melac was always weak. We'll keep the border guarded and have nothing more to do with either of them."

Rael was not convinced. From things he'd overheard in the last few hours, he suspected Melac's counselor would remain a threat. But that was for the future to deal with, here and now he had other worries. "So what do we do with the prisoners?"

"Divide them up and scatter them amongst the dukes." The crease between the king's eyes deepened as he remembered the mass graves that held the flower of Ardhan's youth. "We'll all be a little shorthanded for a while. I'm sure they can find ways to put them to use. If they truly don't want to go home, they can begin to work off the lives they owe us."

"And the battle commander and his officers?"

The king sighed. "Well, they *can't* go home. Melac can always get more spear-carriers and crow-fodder, but returning his officers would be asking to do this all over again. Have them take the standard oath about laying down arms and ever after cleaving to the soil of the land they invaded."

"They won't." Rael sighed as well, and rubbed a grimy hand across the bridge of his nose. "They say they've taken blood oaths to fight for Melac and the Empire until death."

"Empire!" Raen snarled and tried to sit up. "What Empire?"

Rael pushed him gently back. "The one we were supposed to be the first part of. They're fanatics, Father. When we took away their weapons they attacked with bare hands. We practically had to bury them in chains before they stopped. They fought like men possessed." He paused and his eyes narrowed in memory. "Or men in mortal terror."

"They'll have to die."

"Father!"

"How many men did you kill last night?" Raen asked gently.

"I told you, we torched the camp. It's likely hundreds died."

Raen held his son's eyes with his own. "No. How many did you kill? Yourself?"

Rael yanked his gaze away and stared at the carpet. "I don't know. Eighteen. Twenty maybe. I lost count."

"And Rutgar's still dead."

The terror; the reaching hand; his name screamed.

"Yes."

"It didn't bring him back, so the killing is over."

Rael lifted his head and green embers stirred. He'd fought last night blinded by anger and pain and with every life he sent to Lord Death the anger bled away until there was only the pain. "Yes," he said. "There's been enough."

"Unless those seven die, the war isn't over and we've won nothing. Rutgar died for nothing. The men you killed last night died for nothing." Raen lifted a hand and touched his son's arm. "A king has no conscience, lad, he gives it to his people."

"That's garbage, Father, and you know it. The people do what you say."

Raen let his hand fall back onto the blanket. "Then do as I say, Rael, and carry out my command."

Rael searched the stern, closed face on the pillow for his father but saw only the king. He stood so quickly his chair tipped and fell and he almost kicked it out of the way as he spun and headed for the door.

"Rael."

He paused but didn't turn.

"Last night you let your anger define the thin line between justice and murder; a king never has that luxury."

"A lesson, Father?"

"If you wish, and here's another. You'd rather I gave this task to one of the dukes, but the king must be willing to carry out the king's justice. As I am not able, you must stand in for me."

"I don't think I'm ready to be king."

Raen's teeth flashed white amid the dusky gray of his beard and the lines of his face lifted with the smile. "Good."

Doan was waiting when Rael left the king's tent. The night's work had added a limp and several new scars to the Elite Captain's inelegant appearance. He fell into step beside the younger man.

"You were right," Rael said at last.

Doan kept silent. He appeared to be watching the rain drip off the edge of his helmet.

"We're to divide the men amongst the dukes, but the commander and his captains die. I'm to see that it gets taken care of."

Doan merely pulled his cloak tighter to stop the rain from running down his neck.

Rael's laughter sounded a great deal like choking. "Life would certainly be a lot easier if my father was a woodsman or a farmer."

The captain grunted, there being little he could say to his own words.

"If it must be done, then let's do it now."

"I'll call for volunteers, Commander." As Rael's head jerked around to face him, he added. "You must only be present, Highness. You don't strike the blows yourself. And it's not a job you can command a man to do."

By the time the Guard was formed, the rain had stopped. The sun came out, and seven men died.

And the war was over.

"At least I never enjoyed it, Mother," Rael whispered as the breeze lifted his hair from his forehead and blood soaked into the ground at his feet. "At least I never enjoyed it."

The fire reached the grimy foot of the elderly woman tied to the stake and began to lick daintily at the blistering skin.

" 'Ware the child," she screamed in a mad voice raw with much shrieking. " 'Ware the creation of Lord Death's children."

"Lord Death's children?" Lord Elan half turned, enough so he could see the king's counselor but not so much that he must look at the king. That pain at least he would spare himself. "What does she mean, Lord Death's children?"

The golden-haired man lounged back in his chair and sighed. "The race of Man was created for Lord Death's benefit. Thus Man," he inclined his head toward the stake with chilling courtesy, ''and Woman also, are Death's children.''

''It burns! Brilliance within! Brilliance without!'' And then not even madness was enough to overcome the effects of the flames. The old woman sagged against the ropes and prophesied no more.

The king shifted on his throne, hips rotating with each spasm of the body on the pyre.

''She wasn't very clear,'' Lord Elan grunted.

Full lips molded themselves into a smile. ''She was clear enough earlier and more than willing to repeat the entire prophecy as often as I chose to listen.'' Even the most obscure prophet could be convinced to find clarity and while there was no real need in this instance, the convincing had filled a few otherwise tedious hours.

''Then what does it mean?'' The old lord sounded tired. The greasy smoke stung his eyes and coated his throat. He hated executions, even the most necessary, and had attended this one only because he'd vowed that the king would spend as little time alone with his counselor as possible. Others of the nobility, those who had not died with the army—he saw their faces wide-eyed in the firelight—seemed to be taking their idea of pleasure from what pleasured their liege. He gritted his teeth and glanced quickly at the king.

He was beginning to lose interest now that the body had stopped moving.

The voice of the king's counselor was closer to content than it had been in years. He lifted his face to let the evening breeze cool skin flushed by the heat. ''It means, Lord Elan, that I have something to look forward to.''

''But we're going back to Ardhan.''

''No.''

''But . . .'' Lord Elan jerked as sapphire eyes caught his and held. A thin rope of drool fell from one corner of suddenly slack lips. He jerked again as he was released and would have fallen had he not clung, panting, to the arm of the king's throne.

''I said no,'' the counselor repeated quietly. He stared past the pyre, out over the remains of the army. So clever of him to have kept the cavalry back; they would replace the officers killed and, well, one could always get more peasants. *South and east,* he thought. *I will create an Empire to the south and east, giving Ardhan enough time to fulfill the prophecy.* Glancing down at the smoldering pile of meat and bone, he rubbed long fingers against the silk covering his thighs. ''Well,'' he purred in a voice barely audible over the sizzle and crackle of burning fat, ''almost enough time.''

The army returned triumphant to the city, although the king did not ride proudly at its head but was carried on a litter. Rael, with the Elite behind him, led the army home.

The war quickly became a thing of the past. Men went back to holdings and fields, battle armor was polished and put away, and Rael received a most unexpected welcome home from the Duke of Belkar's blue-eyed daughter—who had supposedly ridden to the palace to meet her father. Rael was pleasantly surprised to find that blue eyes held depths as well as green and that the eyes of mortal women also glowed.

The king did not recover.

Glinna now slept in the room next to the royal bedchambers, when she slept at all. The infection had returned and spread, and now the king's whole lower body strained against its increasingly heated covering of skin. She did what she could but finally, no longer able to deny what training and common sense told her, she admitted defeat.

''His life is now in the hands of Lord Death,'' she told the prince. ''I can do nothing more.''

''My father doesn't believe in Lord Death,'' said Rael bitterly.

''Well, Lord Death believes in him,'' replied the surgeon and left Rael alone with his thoughts and his dying father.

But Lord Death, never predictable, stayed his hand and the king did not die; although he didn't exactly live. Affairs of state were left in the hands of the council and royal decisions increasingly fell to the prince, for the king tired easily and Glinna demanded he rest.

"Why have a council," she snapped, prying dispatches from his hand and shoving them at an embarrassed Belkar, "if you don't use it?"

Raen raged against the weakness that held him to his bed, and the raging left him weaker still, until he was only a shadow of the man he had been.

"I am no longer a man."

"You're more of a man than anyone in the kingdom," Rael told him, his eyes filling with tears he refused to shed.

The king laughed humorlessly and stared down at his wasted body. "That doesn't say much for the other men in the kingdom."

The king was dying and everyone knew it. Already a funereal hush hung over the land. The dukes, down to crippled Lorn and ten-year-old Hale, gathered in the King's City, waiting. Rael went numbly about the task of learning to rule. He knew he should go to the Grove and tell his mother that the mortal man she loved lay dying, but he couldn't. He just couldn't. He told himself that Milthra, being who and what she was, probably already knew. That didn't help very much.

One morning, in the quiet hours just past dawn, some five weeks after the war had ended, the Duke of Belkar came to the king. The two men shared an age, but the man on the bed made the other seem obscenely healthy.

Belkar looked down at his liege and his friend and wondered where to begin. Raen spoke before he got the chance, anger turning the words to edged steel.

"It would have been so much easier had Lord Death collected me on the battlefield. Then those I love would not have had to watch me die by inches. And I would not have had to watch their pain as they watched me."

"Raen, I'm sorry, I . . ."

"No." The word was faint but still very much a king's command. "It is I who should be sorry. You didn't need that on top of everything else. I was feeling sorry for myself and you bore the brunt of it." His face twisted in a skeletal caricature of a smile. "Forgive me?"

Belkar nodded, not trusting his voice, although what he thought to hide when tears ran unheeded down his face, he had no idea.

"So," Raen's voice became as light as he was still capable of making it. "To what do I owe your presence so early in the day?"

More than anything in his life, the duke wanted to follow Raen's lead, to try to banish the darkness for just a little while, but he was desperately afraid there was no time for even that small amount of comfort. "The people talk."

"They always have. Death, taxes, and the people talking, the three things you can count on." Raen shifted into a different but no more comfortable position. "Sit down, Belkar, and tell me what they say."

Belkar sat, spread his hands and stared at their backs. It was easier than meeting the king's eyes. "They're speaking against the prince, saying he isn't human."

"They always knew that; I told them who his mother was when I declared him my heir."

"To most of them, the Lady is something to fear. The Elder Races have never been friendly to man. People fear and distrust her power and they fear and distrust her power in him."

"He proved himself in the war."

"Yes, but the war is over. And . . ." Belkar sighed. ". . . he proved himself different."

"He won the war!"

"He used his mother's power to do it. Half of the talkers see the danger in that alone. The other half wonder why he waited so long to use it and ask what game he played."

Tendons in Raen's neck stood out as he ground his

teeth. "And those titled vultures who circle about my deathbed?"

"The dukes," Belkar reminded him gently, "have the right to see the crown passed." Raen dipped his head a barely perceivable amount, as much of an apology as he was willing to make. Belkar continued: "They worry about his mother as well, and the effect her blood will have on the way he rules."

"They've never worried before."

"He's never been so close to being king before."

Raen squinted up at his oldest friend. "They remember that soldier? The one my son killed?"

Belkar nodded.

"And what do they say about me?" The king's eyes held a dangerous glint.

"They say you don't heal because he bewitched you as his mother did."

"And what do you believe?"

"I," Belkar pointed out, "have met his mother." Once, many years before, the duke had gone with Raen to the Grove. He still held the memory of the hamadryad like a jewel in his heart. Occasionally, he held it up to the light to rejoice in its beauty.

"Then," said the king, "you shall stand with me when I speak to the people."

Belkar shot a startled glance at the surgeon, sure she would not allow such a thing.

Glinna shrugged.

"He is dying. Let it at least be where and how he chooses."

Raen smiled, his first real smile in weeks. "An honest woman, Belkar. Every dying man should have one." And then the smile slipped and his eyes looked into the future. "At least the Elite will stand by him. We've seen to that, he and I."

"They'd follow him into the bedchamber of Lord Death," Belkar agreed. "But would you throw your country into civil war if people decide he is not to have the crown?"

"He is my son and my heir. Five generations ago

my house was chosen to rule. We gave our name to the land. He was trained to rule and there is no one else.''

"If you'd only had more children . . .''

"He would still be eldest and my heir.''

The two men locked eyes. Belkar's gaze dropped first.

"I know. I will support him and do what I can, but the people will make up their own minds.''

"Then I'll just have to convince them. Now," he waved the duke over to his desk, "write me a proclamation and see that the criers get it immediately. I want everyone, from the lowest beggar to all six dukes, in the People's Square by noon." His voice grew quieter and he sank back on his pillows, exhausted. "I must ensure the succession for my son.''

And how can you do that when such little speech as you've had with me nearly kills you, Belkar wondered. But all he said aloud was: "Shall I have the prince sent to you?''

"Not now. Let him have this morning to himself. Send him at noon.''

Noon.

The people gathered in the Square.

Rael entered his father's chamber slowly, his heart so heavy it sat like a lump of coal in his chest. This would be good-bye, he knew it. It took a moment to penetrate his grief, but instead of his father lying wasted on the bed he saw the king being dressed in royal purple. Even the crown, massive and ugly, stood close at hand.

He grabbed Glinna's arm and dragged her out of the milling crowd of servants.

"What's going on? Is he better?''

"No. If anything, he's worse.'' The surgeon's tone made it quite clear that she took the king's condition as a personal affront. "But he insists on speaking to the people.''

"Why?''

"The people say they won't have you as king.''

"I don't care what the people say."

"He does."

Rael studied his father standing supported between two burly footmen as a valet pushed his feet into boots. Raen's skin was gray and his eyes had sunk deep in indigo shadows. The column of his throat stood out in a bas relief of ridges and hollows. "Will he survive it?"

"No."

"And you're just letting him die?!"

"Yes." She held up a hand and stopped Rael's next words. "Before you say anything, consider this: he is still the man he was. Would you have that man die in bed?"

Rael released her arm and shook his head. His father might have no fear of Lord Death, but he would refuse to meet the Mother-creator's true son lying helpless in bed.

"I thought not. Now, go to him. He needs you."

Dressed, the king reached for the crown, but his hands shook so they couldn't grasp it. Rael's hands covered his. Together they lifted it from the table.

"A crown," said Raen as it settled on his brow, "is a heavy burden." He grinned a death's head grin as he struggled to straighten his neck under the weight. "There's more than a little truth in these old cliches."

"Yes, Father."

"I'm going to see that this burden goes to you. Perhaps I'm doing you no favor." He sighed. "A king has no conscience, my son, he gives it to the people."

"I will remember, Father."

Raen snorted. "They're not likely to let you forget."

Attendants moved the king to a litter and carried him through the halls of the palace, Rael keeping pace alongside. Although they tried, it was not always possible to keep the litter even and once, when it jerked on a stair, Raen bit back a pained cry. Choking back a cry of his own, Rael reached out a hand and his father's wasted fingers closed gratefully around it.

Belkar, in the formal, ornate robes of a Duke of Ardhan, stood by the Great Door.

"My liege." He knelt and kissed the shadow of a hand stretched out to him.

"Just help me off this thing," Raen snapped. Friendship could weaken him now as easily as pain and he still had much to do. "I'm not dead yet!"

The king had not stood unassisted since he had been carried off the battlefield for the second time, but when he was on his feet he shook off the supporting hands of his son and his friend.

"This I must do alone," he said through gritted teeth. "Let it begin, Belkar."

Belkar shook his head at the prince's pleading look, a look that said as loudly as if Rael had spoken, *You can't let him do it alone!*, and gave the signal. Trumpets called and the great doors swung open.

The People's Square was full and overflowing with the entire population of King's City and, as commanded, all six dukes. They represented only a small percentage of the population of Ardhan, but they would spread the news and by the end of the week, the whole country would know. And then the people would judge.

Raen did not call up deep reserves of hidden strength so that he walked proudly, shoulders back and head erect to the edge of the dais—he had no reserves to call. He tottered that twenty feet, sweat running and lips snarling against the pain. One foot went in front of the other by strength of will alone.

The people saw what it cost him and began to cheer. First those near the dais and then the noise moved back through the crowd until the walls shook with it and Raen felt it through the stones under his feet. He stopped and raised his hands for silence, but the crowd refused to quiet until he swayed and collapsed.

"Father!"

Rael, Belkar, and the king's attendants rushed forward, all expecting the worst, but the king still clutched at life.

"Get me on the litter," he rasped, "and raise it so I can see and be seen. I must say what I have come to say."

"Father, it isn't important, I . . ."

"This isn't just for you. I will not have my country torn by civil war!"

With gentle hands, Rael lifted his father and laid him carefully on the litter. Some of the crowd hissed at this show of his strength—wasted or not, the king was a large man still—but Rael didn't care. His only thought was for the man he loved who lay dying.

Two of the attendants hoisted one end of the litter to their shoulders. Raen stared out at the Square from the dark hollows his eyes had become.

"I am still your king!" he cried in a voice surprisingly strong.

The people cheered.

"This," he continued, taking Rael's hand, "is my son."

Only a few cheered. Most muttered sullenly and one, a weaver, apparently the chosen spokesman, twisted his cap in his hands and called out: "We don't doubt you are his father, Sire, but we have concerns about his mother."

"You know who his mother is."

The weaver squirmed and reddened but he persisted. "And that's the problem, Sire. He isn't human and who's to say with you gone that he won't turn on us. You can't trust the Elder Races, they've never had what you'd call good will toward man. If he should take after his mother . . ."

'If you knew his mother," Belkar's voice rang out over the muttering that signified agreement with the weaver's words, "you wouldn't . . ."

His last words vanished under the noise that rose from the far side of the Square. There was no need to strain to see the cause of the commotion, for Milthra's silver head shone like a star amongst suddenly drab browns and reds and yellows.

"The Lady," ran the awed whisper as the crowd

parted before her. "The Lady of the Grove." Those who had lost their ability to believe in the wondrous found it again. Those who had doubted, couldn't remember why. A young woman reached out and let a lock of the Lady's shining hair caress her fingers and then stood gazing at her hand in amazement as if it belonged to another. Peace walked with the Lady and the smell of a sun-warmed forest grove filled the air.

She looked neither to the left nor the right as she approached the palace, her eyes never moved from the man on the litter or the youth standing beside him. At the steps of the dais she paused, as if gathering strength—the fragrance of the forest became stronger and a breeze danced through her hair—then she lifted her skirts in her hand and climbed the steps.

With a strangled cry, Rael threw himself into her arms. She held him to her heart for a moment, stroking his hair, and then gently pushed him away. Green eyes gazed into green.

Rael wondered how he could ever have thought of his mother as young. He saw wisdom, understanding, compassion to a degree most mortal minds could not accept, let alone achieve, resting in the depths of her eyes. She had walked with the Mother-creator at the beginning of the world. She had seen the creation of man. And she loved him. Rael felt her love wrap around him, a warmth, a protection he would always wear.

Milthra saw that her son would make a fine king. His heart sang with courage and pride and his eyes were filled with hope. He might stumble and fall, but he would try and no mother could ask more. She had no regrets.

The people in the Square saw only the Lady of the Grove and the young man she claimed as her son, but it was enough. The unworldliness of their future king turned from a thing to be feared to one to be treasured. Not one of them realized what Milthra had done in leaving the Grove.

"Mother," Rael's voice grew heavy with a new anguish, "you've left your tree."

"I have left my tree." She touched his cheek softly. "How could I live when my love died? My sisters sleep and someday a child of your children's children will wake them, but my day is done."

She kissed him and turned to the king.

Raen looked up at her with such a mixture of longing and pain that those in the crowd who saw it, wept.

"Why have you come?" he cried.

"You would not come to me, beloved, so I have come to you."

"Then you will die."

"Yes. But what is my life without you?" She tried a smile, but it faltered and the brilliant green of her eyes dimmed for an instant as they filled and overflowed. Her hands were caught in his, fingers too tightly woven to be parted, so she let the tears drop where they would.

They fell almost slowly, taking form and beauty in the air, and then lay shimmering like jewels on his breast. Instead of drying in the sunlight, they caught it, bound it, and gave it back. Their light grew and grew until everyone save Raen and Milthra covered their eyes. Even Rael stepped back and shielded himself from the glory.

When eyes could see again, an old and dying king no longer lay on the dais. In his place was a young man with hair of jet and smooth golden skin over corded muscle.

"The king," sighed the crowd. "His youth has returned."

Rael's eyes widened, joy beginning to surface, but Milthra shook her head.

"It is an appearance only, my child," she said. "Death is the true son of the Mother and not even I can stop him." And then she looked beyond Rael, to the young man who stood in his shadow. The young man that only she, of all the hundreds in the Square, could see.

Under the weight of her regard, Lord Death bowed his head and when he raised it again said softly: "I would spare you both if my nature allowed it, Eldest."

Raen looked down at his body and raised his hands to his face.

"It's true!" His voice throbbed with passion. "I'm a man again. I am as I was in my prime!" He held out his arms and Milthra lay down beside him, her head pillowed on his chest.

"As you always were to me, beloved, and as you always will be now."

He kissed her once, softly, and then together they died.

The silence was so complete, the crowd so quiet and still, that the sunlight bathing the bodies in golden luminescence could almost be heard. From the distance, from the forest, came the sound of thunder.

Belkar stepped forward and three times opened his mouth to speak. Finally, his voice got past his grief and filled the Square.

"The king is dead!"

And then he dropped on one knee before the tall young man with eyes the green of new spring leaves.

"Long live the king!"

Rael buried his mother and father in the Sacred Grove under the remains of his mother's tree. It had been hit by lightning and then consumed by fire until only a charred stump remained. Not one of the other trees, or even so much as a blade of grass, had been touched.

"This stump shall be your headstone," he said softly, patting the last bit of earth into place. "And I will see that none disturb your rest."

"I won't cry for them," he had told Belkar, "for they're together at last and even in death that is no cause for grief."

As the young king left the Grove, he thought he

heard women's voices, lamenting, soft with sorrow, but when he turned, he saw only the wind moving through the circle of trees and leaves falling to cover the grave.

Interlude One

Rael joined with the Duke of Belkar's blue-eyed daughter and their years together were filled with love and laughter and children. He never found the common touch that had so endeared his father to the people, but he ruled well and was always after remembered as just.

For all the years of Rael's reign, Doan, the Captain of the Elite, stood by his side. His unaging presence became a part of the king: two arms, two legs, and the captain. And when he buried his sword in Rael's grave and vanished from mortal lands, that too was accepted with no surprise. It could not be imagined he would serve another.

The death of the Eldest became the subject of a thousand songs and in her honor, or perhaps to save her sisters from a like fate, Rael, as his first act as Lord of Ardhan, forbid all mortals entry to the Grove, swearing those who knew its direction to oaths of secrecy. Over forty years later, when his son took the throne, time had erased the reality of both the Lady and the circle of silver birch and left only the songs.

The dwarf stepped back from the sapling and nodded once. "Just like you said."

The great black centaur that stood beside him returned the nod, although both kept their eyes on the tiny tree. Around them, the Sacred Grove was silent and still. No leaf rustled, for no breeze dared to intrude.

"Can They hope to succeed?" the centaur asked at last.

Doan shrugged. "I don't see why not. This," he waved a hand about the Grove, "is the oldest magic in the world and They've woven themselves into it. Sacrificed Themselves to do it. They've succeeded, C'Tal, that tree holds a life as real as any in this place. But after . . ."

"So much rests on the Mother's youngest children." C'Tal folded his arms across his massive chest, the black beard flowing like silk over them. "And the Mother's youngest children have never been strong."

"Strong enough to begin this mess," Doan snorted. His gaze dropped to the lichen covered mound the young birch grew from, all that remained of Milthra's tree. "Strong enough to draw out the Eldest and take her from us."

"True," murmured the centaur and the trees around them stirred and moaned. "But you must never forget, she chose her path."

"Forget!" Doan whirled and his eyes blazed red, not with power but pain. "As if I could!" He turned again to the sapling. "I could end this, here and now." He grabbed a tender leaf and ripped it free. The small tree shuddered. "They've risked it all on this one toss, and if I destroy Their vessel it's over."

"Perhaps for us as well."

Doan's arched eyebrows invited C'Tal to continue.

"He has no checks on his power this time. Who is to say when he is done with the mortals he will not turn at last to the Elder Races?"

"So *that's* why you finally stuck your noses in." Doan's laugh was bitter. "Fear."

"Unlike other races, we do not become involved in that which does not concern the centaurs." C'Tal's voice remained calm, but the points of his ears lay back against his head and for an instant great slabs of teeth showed startlingly white against the black of his beard. "Nor, given the evidence, is it unreasonable for us to fear what he may do and wish to stop him."

Doan looked thoughtful. He rubbed another leaf between thumb and forefinger, but this time the action was almost a caress. "I could end it now," he murmured, his voice unusually gentle.

"But you will not." A huge black hand reached down and engulfed the dwarf's shoulder.

"No." He pulled himself out of the other's grasp and stood flexing the shoulder the centaur had held. "And you needn't snap bones to convince me either," he added peevishly. "For the little of her that's woven here and greater part of her yet to come, I'll let Them try to right the wrong Their brothers did."

"You must do more than that." C'Tal ignored both glare and clenched fists and continued. "As you infer, They cannot protect themselves now; if you can destroy Them, so too could another. Until the seed is sown, They must have a protector."

"Go on." Doan's voice was the rasp of moving rock.

C'Tal looked surprised. "You have been protector once before."

"And I don't choose to be again. I am needed in the caverns."

"Your brothers can guard what the caverns hold. You are needed here."

"No." A muscle jumped in his cheek; the Lady lost to love, her son to Mortal time and he could protect them from neither. "Do it yourself." Moving jerkily, stamping indentations into the velvet grass, Doan pushed past the centaur and out of the Grove.

C'Tal stood quietly, an ebony monument, framed by green and gold. He did not appear distressed by the refusal of his chosen guardian. He merely waited.

"All right." The pain was safely masked by irritation. "But only until the seed is sown. I've raised one child and I don't care to repeat it."

"Until the seed is sown," C'Tal agreed as Doan

stomped back and stood snarling down at the tree.
"Then we will return to the mortals' ranges . . ."

"Big of you," Doan interjected sarcastically.

". . . and as we did with the others, we will instruct
the child."

"Yeah? Well, get it right this time."

It was C'Tal's turn to glare, but all he said was: "We
shall."

"If there is a child."

"You think the Eldest's line will not be able to accomplish what they must to fulfill the prophecy?"

The dwarf threw his hands in the air, then, catching
sight of C'Tal's face, he closed his mouth on the cutting remark that had risen to his tongue. The centaur
was truly worried. "You want my opinion?"

"Yes."

Doan remembered. He'd been standing in the
Square, with the rest of the Elite when Milthra had
given herself to Death so many years before. He would
never, for the eternity he might yet live, forget the
look on her face.

"The Mother gave each of the Elders one role to
play in the lives of her youngest."

"She did," agreed C'Tal.

"Dwarves guard. Centaurs teach. But the Eldest . . ."

The sapling's roots were deep in the remains of
Milthra's tree, deep in the earth where Milthra and
her beloved had been returned to the arms of the
Mother.

". . . but the Eldest loved. And the Youngest were
strong enough to bear that. In my opinion They have
not sacrificed in vain. The weapon will be forged.
There will be a chance to defeat the ancient enemy
and maybe, just maybe, we'll have peace for a time."

The centaur sighed and once again the great hand
closed on the dwarf's shoulder.

"Thank you," said C'Tal, and almost the trees
around echoed him. Then, with the uncanny speed of
his kind, the centaur was gone.

For a moment, Doan stood quietly, looking down at

the miniature silver birch, considering the life within it. The moment passed, his face fell back into its accustomed scowl, and he kicked at a nodding buttercup.

"Seeds, bah! They need a gardener not a guardian."

Six

"Tayer, we're lost. We'll never find our way back."

"Oh, do be quiet, Hanna. I'm trying to think."

"But what about bandits? We could be killed. Or worse!" The girl's voice rose to a piercing wail.

"Hanna!" Tayer turned in her saddle and glared at her cousin. "There are no bandits in the Lady's Wood. And if you'll just be quiet for a moment, we may be able to hear the horns and find our way back to the hunt."

Hanna sniffed but stopped wailing. All her life she'd followed the older, stronger-willed girl and now habit conquered fear.

"If we could only see the sun," Tayer mused, standing in her stirrups and squinting up into the thick summer foliage, "at least then we'd know which way we were heading." But the sky was overcast and what showed through the leaves was a uniform gray.

"It'll probably rain."

"Oh, Hanna!" Tayer's laugh lightened the wood's darkness for a moment, and it almost seemed the birds fell silent to hear. Songs without number had been written about the laugh of the Princess of Ardhan. Every bard in the kingdom, and not a few from outside, had tried to immortalize the sound. They'd never quite managed it. As had been said more than once, the sound, although beautiful beyond compare, was nothing really without the princess. Strands of gold wove through the thick chestnut of her hair, flecks of

93

gold brightened the soft brown of her eyes, and a sprinkle of gold danced across the cream of her cheeks. She was the youngest of the three children of the king, the only daughter, and the image of her dead mother. The king counted her amongst the treasures of his kingdom.

Hanna's pale, delicate beauty had always been overshadowed by her cousin's—what chance had a violet against a rose, even one just barely budded—but she appeared content living in the light of reflected glory.

The four generations since the death of Milthra and Raen had wiped out all overt physical resemblances to the hamadryad in the Royal House of Ardhan, but nevertheless differences remained. When Rael, at sixty-four, took his mother's road and followed his beloved into death, he had looked like a man of less than forty. His son was seventy-five when he finally married and one hundred and thirty-five when he died. The blood of the Eldest could not keep Lord Death away indefinitely, but it certainly delayed his coming.

In those four generations, the Lady's Wood had become just another forest, distinguished only in that Royal Law forbade the cutting of any living tree within its boundaries. In this generation, it had become the favorite hunting ground of the Court.

A bird with snowy white plumage, startling against the deep green of the forest's summer canopy, had separated Tayer and Hanna from the rest of the hunt. Tayer had thought it so unusual, and so beautiful, she rode off after it to get a better look; Hanna trailing, as always, along behind. When the bird disappeared, seemingly between one tree and the next, they were in a part of the forest completely unfamiliar to them and hopelessly lost.

A certain heaviness in the air, a waiting stillness, said Hanna's fear of rain was not wholly brought about by depression. The horses' ears lay flat and the animals had to be urged down the trail. Heavy underbrush clutched at the girls' clothing and the horses' legs with sharp, damp fingers. No birds sang and even the leaves hung still. The sounds of the horses' hoofs on the forest floor were muffled and indistinct.

Silence shrouded the forest.

Thunder shattered the air.

The horses went wild. Hanna screamed and dropped her reins, but Tayer hung grimly on and fought to control her plunging mount.

For what seemed like hours, Tayer's world collapsed to the space between her horse's ears, the reins cutting into her fingers, and the saddle trying to escape from between her legs. Finally the mare stood, trembling but calm, and Tayer turned to check on her cousin.

She wasn't there. She wasn't anywhere in sight.

A trail of broken branches and crushed underbrush showed the direction Hanna's horse had taken in its panicked flight and Tayer thought she could hear, very faintly, her name being called in desperation. Over and over.

Concern and anger chased each other across Tayer's face as she stared at the destruction. Finally, she sighed and swung out of the saddle to better guide the mare around on the narrow trail. She dearly loved Hanna but sometimes wished the girl would learn to cope on her own. It never occurred to her that she dominated Hanna's life so thoroughly there was rarely anything, besides Tayer, for Hanna to cope with.

"She rides as well as I do," Tayer muttered to Dancer, the mare, maneuvering until they could get off the trail at the same place. "There's no need for this." She remounted and urged the horse forward.

Dancer picked her way delicately along the line of destroyed underbrush, avoiding the spiky ends of broken branches. Tayer kept her eyes on the forest ahead, hoping for a view of her cousin's pale blue jacket amid the greens and browns.

The second crack of thunder was, if possible, louder than the first. This time Dancer would not be controlled and she took off on a panic-stricken flight of her own. Tayer could only try and keep her seat and pray the horse wouldn't stumble and fall. A branch whipped her across the face and her eyes filled with tears.

When she could see again, it was too late to avoid the heavy limb hanging low in the path of the frightened animal. Tayer had only a brief glimpse of bark and moss and leaves and then the branch swept her from the saddle. Gasping for breath, and more frightened than she'd ever been in her life, she was miraculously unhurt by the blow and would have walked away only badly bruised had the trees not been so close together where she fell. She screamed as a stub of wood slammed needle-sharp into her shoulder and then the back of her head came down on a protruding root, almost as hard in its gnarled age as stone. For a while, she knew no more.

Drifting in the gray mists just this side of unconsciousness, Tayer felt strong arms lift her effortlessly and cradle her against something that smelled of leather and earth. She giggled weakly, for although she was securely held, the tip of each foot dipped to touch the ground with every step her rescuer took and it struck her as funny that one so strong could be so short. She tried to open her eyes, but the lids refused to obey. Her head lolled back against the stranger's shoulder and the gray turned black.

When the darkness lifted for the second time, she felt herself upon the softest of beds where gentle hands cleaned and treated her throbbing shoulder. These were not the hands that had carried her; she was sure of it although she had no idea of how she knew. Beneath these hands her body trembled and it seemed she had waited all her life for their touch. She gave herself up to the golden glow they wrapped about her, but the reality of her injuries could not be denied for long and pain pulled her from that sanctuary.

As she became aware of the ache in her shoulder and the fire that burned in her head, she also became aware of an arm across her back raising her lips to touch the edge of something wet and cool.

"Drink," said someone softly, and she did, never even considering questioning the voice.

The cup held only water, but drinking it she thought she had never tasted water before. It was like drinking light, or liquid crystal, and it washed all the pain away.

The sound and smell of the forest was around her still but, rather than feeling the terror her recent experience should have demanded, she had never felt so safe. It reminded her of being very young and held securely in the circle of her mother's arms. As her head was gently lowered, Tayer opened her eyes.

Sunlight slanted down through the leaves of the tree that towered above her. She struggled to her elbows—helped by that same arm across her back, which withdrew as she steadied—and looked around.

She lay in a clearing ringed with silver birch in their full summer glory and filled with soft golden light. Either the storm had ended or it had never penetrated the circle. The stillness here was peaceful, not ominous. Thick grass covered the ground where she rested—soft and springy and unlike any she had ever seen before.

And he who went with the voice . . .

Never had Tayer seen a man so beautiful. His hair fell to his shoulders in a white so pure it surrounded his head with a nimbus of light. His skin was the color of old copper and his body was so well proportioned he seemed more an artist's conception than a real man. And his eyes . . . Tayer caught her breath when she met his eyes. It looked as if the sunlight poured through them as it did through the leaves of the birch above her and she felt herself sinking into the glory of the other world they showed.

She could have stayed within those eyes forever, but her arms gave out and she collapsed to the grass, the spell broken.

"You are weak," he said, stroking her forehead. "Rest."

Tayer felt his touch resonate through her body. Her

soul sang, a harp string he had played upon, only she did not, as yet, understand the song.

"Who are you?" she sighed as her eyes closed.

"I am Varkell," came the answer. "I am a part of the Grove."

She wanted to ask if she would see him again, but her mind felt wrapped in amber and she couldn't get her voice to work. The last thing she saw was a compassionate smile and then she slept.

When she awoke, she was in her bed in the palace.

"But you believe me."

"Of course I believe you." Hanna adjusted her sling and settled more comfortably amongst the pillows on the lounge. "It's exactly the sort of thing that would happen to you." The faintest shade of resentment colored her voice and she punched at an overstuffed pink square with her good arm. "Like something out of a fairy tale."

Tayer turned from the window, where she'd been straining her eyes to see the distant line of trees, and smiled dreamily. "That's exactly what it was like. Like something out of a fairy tale."

Hanna sighed. The healer, a man of undeniable skill but little imagination, had explained that the silver-haired man with the leaf-green eyes was probably a hallucination caused by the bump on her cousin's head. He'd also said that the scar puckering the smooth curve of Tayer's shoulder was an old wound, long healed. Hanna hadn't argued, because it wasn't her way, but she knew there had been no scar when they rode out for the day's hunt. And if the part about the wounded shoulder was true, she saw no reason to doubt the rest.

"Maybe he was a woodsman," she said in her most matter-of-fact tone, knowing full well that no woodsman would dare to venture so far into the Lady's Wood.

"He said he was a part of the Grove," Tayer declared, soft lips curving at the memory.

"But no one has been to the Sacred Grove for years, not since the Lady died. No one even knows where it is! And I should think,'' Hanna added, remembering long hours of lessons, ''that if a priest tended the Grove, the Scholars would've told us.''

''There were birch trees all around, and green and gold sunlight, and the music of the wind in the leaves.''

Hanna gazed at her cousin in astonishment. Tayer was staring into space, her eyes focused on something Hanna couldn't see, her head cocked to hear a song Hanna couldn't hear.

''He was so beautiful.'' Tayer's voice caressed the words. Her hand reached out to stroke a cheek that wasn't there. ''He looked into me.''

''The Lady was very beautiful,'' Hanna said thoughtfully, trying to bring Tayer's experience into line with what they'd been taught about the Grove, ''and tall, with silver hair and green eyes and her sisters were the same. Maybe it was one of the other hamadryads who tended you. Are you sure it was a man?''

Tayer's eyes lost their dreamy look and gained a mischievous sparkle.

''Oh, I'm very sure,'' she said, standing and shaking out the red velvet folds of her skirt. ''He was naked. I can't stand to be inside any longer, I'm going for a walk in the garden.''

''Naked! You never mentioned that before!''

The princess turned in the doorway and ran a finger up and down the vines carved around the frame. ''Would you have mentioned to your father and brothers that the man who found you unconscious in the woods was naked? Besides, it didn't seem important at the time.'' Then she laughed and was gone.

''Well it would have been important to me,'' Hanna muttered at her cousin's departing back.

''What would've been important to you, little one?'' asked Mikhail, entering the room through the other door.

''The man Tayer met in the woods was naked.''

''The hallucination?''

Hanna got to her feet. "I don't think she was seeing things," she said with a conviction that was quite unlike her.

Mikhail took his sister firmly by the shoulders and sat her back down. "Tell me about it," he commanded.

As he listened, Mikhail paced. He was fair, like Hanna, but where she was the pale gold and blue of early morning he was the tawny gold and violet of a sunset. Like all the children of the Royal House, he was tall, for height was one of the Lady's gifts, but where Hanna and his cousins were sapling-slender he had the bulk of an ancient oak. Although generations removed and thinned by marriage, the power of the tree was still his. Coupled with his massive frame, this heritage gave him the strength to create legends. His black sword was dwarf-crafted, the only such blade in the kingdom, and the tale of how he won it was sure to be told any time men gathered and ale flowed. Mikhail found the tales an embarrassment and would retreat, ears burning, from any praise. As he told Tayer's brothers; "It's no great feat to split a man in half with one mighty blow when you're twice his size with the strength of the Lady and a magic sword to boot." As the only warrior in the royal family, both by choice and inclination, Mikhail commanded the Elite.

He moved restlessly from window to window as Hanna told him of the scar and of all she and Tayer had discussed that morning. From the way he twisted and crushed his heavy leather belt, Hanna could tell he wasn't pleased with Tayer's strange experience.

"Has there ever been a man in the Sacred Grove, Mikhail?"

"Not that I ever heard of, only the Lady and her sisters. And the Lady is dead and her sisters are asleep."

Hanna sighed and shook her head. "So if it was a man, Tayer must have been seeing things." And if those were the kind of visions a bump on the head caused, she would be more inclined to fall off her own horse in the future. The visions caused by a broken arm were tedious in comparison. "Still, we could've been in the right part of the forest."

"By King's Law," Mikhail reminded her, "no one has been to the Grove since the Lady died." He raised a foot to kick a delicately carved footstool out of his way, thought better of it and stepped around. "Not even those of us who bear her blood know its location."

"But we all know it's in there," Hanna insisted. "We all know it isn't just a story."

"Aye." Mikhail stopped his pacing and stood at the window where Tayer had stood earlier, his gaze also trying to pierce the dark line of trees. "But I've hunted all over that area, been through the forest and to the Great Lake on the other side, and I've never found the Grove."

"Perhaps it didn't want to be found."

"Perhaps."

"Do you think Tayer was seeing things?"

He turned from the window and looked down at his sister. His face was troubled.

"No."

And they both remembered the scar. The healer had insisted that Tayler had carried the mark since childhood, but they knew better.

"Where is she now?"

"She went for a walk in the gardens."

Hanna watched her brother's departing back with concern. He thought no one suspected, but she knew him too well to be fooled. There were times when his love shone from his eyes like a beacon and Hanna wondered how Tayer had not been blinded by the intensity of the light.

Tayer, used to being adored, had never noticed.

On his way to the garden, Mikhail considered all that Hanna had said. Tayer was vain and willful, he was not the sort to let love blind him to another's faults, but she had never been a liar. She'd never even had to resort to the small lies children use to make themselves important; from the day of her birth she'd been the darling of the court. If Tayer said she saw a naked man in Lady's Wood, then that's exactly what she saw.

But why did she not want her father and brothers to know? He could think of only one reason.

He scowled and growled low in his throat, so frightening a young servant hurrying by on some errand of her own, that she dropped the tray she carried and pressed herself against the wall one fist in her mouth to stop a shriek.

Mikhail stared at her in astonishment, then, realizing that her terror was directed at him, blushed and bent to retrieve her tray.

"You mustn't mind me," he said, wincing inwardly as the girl continued to stare at him with wide eyes.

"No, milord?" She gave a tiny, jerky bow as she took back her tray.

"No. I was thinking of something else and didn't even know you were there." He smiled down at her, the last of his anger fading behind his embarrassment.

She tried a tentative smile in return. "As you say, milord."

It suddenly occurred to him that he had no idea of which garden Tayer had gone to and there were at least half a dozen scattered about the palace. "You, uh, haven't seen the princess, have you?"

Although Hanna was equally *a* princess, *the* princess could only refer to Tayer.

"Yes, milord. I saw her enter the small walled garden behind the new archives in the south wing."

"Thank you." Mikhail smiled again and headed toward the maze of corridors that would take him to the recently added south wing.

The servant stood for a moment, watching him go, her expression remarkably similar to that Mikhail's sister had worn moments before. The emotional entanglements of royalty were not her concern, but the look on his face when he mentioned the princess sent shivers down her spine. She sighed and went on her way, wishing that someday, someone, would look at her like that.

Mikhail stepped into the late afternoon sunlight of the garden and the color drained from his face. Tayer lay crumpled on the path, pale skin made paler by the deep crimson pool of her skirts. He dove across the tiny courtyard and threw himself to his knees by her side, a trembling hand reaching out to touch the smooth column of her throat. Beneath his fingers, her life throbbed fast but sure.

"You called, milord?"

"No, I . . ." Mikhail looked up at the gray-robed Scholar. The noise he'd made as he moved had not been a call exactly, but . . . "Uh, I mean yes, I called. Get a healer. The princess has fainted."

"In bed for a week? But I feel fine!"

"Of course you do, Princess, which is why you were taking a nap in the roses."

"I just fainted."

"Precisely my point." The healer motioned for the maid to close the heavy brocade curtains and, with the room darkened, waved a candle before Tayer's face. "Follow the light with your eyes, please."

"The Lord Chamberlain's wife faints all the time and she doesn't have to stay in bed."

"Just with your eyes, Princess. Don't turn your head. The Lord Chamberlain's wife is a weak, foolish woman who thinks fainting makes her interesting. *You* have received a nasty blow to the head. Not the same thing at all." He blew out the candle. "In bed for a week. No riding for a month."

"A month?"

"A fall from a garden bench is one thing, a fall from a horse is something else entirely. It is, if you recall, what got you into this mess in the first place."

"Oh, please, you can't mean it." Tayer looked up at him through her lashes, her lower lip beginning to quiver. Women less beautiful than Tayer had destroyed whole countries with that look. The healer, however, was more concerned with the way her pupils were dilating as the maid threw back the curtains and flooded the room with light.

"Of course, I mean it," he said, apparently satisfied for he turned to go. "I always say what I mean. No riding for a month."

Tayer pleaded, pouted, and petitioned her father, but the verdict stayed the same: visits around town in a litter were permitted but riding was not.

One could not go to the forest in a litter.

Used to being active, the princess was unbearable as an invalid. With riding denied her, there just wasn't that much that she could do. She had little interest in statecraft and the public duties of the third child of the Royal House were few and far between.

"If I have to set one more stupid tapestry stitch, I shall scream!" Tayer leaped to her feet and darted about the room, almost bouncing from the walls. "There must be something else I can do."

Hanna sighed and bent to retrieve the skeins of silk now widely scattered and hopelessly tangled.

"I know," the princess dropped back into her chair in a most unprincesslike manner, "I shall garden."

"Tayer, what are you doing?"

Tayer glared up at her brothers and jabbed her ivory handled trowel into the damp earth. "Even you two should be able to figure that out. I'm planting roses."

Davan pursed his lips. "They'll never grow there; not enough light. Why don't you leave gardening to the gardeners and do something you're capable of?"

She threw the trowel at him. Then, just to be sure he knew she was truly annoyed, followed it with the tray of seedlings.

Eyrik laughed.

She stood and dumped the contents of her watering pot over his head.

* * *

Only Hanna noticed how often Tayer went to the one window in the palace where the dark line of the forest could be seen in the distance.

No one heard her call out his name in her sleep.

Hanna bore the brunt of Tayer's dissatisfaction. She was expected, not only by Tayer but by everyone else in the palace, to keep her cousin entertained and cheerful. She not only suffered from Tayer's moods but from the accusations that she could have done something to prevent them.

"I love Tayer," she sighed to Mikhail one evening, "but there have been times lately when I haven't liked her very much."

"How can you say that?" Mikhail protested. "You've always been like sisters. You should be glad you can help her."

"There are times," Hanna said sharply as she hurried down the hall in answer to an imperious summons from the invalid, "when I don't like you very much either."

Mikhail stood and stared in astonishment as Hanna slammed the door to Tayer's room behind her. "What did I say?"

When the month finally ended, a great picnic was arranged in celebration of Tayer's official return to health. The king allowed Tayer to convince him that such a picnic could only be held in the lee of the Lady's Wood. Officially, because the shade beneath the trees would be welcome in the heat of the afternoon. Actually, because, unlike the healer, the king was not immune to his daughter looking up through her eyelashes and quivering her lower lip. He knew his weakness, however, and he was grateful she wanted such an insignificant thing.

If any of the court considered a two-hour ride for a picnic a little extreme, they kept silent. As the king had allowed himself to be convinced, so did the court. And if truth be told, after the last four weeks, the court was as glad Tayer was mobile as Tayer was herself.

A large and merry company set out from the palace in the early morning. In the midst of the crowd, the laughter, and the sunshine it was easy to miss seeing that Tayer's gaiety had a brittle edge and that Mikhail smiled grimly if at all. Hanna noticed, but, as usual, no one noticed Hanna.

Mikhail didn't know who, or what, Tayer had seen in the forest that day but he knew that whether spirit, demon, or mortal man, it had bewitched her. He had no doubt she would try to lose herself in the woods that afternoon and attempt to find the creature. Silently he vowed, and swore on his sword, that he would not take his eyes off her until she was safely back in the palace and far away from the naked man with silver hair and green fire in his eyes.

Keeping an eye on Tayer turned out to be difficult; she flitted from person to person like a nervous butterfly. Mikhail's efforts were further hampered by the duties expected of him as a Prince of the Realm. It wasn't easy being charming, witty, and vigilant all at once.

When the sun was at its zenith and its warmth—combined with a large and excellent lunch, sent on its way with several gallons of good wine—was putting many of the party to sleep, he noticed Tayer disappearing amongst the trees. With a curse, he leaped to his feet and, paying no attention to the drowsy protests rising from those about him, ran after her.

The forest seemed unnaturally still. Not a leaf rustled, not a bird sang, and although Mikhail was barely thirty feet from the meadow—and could, in fact, still see brightly colored robes and gay pennants—not a sound from that direction could he hear. Motes of dust danced in rays of sunlight, but they danced alone. There was no trace of Tayer.

Loosening his sword in its sheath, Mikhail bent to study the ground. Very faintly, for the moss and leaves were already shifting to fill the track, he saw the print of his cousin's foot. And then another. The trail shifted, and twitched, almost as if it had a mind of its own, but Mikhail was one of the best trackers in Ardhan and this was no ordinary hunt. Soon he was running, his eyes never leaving the ground.

He didn't see the root that tripped him. He would've sworn there was no root there. It came as a great surprise to find himself suddenly stretched full length upon the forest floor, the wind knocked out of him and his chin digging a trench in the sod. He lay there for a moment catching his breath, and then for another moment strangely unwilling to rise. The silence and sunlight washed over him in green-gold waves.

The forest had welcomed Tayer. The moment she stepped beneath the trees the force which had pulled her this way and that, keeping her on the knife's edge between fear and longing, disappeared. Only the longing remained and a gentle tugging which directed her feet.

As she walked deeper into the Lady's Wood, on paths she had no doubt were created just for her, a breeze came out of the stillness, caressed her bare arms and ran unseen fingers through her hair. When the path disappeared, she unquestioningly followed the breeze. It drew her through a ring of silver birch and then left on errands of its own.

Tayer had never seen a more beautiful place. The sunlight poured down into the clearing like liquid gold. It had a tangible presence in the air and spilled out of the buttercups scattered in the thick grass. As Tayer stepped into the center of the circle, she felt the light fill her, like rich wine in a crystal goblet. The birches that surrounded her, all but one majestically old, glowed with their own inner light.

"You have come."

From the one tree still straight and smooth he stepped, and for Tayer the light in the clearing dimmed in the glory of the light that flowed from him. He was just as Tayer remembered.

She stepped forward to meet him, hands outstretched and trembling.

"You were not a dream," she said softly, thankfully. "You were not a dream."

And Varkell, who was a part of the Grove, with silver hair and eyes that held an unworldly green light, looked very human as he drew her into his arms.

"Nor were you."

She'd left Varkell's side only because he'd told her she must, but every part of Tayer's body still sang with his presence. Even outside the Grove, there was a lushness in the air; a glory in the ordinary things; in trees and shrubs and moss.

New words, she decided, *will have to be created to describe how I feel.*

"Princess."

Any other day, the ugly little man perched on the fallen tree would have sent her screaming for her guards but today, today he couldn't possibly be a threat. She paused and fearlessly met the glow of his eyes. Her nose wrinkled as the fires damped down to an unusual shade of red-brown.

"Do I know you?" she asked, struggling to hold the teasing edge of a memory.

He spread rough hands and scowled. "Is it likely?"

"No," Tayer admitted. He was obviously not a member of the court and she knew few others, but still there lingered the thought that she had met him before.

"If you go past that big pine, Princess, you'll find your cousin. Perhaps you should gather him up as you go."

"Thank you." She smiled and followed his pointing finger, barely five steps beyond him before the lingering radiance she moved in drove the meeting from her mind.

"Not yet," Doan snorted, watching the slender figure disappear, "but soon."

Struggling through the green and gold wrapped about him, Mikhail first became aware of bird song—second of a woman's laughter more beautiful than the song. He opened his eyes to see Tayer standing over him.

"You've picked a strange place for a nap, Cousin," she said, extending a hand to help him up. "Did the ladies of the court prove too much for you?"

"I didn't choose the place," Mikhail replied, rubbing his eyes and glaring about him suspiciously. The forest, so still before, had come alive with sound. The sunlight no longer fell heavy and somber but slanted through the trees at a rakish angle.

"The time . . ."

"It's late afternoon. Come," she tucked her hand in his, "we'd best get back if we don't want to be left behind. Listen, they're blowing the horns for us."

Mikhail listened and in the distance he heard the king's horn.

"I don't understand," he began, looking down at Tayer as they started to walk, and then he stopped and grabbed her shoulders. "Your clothes! They were red and brown this morning!"

Both tunic and pants were now a pale green with golden trim.

Tayer smoothed the cloth over her hips and smiled. "He made this for me, out of new leaves and sunshine."

She had never looked so beautiful, nor, Mikhail realized, so complete. Her eyes shone and there was a gentleness about her that had not been there before. She looked as if a great artist had taken the unfinished canvas of her and made it into a masterpiece.

A little overwhelmed, and not sure he liked the change, Mikhail allowed her to lead him from the forest. He didn't mention the clothes again and neither did she. No one else noticed, although their absence provided food for the palace gossip mill and evoked more than a few thoughtful glances from the king.

Over the next few weeks Tayer sang around the palace. Nothing could dampen her good spirits. Rumor had it that she was in love. Rumor didn't know the half of it.

One afternoon, when Mikhail was on duty, for even in peace the Elite still trained and its commander was expected to attend, the ladies of the court went to the forest for wildflowers. They returned that evening so heavily laden, those who had remained behind laughingly accused them of having stripped the Lady's Wood of blossoms.

Tayer brought back only a single buttercup that glowed with an inner light. A light that endured until Mikhail ground the delicate flower under his heel.

Hanna was at first pleased with the change in her cousin—Tayer had never been less demanding nor more affectionate—but as the weeks passed her pleasure dimmed. Tayer made it clear she no longer needed anyone but the creature of light she carried in her heart. With no real position in the palace beyond that of Tayer's companion, Hanna found herself completely unneeded and even longed for the days when Tayer had blithely ordered her life. More than ever, she felt mousy and insignificant beside her cousin. Whether this was due to the new depth and gentleness in Tayer's manner or the sudden mature light of her beauty, Hanna was not sure, but she found she didn't like it.

Seven

As the glorious summer drew to an end, a shadow fell on the kingdom. Word came from Riven and Lorn on the western border that Melac's raids had begun again.

"Why do they bother!" roared the king, slamming down his fist and causing the Messenger who'd brought the news to flinch and wonder if she was supposed to know.

"It's fairly obvious, isn't it, Father?" Davan, the heir to the throne, steepled his fingers in an unconscious imitation of his father's habit. "Melac's armies have gotten so large, the Empire's conquest is moving so fast, that there's no one left to grow food and they must raid us for supplies."

"That's exactly what they want us to think," said Mikhail shortly, turning away from a detailed map of the west to face his cousin.

Davan snorted. "Are you still on about that?"

The king, who had been asking a purely rhetorical question brought on by frustration, raised bushy eyebrows at the discussion between his son and his nephew.

"They raid to gather information," Mikhail insisted, "not grain and cattle. Those men are soldiers, not brigands. Our land, our people, our way of fighting, is being studied."

"Studied?" Davan scoffed. "What for? Melac's armies move south and west; the emperor has no intention of attacking us. He tried that once, remember, back in the Lady's time, and was soundly trounced.''

Mikhail shrugged. ''We are being studied,'' he insisted, wondering why he seemed to be the only one in the country who could see it. ''Melac is waiting for something.''

''For what?''

''I wish I knew. Sire,'' Mikhail turned to the king, ''every year we drive the raiders back, but every year we lose young men and women to Lord Death before their time. The western border is like an open wound that bleeds with the lives of our people.''

''Eloquent,'' muttered Davan.

Mikhail ignored him and once again made the plea he'd made yearly since taking up arms. ''Melac's Empire stretches far to the southwest, but it is directed still from the towers of the old capital, not three days' march from our western border. Let me raise the country, Sire. I'll destroy the head of the Empire and see that Melac never bleeds us again.''

And, as every year, the king denied the petition.

''If Melac ever turns all of its armies against us, we stand no chance; Ardhan as a country would be wiped from the memory of man. These raids are a small price to pay for the survival of our nation. Someday, Melac will have to be dealt with, but there will be no war in this land while I am king.''

By the time you're not king, there'll be no men left to fight, Mikhail thought bitterly. He knew Davan held the same beliefs as his uncle; there would be no war when Davan was king either. It looked as if the wound on the border would bleed for generations more.

''I understand how you feel, Mikhail,'' the king said kindly, and he thought he did for his brother and brother's wife, Mikhail's parents, had died in a border raid. ''I will not risk war, but I do have plans to strengthen our defense.''

Mikhail choked back a final plea, bowed to his liege and left the room. It would, he knew, do no good to argue further. In years of trying he'd convinced neither king nor heir of what appeared so obvious to him. Both had a blind spot concerning Melac that he'd never been able to breach. He could only cause as much damage to the enemy as possible with the relatively few men they'd given him and hope, when war finally came, Ardhan would not be taken totally by surprise.

Leaving his feet to find their own way to the training yards, the Commander of the Elite wrapped himself in battle plans and troop deployments and almost missed seeing Tayer sitting with the Duke of Belkar's wife in a sunny corner of one of the small gardens.

Almost.

All thought of battle, of war, of Melac, vanished. It had been days, he realized, since he'd seen her and only the Mother-creator knew how long it would be until he saw her again. He stopped and stared, imprinting her on his mind; the sunlight dancing through the gold in her hair, her lips slightly curving, the soft swell of her breasts beneath ivory silk. This would be a vision to carry him through the long days and nights ahead.

Tayer, oblivious, continued dangling a blossom over the chubby face of Belkar's infant heir. Lady Belkar, perhaps feeling the weight of Mikhail's gaze, looked up, started, smiled, and beckoned him closer.

"Milord Mikhail," she greeted him graciously when he approached. "I'd thought you on the border by now."

"Soon, milady." He bowed over her hand. "Tomorrow."

"Tomorrow. . . . We'll miss not having you about the court." She peered sideways at her companion, her tone carefully neutral. "Won't we, Tayer?"

Slowly, Tayer raised her head and Mikhail's heart gave a sudden lurch. He gritted his teeth and forced a friendly smile through the longing.

"Oh, yes," she said, "it'll be . . . different . . . around here without Mikhail."

Different. He could only hope she'd even notice he was gone. Then a sudden flush of jealousy caused his hands to curl into fists—she'd notice all right, for without his watching, who would stop her from riding off to be with . . . Him? The thing she'd met in the Grove. The creature that had bewitched her. The thought had occurred to Tayer as well; he'd grown up with her, he knew the speculative expression she now wore.

Lady Belkar looked from one to the other and felt like shaking them both. Mikhail stood staring down at Tayer, longing, pain, and anger mixed in about equal proportions on his face. Tayer sat staring off into the distance, longing and things harder to pin down mixed on hers. Not being privy to either's thoughts, Lady Belkar jumped to entirely the wrong conclusion on everything save what Mikhail longed for, and that had been an open secret about the court for almost a year. The tension thickened and she wondered if she should speak, then the baby on her lap suddenly howled and the moment was lost.

"Oh, dear, he's wet." Murmuring soothing sounds into the baby's hair, she stood, and placing her free hand on the rigid muscles of Mikhail's arm said: "Perhaps you would walk me from the garden, milord?"

With an effort, Mikhail drew his eyes from Tayer and managed a jerky nod.

At the edge of the garden, they paused and looked back.

"You should speak to her, Mikhail," Lady Belkar said softly. "You simply can not go on like this. Neither of you can."

"Speak to her of what?" He was amazed how steady his voice sounded. Surely the turmoil that seethed beneath the surface should show more.

Lady Belkar sighed. "Speak to her of how you feel. Tell her you love her." At his sudden startled expression, she added. "Everyone knows."

"Everyone?" he asked.

She smiled at his tone of stunned disbelief and reached up to pat him lightly on the cheek. "Everyone except Tayer." Then, under the prompting screams of her son, she left.

Mikhail looked again at the distant figure of his cousin, his love, his brows drawn together as he considered how he felt. Perhaps it was time for him to speak.

But he didn't. And the next morning he left for the western border.

Over the last few weeks of summer, and the early weeks of fall, Tayer almost daily answered the call from the Grove. The summons beat in her blood, day and night, and left unanswered too long it grew until it filled her every moment and she thought she would go crazy with need. When she was missed, all assumed she was with Hanna. Hanna, for reasons of her own, kept silent.

The day Mikhail returned, with a limp and a new resolution in his heart, Tayer was not in the palace. Although the need to ride after her beat at his thoughts—and he had no doubt of where she could be found—his duties kept him tied to his men and his reports.

But he was in the stableyard when she rode in.

He opened his mouth to tell her, the words cut and polished over long nights alone in his tent when she was the only thing on his mind, in his dreams. Then he saw her face and the words shattered. He had seen that expression too many times in his mirror to mistake it now. Tayer was a woman very deeply in love. He had waited too long.

He should leave, he knew, hide somewhere and lick his wounds. He hadn't thought he could be in so much pain and still live. But he stayed. Whether to hurt her in return or hurt himself further, he wasn't sure.

"Where are your guards," he growled as she swung from the saddle.

"The guards rode with you."

"Well then, servants," he snapped. "You know you're not to ride out alone."

"I can take care of myself," Tayer sighed. "Please, get out of my way." She pushed past him and led

Dancer into the stable. A groom came forward, took one look over her shoulder at the glowering prince, and retreated with the mare as quickly as he was able. Tayer sighed again and slowly turned.

Mikhail noticed that in the two months he'd been gone, Tayer's face had lost all memory of childhood. Its beauty was startling; the curve of her cheek was a song, but sorrow lay close to the surface and the sparkle in her eyes had been replaced by the reflected glow of an other world. With one hand he held her shoulder in an iron grasp and with the other he lifted a red-gold leaf from her hair.

"So, it's not all happiness in the Sacred Grove," he snarled, and crushed the leaf to powder.

Tayer met his gaze and he flinched before the radiance.

"No," she said. "It is not."

The pain in her voice hit Mikhail like a bucket of cold water, washing his anger away and leaving him trembling. He released her shoulder and took an unsteady step back. He wanted to take her in his arms and comfort her, but he feared her reaction. He didn't think he could stand it if she pushed him away.

"I'm sorry," he said finally.

She touched his cheek gently as she passed.

"So am I."

He watched her walk away and could think of no reason to follow.

The next morning, a great shouting in the courtyard dragged Mikhail up from an uneasy sleep. Briefly he wondered why he felt so rotten, then he remembered: he'd lost Tayer, lost any hope of her ever returning his love, and had tried to forget in every tavern in the city. The memories of the taverns were dim, but the memory of the pain was still sharp and clear. Holding his throbbing head, he stumbled to the window to see what all the noise was about. From the pennants and the livery, the seething mass of men, women and horses appeared to be a Royal Envoy from Halda, a small country that shared borders with both Ardhan and Melac. As Mikhail watched, the Lord Chamberlain appeared, ushered the men and women ceremoniously inside, and had the horses removed to the stables.

"They arranged it while you were away."

Mikhail turned. Hanna had come into the room and now perched on the edge of his bed.

"Arranged what?" he demanded, pouring some wine to clear the fog from his head.

Hanna looked down at her entwined fingers.

"Tayer's joining."

"What!" Mikhail threw the goblet to the floor, dove across the room, and yanked his sister to her feet.

"Tayer's joining," Hanna repeated with remarkable calm, considering that she had just been shaken vigorously. "The king has arranged for her to marry the Crown Prince of Halda."

"But why?"

"For mutual support against Melac obviously. The crown prince has no sisters and Tayer is the only daughter the king has."

"Why so quickly? These arrangements usually take months. Or years."

Hanna looked pityingly up at her brother. "The king has seen the way you look at Tayer. This is a very important state joining and he wants it done before she has a chance to fall in love with you. And she has been acting rather strangely of late."

Mikhail suddenly remembered the king speaking of plans to strengthen Ardhan's defense. This, then, was what he had meant.

"What does Tayer say about it?"

"I doubt she was asked. Princesses are expected to go along with this sort of thing as part of their duty to the kingdom. Besides, what could she say; I can't join with Halda because I'm in love with a hallucination?"

"No." Mikhail set his jaw and dropped Hanna back onto the bed. "I won't allow it." He dug his breeches out of a pile of discarded clothes and yanked them on. "I won't allow it." He couldn't believe he'd almost given up without a fight. It wasn't over yet, of that he was suddenly certain.

"There's not much you can do," Hanna said quietly. "And Tayer's gone. I just came from her room."

Tayer had ridden out before dawn according to the stable boy, but he had no idea of which way she'd gone.

"Beggin' your pardon, sir," he apologized to Mikhail, "but I ain't the one to be stoppin' the princess if'n she wants to go, and I ain't the one to be keepin' watch of where she went."

Mikhail knew exactly where Tayer was and he knew if he didn't catch her before she entered the forest he'd probably never be able to find her. *To the Grove*, pounded the hoofs of his galloping horse. *To the Grove*, pounded his heart. *To the Grove*.

When he reached the Lady's Wood, Dancer stood grazing in the long grass of the meadow, but Tayer was nowhere in sight.

Leaving his horse with the mare, Mikhail drew his sword and stepped beneath the trees. He was no longer truly in control of what he did. A force he couldn't explain drove him and he only knew that he had to find Tayer.

He began to run, crashing through the underbrush, using his sword to clear a path. All logic, all woodcraft, left him.

Sword first and panting, he stumbled into the Sacred Grove.

The birches wore their autumn dress of old gold and bronze, their leaves whirling free, carried and caressed by the breeze. In the midst of this erotic dance, stood a couple in a close embrace. The woman was Tayer. The man . . . Aware of the intruder, they turned in each other's arms to face him.

Mikhail didn't see the hand extended toward him, nor the welcoming smile. All he saw was Tayer gazing up into the leaf-green eyes of the creature who held her. Throwing aside his sword, he charged.

The two men were matched in height, but Mikhail

was heavier and fighting from the depths of his pain. The suddenness of his attack allowed him to get his hands around Varkell's throat and the muscles of his arms bulged as he tried to snap the other's neck. This thing had taken Tayer from him.

Pushing Tayer to safety, Varkell swept Mikhail's feet out from under him and they crashed to the ground.

The fall and his own weight broke Mikhail's hold, but he quickly gained another. From a distance, a saner part of his mind cried out that this would solve nothing, but he couldn't, wouldn't stop. Varkell made no attempt to return the attack, merely defending himself against Mikhail's assaults. A blocking elbow hit Mikhail in the mouth and his lip, caught between tooth and bone, split. As he jerked his head free, six drops of blood arced away—where they landed, the grass died. They thrashed about the clearing, tearing great gouges out of the velvet sod, first gold head on top, then silver.

Finally Varkell gained the top and kept it. Mikhail looked up and fell into the other world that burned in Varkell's eyes. Seeing what Tayer loved, and loving it himself, in spite of himself, he turned his head and closed his eyes in defeat. Tears seeped out through his lashes and left glistening trails down his cheeks. There was nothing left but the pain. There would never be anything but the pain.

"I yield," he said softly. "You have won."

Varkell stood, but Mikhail didn't move. He wasn't sure he could. He knew he didn't want to. The peace of the Grove, too deep to be shattered by the battle just ended, began to lap at the edges of his soul.

"Mikhail." The voice was a summons impossible to deny. "Look at me."

Mikhail opened his eyes. He saw, standing before him, a tall young man with silver-white hair and leaf-green eyes. The other-worldliness was gone.

"No, never gone." Sorrow clouded the words. "Just pushed aside for a time so we can talk."

"Who are you?" Mikhail asked, getting slowly to his feet. "What are you?"

Varkell pointed to the young birch in the circle of ancient trees.

"In that spot, amidst the roots of a tree long gone, were buried the bodies of a hamadryad and the mortal man she loved. Out of their love came the Royal House of Ardhan. Out of their bodies and the roots of the holy tree grew the tree you see here. I came from the tree."

"Are you a god?"

"No, only a messenger."

Varkell turned and smiled sadly at Tayer. His eyes blazed as she came into his arms. "And, may the Mother help us all, the message has been delivered."

The look he then turned on Mikhail was far removed from mortal understanding, but a greater part of it held the full weight of pain Tayer had only reflected.

"She carries my child, Mikhail. This is the last time I shall see her."

"It burns, cousin," Tayer said softly, "this brightness within and brightness without. I can no longer bear them both."

Mikhail stared at them. He felt large and stupid. "What can I do?" he asked, knowing he would do whatever they wanted but not knowing what he could possibly do that would help.

"The joining planned for Tayer must not happen. You must join with her yourself."

"She doesn't love me."

"No, she doesn't." Varkell could not lie. "But when I am gone, she will."

Mikhail looked at Tayer and then within himself. The flame of love he had carried for so long still burned, perhaps now more brightly than ever. Tayer had been chosen for glory; he could love that as well. He nodded and held out his arms.

Walking like one in a dream, Tayer came to him and rested her head against his chest with a sigh. Holding her gently, as if afraid she would break, Mikhail bent and laid his face upon her hair. When he looked up, they were alone in the Grove.

On the ride back to the palace, Mikhail pondered how much to tell the king. In the end, he decided not to mention the Grove. He'd not have believed it himself without proof. As everyone seemed to know of his love for Tayer, Mikhail felt his best chance lay in convincing the king that Tayer cared for him in return, hoping the older man's love for his daughter and his desire to see her happy would cause him to call off the arranged joining.

He glanced at Tayer riding serenely beside him. It could only help that she was so obviously a woman in love.

Hanna met them in the stableyard.

"He's been asking for you both," she told them. "You'd better hurry. He's waiting in the small audience room."

Mikhail took Tayer's hand and together they went into the palace, Hanna trailing along behind. Heads turned as they passed and the halls filled with rumor. Tayer, listening to the song of another world, didn't hear. Mikhail set his jaw and pretended not to.

"Sire, I have to speak with you."

The king looked at his nephew and then at his daughter.

"Yes," he said dryly. "I should say you do."

His Majesty had not been impressed when Tayer's absence had been discovered and he was less impressed when she showed up five hours later with Mikhail. What must the envoy from Halda be thinking?

"Sire, your daughter and I wish to be joined."

Keeping his face carefully noncommittal—he'd been afraid something like this would happen since the first time he'd seen the light in Mikhail's eyes—the king sat down and peered over steepled fingers at Tayer. "Is that what you wish, child?"

"Yes, Father."

"This talk of your joining is a little sudden, is it not?"

"If I'd known you were arranging a joining, Sire, I would've spoken sooner, but I was away on the border . . ."

"Defending the country. You grew up in my household, Mikhail, I know your worth. However, nothing prevented Tayer from speaking when I made her aware of my plans." Although he'd carefully kept Mikhail from finding out, he'd made sure Tayer had no objections before he sent the Messenger to Halda.

Mikhail held his breath and sent a short prayer to the Mother that Tayer remained enough in the world to lie.

"I was unsure of my feelings, Father," she hesitated then looked almost shyly up at Mikhail. "It wasn't until I saw him on his return that I knew."

Mikhail smiled at her and gently squeezed her hand. It seemed very small in his and very cold. Then he gave his attention again to the king.

"If Tayer joins with Halda," the older man said thoughtfully, "Ardhan gains a valuable ally. What does the country gain if she joins with you?"

"The country would gain less, it's true, but you would have comfort in the knowledge that your daughter was happy. Sire."

The king raised a bushy eyebrow.

"And you don't believe she will be happy in Halda."

"No, Sire." Mikhail met his gaze steadily. "If she joins with the Crown Prince of Halda, it will be a joining without love."

"Do you love her?"

"Oh, yes, Sire! With all my heart!"

Only a fool would doubt the sincerity of Mikhail's response. The king was no fool.

"Tayer?"

For the first time since she had entered the room, for the first time in many months, Tayer looked at her father directly. He drew in his breath sharply under the full impact of her eyes. He couldn't question the love they held—he couldn't know the love was not for Mikhail.

"If love is the way of it," and he wondered how he could've been so blind to think that Tayer had no more than a sibling's affection for her cousin, "you have my blessing. I will do what I can about Halda."

"I will join with him, Sire."

"What?" The king spun around, Mikhail stared at his sister in astonishment, and even Tayer rejoined the world long enough to look surprised.

Hanna got up from the stool where she'd been sitting and stepped forward.

"Hanna, child, I didn't know you were there."

Hanna smiled strangely. "Yes, Sire, I know."

"What's this you've said?"

"I am willing to join with the Crown Prince of Halda. If he approves, you'll still have an ally and Tayer will be happy." The Mother forbid, said her eyes, that Tayer should be unhappy.

"That's a very noble sacrifice you're making for your cousin," the king began kindly, wishing that either Hanna's mother or his beloved queen still lived. "And we are all touched that you're willing to put her happiness ahead of yours but . . ."

"I'm not doing it for her," Hanna explained, wanting someone to understand, just this once. "I'm doing it for me."

"To go away from your family, to join with a man you've never met." Mikhail took a step toward his sister, his hands spread in puzzlement. "What is there in that for you?"

"A place of my own," Hanna answered softly, turning to face him. "Where I am not overlooked. Where I am myself, not Tayer's cousin or Mikhail's sister or the king's niece. You and Tayer have each other, why can't this be for me? All my life I've been the second princess, I'd like to be first for a change."

The king's heavy brows drew in over his nose and he studied his niece as if seeing her for the first time. "We never knew you felt this way . . ."

"That," said Hanna, "is part of the problem. Please, Uncle."

And the king nodded.

"If Halda agrees . . ."

A Messenger was sent and Halda agreed. One unknown princess would do as well as another in the opinion of the crown prince, who had little interest in being joined at all. At the end of a week of state festivities, a proxy joining was held on the dais of the People's Square. Hanna managed to look regal in the ridiculous clothing demanded by the occasion and gave her responses in a strong, clear voice that carried to the meanest viewpoint at the back of the Square.

"I still don't understand why you have to do this," Mikhail said, as attendants carried her back into the palace and the Great Doors closed.

"If you'd understood," Hanna told him sharply, removing the cumbersome headdress, "I wouldn't have had to do it."

Mikhail looked to Tayer for support, but she only smiled sadly and shook her head. With the light she carried had come understanding, but it was far too late to start making amends.

The next day, Hanna left to live with a husband she had never met and, although Mikhail and Tayer both watched until she rode out of sight, she never once looked back.

Tayer and Mikhail were joined by the king in a quiet ceremony; a ceremony they both considered to be unnecessary. In their hearts, they knew they had been joined that day in the Grove. Tayer's condition soon became obvious and her father was delighted.

"The Mother has blessed this union," he declared, so enchanted by the idea of a grandchild he ignored the unusual aspects of the pregnancy.

For the most part the rest of the court took their cue from the king. Tayer was insulated from gossip and Mikhail heard little of it, for only a fool would speak in Mikhail's presence, but what he heard caused him great uneasiness.

"Tayer?"

With a visible effort, Tayer brought herself back from the light. She smiled at Mikhail, who knelt at her feet, and gently touched the tumbled mane of his hair.

"Tayer," he hesitated, considered what he was asking and found, with no little surprise, that the question was painless. To think of Tayer with another man would have torn him to pieces, but to think of her with Varkell brought only a renewed sense of wonder. "Tayer, the child you carry, when did you conceive?"

"A month after you left for the border."

Mikhail cursed beneath his breath and Tayer looked at him in puzzlement.

"What's wrong?" she asked.

"When the child is born, the court will know it isn't mine. Your time will be either a month too early or a month too late." Convincing the court, and her father, that he'd impregnated her before leaving would've been bad enough but nothing compared to what was likely to happen. A royal child was meticulously examined and then presented to the people, making an eight-month lie impossible to sustain. He didn't want to think of what Tayer would go through then.

"Don't worry." She took one of his hands and placed it on the gentle swelling of her stomach. "It has been taken care of."

And suddenly, Mikhail felt that it had.

Tayer's pregnancy was not an easy one. Throughout the long winter, as the child grew within her, she seemed to fade. Cheekbones cut angles into her face and her hands became thin and frail, almost transparent. She gave all her strength, all her life, to the child. Her eyes still shone as bright, or brighter, but few could meet the unearthly beauty of her gaze. Mikhail, looking beyond the beauty to the glory that consumed her, was himself consumed with worry for his young wife.

Winter finally ended. The grip of ice and cold released and the first greens of spring began to appear.

The time came when, by Mikhail's count, Tayer should deliver; and then it passed. Taken care of, yes, but Mikhail worried that Tayer would not be able to bear the burden much longer. Every day he carried her out to the gardens, but it did little good, for every day she grew weaker. At long last, on a cloudless summer afternoon, the pains began.

The midwives expected trouble. The princess' hips were narrow and she wasn't strong. The birth, they feared, would rip her apart.

"And if it comes to it," sighed the younger as they scrubbed their hands, "who do we save, the mother or the child?"

"Both," came the reply and the voice held conviction that even Lord Death would have hesitated to challenge.

When everything was ready, they let Mikhail into the room. He sat by the bed and held Tayer's limp hand in his. Her grip tightened and she whimpered. He doubted she knew he was there. He'd never felt so helpless.

"Isn't there anything I can do?"

"Give her what strength you can, milord," said one of the women, laying a cool cloth on Tayer's brow. "This isn't going to be easy."

But the babe had other ideas. As if wanting to make up for all the trouble that had gone before, she slid effortlessly into the world and greeted the day with a hearty bellow.

"A girl, milord, milady. A fine, healthy girl."

Mikhail looked at the bloody, wrinkled bundle at Tayer's breast and touched a tiny cheek with one massive finger.

"She's beautiful," he whispered.

A breeze came through the window, bringing with it the scent of trees and forest loam. It gently fanned the mother and child.

"We shall call her Crystal," Tayer said, looking down at her tiny daughter, "For the light shines through her."

When Tayer raised exhausted eyes to Mikhail's face, his heart sang with joy for though the other world had left her they still shone with light . . . only now, at last, as Varkell had promised, the light was for him.

Seated on a moss-covered log, just outside the Sacred Grove, Doan waited. The seed had been planted and nurtured. All that remained of Varkell was the tree and the child. The tree was an empty vessel. The child had her own guardian in Mikhail. One last thing and he could return to the caverns.

"So, little gardener, your job is done."

Doan's eyes narrowed as the speaker sat down beside him. The sapphire robes should have looked ridiculously out of place in the depths of the Lady's Wood; as it was, the Wood looked out of place about the robes. Doan suppressed the urge to move away. "I felt your presence," he growled. "I waited. You're too late."

Slender fingers ran through red-gold curls and the full lips curved. "But I came to talk to you."

"Why?" the dwarf demanded.

One wickedly arched brow rose. "Why to thank you for being such a sturdy guardian, of course."

Doan hooked his thumbs behind his belt and glared. "I guarded against you, not for you."

"But I never had any intention of interfering." He stretched out long legs and settled himself more comfortably against a protruding branch. "I'm a game player, always have been. Your *seedling* is likely to be the last worthy game I'll be able to play."

"Last game?"

"Don't get your hopes up, little man. She can't defeat me, although I won't begin until she thinks she has a chance."

"You'll stay away from the child?"

"I just said so, didn't I?"

"You lie."

"Yes," he agreed, "I do."

Doan could not decide if this amiable admission was

general or specific so he left it. It was enough that the enemy saw only the most obvious scenario, that his vanity blinded him to possibilities other than outright confrontation. "Was that all you wanted to say?" he demanded after the silence stretched to uncomfortable lengths.

"That you've been more than useless here? Yes."

"You came all this way just to annoy me?"

He smiled lazily. "Basically. It's a hobby of mine, annoying people."

A twitch. Another. Then Doan threw back his head and laughed. He couldn't help himself. It was, after all, a hobby of his as well. When his eyes stopped streaming, he was alone on the log.

I almost liked him, he realized, wiping moisture from his cheeks. *Mother-creator help you child; he is more dangerous than we thought.*

Interlude Two

Tayer's baby grew into a child, not outwardly different from other children. She learned to walk early, and then to run. Soon, the entire court, the Palace Guard, the Elite, and a small army of servants were watching out for her as she frequently appeared in places she had no right to be, her harrassed parents and nurses often with no idea of where she'd got to. She learned to talk late, but when at last she did, she spoke in full sentences; never resorting to baby prattle, and never hesitant about expressing her opinion. Green eyes wide and oddly mature, she backed many an adult away from their views.

She was pampered and much indulged and proved without doubt that a child cannot be spoiled by too much love.

For ten years she grew as other children did. And if she moved a little faster, threw herself into childhood with an almost desperate enthusiasm, involved herself in everything she did with a thoroughness and single-minded purpose, it was easy for the adults surrounding her to miss seeing. Or seeing, misunderstand.

Toward the end of her tenth year she quieted and began to spend long hours with Tayer in the gardens, leaning against her mother's knees. She went to Mikhail's office off the training-yards and stood, cheek pressed to his shoulder, watching as he worked. At odd times she stood, head cocked, as though she listened to words carried on the wind.

Two days after her eleventh birthday, the centaur came, appearing suddenly in the garden where Tayer and Mikhail sat with their daughter.

"Crystal." His voice was the rumble of a thousand galloping hoofs. "I have come for you."

Slowly, Crystal pulled herself from Tayer's nerveless fingers, and walked forward until she stood within the shadow of the massive creature. Then she turned and faced her parents.

Whatever protests they might have made washed away in the flood of radiance from her eyes. For the first time in eleven years, they were forced to confront who her father had been; not the mortal man who'd loved and raised her but an enchanted being of power and light. Still, Mikhail might have found the strength to deny it had the child not raised her eyes to his. Once before he had looked into the other world they showed and that time as this, he'd admitted defeat. His angry questions choked off and became a pained nod.

Tayer dropped to her knees and held wide her arms. Crystal hesitated a moment then ran to her mother's embrace. The light poured from them both and Mikhail, refusing to look away, was temporarily blinded by it. Then his arms were full of a warm bundle smelling of sunshine and hidden forest groves and the apricot she'd been eating . . . had it been mere moments before?

"Don't worry, Papa," breathed a quiet voice against his cheek. "I shall take the pony you gave me for my birthday, and I shall remember you, and he shall help me not to be lonely."

Then his arms were empty and when he could see again, Crystal sat perched on the broad back of the centaur. As the creature turned, the sunlight flashed on a single tear running silver down the gentle curve of her face, and then they were gone.

Tayer, who had been brave for her daughter's sake, shuddered and turned to face her husband.

"You knew," he realized suddenly. "You knew that someday this would happen."

She nodded and her tears scattered to fall like dew upon the roses. "I carried that light beneath my heart," she said. "I am sorry, my love, but I could never forget she was her father's daughter."

Mikhail wordlessly opened his arms, much as Tayer had done, and Tayer, much as Crystal had done, ran into them.

He stroked her hair, marveling at the strength it must have taken to hold such pain within herself for so many years.

"What shall we tell your father?" he asked at last. "The king and the court will have to know something."

"We will tell them the truth. The truth from the beginning."

"Will he believe us?"

"It doesn't matter," Tayer cried, her fingers digging desperately into Mikhail's arms. "She's gone."

Doan pulled his hood closer around his face and glowered up through the rain at C'Tal. "This'd better be important," he warned.

The centaur nodded, hair and beard a solid wet mass on shoulders and chest. "It is," he said. "Else we would not have felt it necessary to call you. You are aware that it is raining?"

"No," Doan snarled. "I hadn't noticed."

C'Tal looked confused. "You had not noticed? But . . ."

"Of course I'd noticed, you over-educated carthorse." He scanned the area, stomped to a nearby boulder, climbed to the top and sat with an audible squelch from sodden clothes. This put him eye to eye with the centaur. "I'm cold, I'm wet and I'm fast losing what little patience I have. Get to the point."

"It is raining." C'Tal held up a massive hand as Doan's eyes began to glow red. "Please, hear what I have to say. The rain is, as you have said, the point. It has rained here for eight days now. The child is causing it."

Both Doan's eyebrows rose until they disappeared beneath the edge of his hood. He held out one gnarled hand, palm up, then brought the captured water to his lips. "I'm impressed," he said at last. "How?"

The centaur absently scrapped at the rock with a front hoof. "She is not even aware that she is doing it. But," he added, anticipating Doan's next question, "we are aware and we are sure it is her doing."

"Just what exactly did she do?"

"Eight days ago, her pony died and in her grief she wept."

A slow smile spread over Doan's face. "And the world weeps with her. Sympathetic magic."

"So we feel also. But she has stopped weeping and the world has not. As this is not something we taught her to do, we are not able to teach her to undo it. This is not something any of the others were ever capable of."

"Well, they weren't a very sympathetic lot, were they?"

Great corded muscles stood out along C'Tal's shoulders and arms and his voice was ice as he replied: "We only teach. We are not responsible for what is done with our teachings."

Doan slowly rose to his feet and the two ancient powers stood immobile, gazes locked. With a shudder that ran down the length of his body, C'Tal broke away, his head and shoulders slowly bending under the weight of an impossible burden.

"We are not responsible for what is done with our teachings," he repeated, his voice so low it sounded like the distant rumble of thunder. "We cannot be responsible for the actions of any thinking being. But this time . . ." His head came up and his mighty shoulders squared. "This time we teach where the responsibilities lie." He snorted, an amazingly horse-like sound. "We are no longer so blind as to think the Mother's Youngest will know this on their own."

Doan stood a moment longer, then he nodded, once,

and abruptly sat. "Which brings us back to the rain. Have you tried to comfort her?"

C'Tal backed up a step, his tail flicking from side to side in short, jerky arcs. "We are not . . ." he began. "That is, we do not ever . . . it is not in us to . . ."

A centaur at a loss for words, Doan thought, the corners of his mouth twitching slightly despite the circumstances. *Now that's something you don't see everyday.* Aloud he said, "Let her go home, C'Tal."

"But her learning has barely begun!"

"Not forever, you idiot; just let her visit."

"If that is all you can offer, you may return to your caverns. We hone a weapon and time is short."

"Try to remember that weapon is still a little girl. No, wait!" Doan chopped through whatever C'Tal was trying to say with that staccato command. "You asked for my advice, now listen to it. Responsibility isn't enough. She'll never know compassion if she isn't shown it, nor love either. If you can't give that to her, take her to someone who can."

"Emotion is . . ."

"Emotion caused this." Doan gestured up at the glowering gray sky. "Remember? She's tapped into something here the Enemy doesn't have. I don't know how, maybe it's her parentage, the Mother knows that's strange enough, but if she's to be the key to the Enemy's Doom she'll need all the help she can get. Don't cut her off from this. It may save her life. It may save all our lives."

C'Tal appeared to be thinking it over. More rain gathered in his hair and beard and began to stream over his motionless body.

"It is possible that you are correct," he said at last, spun on one hind leg, and galloped away.

"You're welcome!" Doan snarled as C'Tal's glistening black haunches disappeared into the distance. A centaur at full gallop moved too fast for the eye to follow. "I don't envy that child her next few years with those pompous nags," he muttered, climbing down off the boulder. He scowled as he realized he was wet through, then he smiled suddenly. "Nor," he declared vindictively, heading for home, "do I envy those overblown horse's asses their next few years with her." He snorted. "They'll remember this rain with fondness if she ever gets mad."

Eight

One moment, all was peace and stillness in the Sacred Grove. The next, the muffled boom of a distant explosion sent Tayer into the sanctuary of Mikhail's arms. The sound had barely died when there came another. And then another.

In the quiet after the third blast, the birches of the Grove shuddered and swayed, although no wind moved through them.

"Balls of Chaos," Mikhail swore softly, holding Tayer safe against his chest. "What was that?"

"The beginning of war," replied a clear, young voice. "And possibly the end of Ardhan."

"What . . ." Mikhail's hand went to his side, groping for his absent sword. Not since his first visit, seventeen years before, had he carried a sword into the Sacred Grove. Not until this instant had he missed it.

But Tayer pulled herself from Mikhail's grasp and stepped forward eagerly, scanning the circle of trees.

"Crystal?" she called.

The young woman who stepped out from between the birches seemed to have also stepped out of legend. Although barely more than a girl, she stood as tall as Mikhail, sapling slender, and graceful in a way unseen since the Eldest died and her sisters disappeared from mortal sight. Her hair was a white so pure it shone silver and her eyes were the green of new spring leaves flecked lightly with gold.

She was dressed for travel, breeches, tunic, and riding boots all in black, and she looked like a shadow defying the soft sunlight of the Grove.

"Crystal," Tayer said again and held open her arms.

Crystal went eagerly to the embrace, resting her cheek on her mother's head with a weary sigh. She had come a very long way in the last few days and she had a disagreeable duty still to perform. This temporary haven was welcome.

Tayer broke away first. She pushed her daughter out to arm's length and looked her up and down. "Black becomes you," she said at last with a smile. "But what are you doing home? Have they given you a holiday?"

"No, Mother. My time with the centaurs is done. They sent me to help."

"Help what, child?" Mikhail asked.

Crystal looked over at her stepfather, her face grim enough to wipe away his smile of greeting. "From the time of the Eldest, through the raids we have fought every harvest, we . . ." She waved a long-fingered hand. ". . . Ardhan, has been part of a most deadly game, put through our paces by Kraydak, the wizard who has controlled the throne of Melac for the last four hundred years."

"Wizard," Mikhail grunted, his brows drawing into a golden vee as he considered it. "That would," he muttered to his memories, "explain a great deal."

Tayer shook her head. "You must be mistaken, child. The wizards are all long dead."

"No, not all. Two remain. The sounds you heard were Kraydak's work." Crystal paused and took a deep breath, the rest was difficult to say. "We must go back to town at once. The palace and everyone in it has been destroyed. We three are the only survivors of the Royal House of Ardhan. Mother, you are now queen."

The distant cry of a bird was the only noise as shock, anger, sorrow—a cacophony of emotion—roared through the Grove. But no disbelief. No denial. The truth in Crystal's voice was stronger than those.

"Everyone?" Tayer asked at last, her eyes wide, her voice trembling.

"Yes, Mother. Everyone."

Mikhail looked out at Crystal through the numbness that thankfully seemed to be cushioning the despair. "You were in the Grove seconds after the sound died. How can you know what happened?"

"The centaurs foresaw Kraydak's attack. As I could do nothing to stop it, they sent me here to you." She looked earnestly at her parents. "Although I'd have tried if there'd been time . . ."

"You could do nothing to stop it?" Mikhail interrupted, a dawning light of understanding showing on his face. "What could you possibly have done?"

Crystal backed up a step, laced her fingers together, and stared down into the pattern.

"I," she said softly, "am the other wizard."

When Tayer, Mikhail, and Crystal brought their lathered horses to a stop in the People's Square, they were instantly surrounded by terrified men and women. Hands clutched and pulled at their clothing and the horses' harnesses. Voices wailed, sobbed, and cried out in despair. Tayer and Mikhail sat like statues in the midst of chaos and stared in shock at the smoldering pile of rubble that had been the palace. Even Crystal, who had known what they would face, sat silent and disbelieving.

The blow had been well aimed. The outbuildings—the stables, the barracks, the servants' quarters—had not been touched. The old palace wall, with its seven new arches opening the palace up to the people, still stood. Only the palace itself had been destroyed. The great hulking stone edifice that had squatted ugly and supreme in the center of King's City was no more. It looked as if a giant had lifted his massive fist and squashed it flat.

A score of people—those of the Guard who had not been in the building at the time of the attack, as well as nobles, servants, and townsfolk—crawled over the wreckage. In several places, small groups marked another body being lifted clear. On the pile of debris that had once been the West Tower, a girl, no more than ten or twelve years old, crouched and rocked a broken, bloody body in her arms. The body had been so badly crushed it was impossible to tell at a distance if it was male or female, mother or father. The girl's face was wet with blood from pressing her lips against her grisly burden. Her eyes were wide with shock, staring ahead at nothing. She wailed, a thin high cry, sorrow and fear mixed together. It rose and fell to the cadence of her rocking.

On the very edge of the Square, atop the rubble of what had been the sunroom wall, four bodies lay. Around them stood a Guard of Honor. The guards' arms were red to the elbow and their uniforms were spattered with blood. Dull crimson stains marked the sheets that covered, but did not hide, the identities of the four dead.

When Tayer's anguished eyes rested on what lay guarded there, she moaned softly and tried to swing off her horse. The mob clung to her in desperation, and she retreated, trapped. Mikhail peeled his hand from the pommel of his sword—it had gone there in a truly useless gesture of defiance when he first saw the destruction—and reached for Tayer's reins, his intention clear. If the crowd would not let them dismount, then he would force a way through on horseback.

Crystal laid her hand on his arm and, when he turned to look at her, shook her head. She dropped her own reins, took a deep breath, and sang.

If the song had words, no one afterward remembered them. It was more a song of feelings. It was reassurance, security, hope. It was the song a mother hums to her child as she tucks it in at night. It was powerful, universal, calming.

One by one, the crowd quieted as the song poured over them. Some began to weep bitterly, but the panic stilled. Even the young girl stopped wailing and turned to stare at Crystal with wounded eyes.

Crystal's gaze swept the crowd, resting briefly on each mourner. Not until all who needed it had drawn strength from the green fire of her eyes did she stop singing. The breezes carried the melody for a few seconds more, then they too were still.

Mikhail swung down to the pavement, the creaking of his saddle leather sounding unnaturally loud. He held up his arms to Tayer. She collapsed into them, paused for an instant in the security of his embrace, then, keeping a tight grip on his hand, started the long walk to the edge of the Square. The people parted to let them through.

When she reached the bodies, Tayer knelt and lifted the edge of the sheet. They were all there: her father, the King, Davan and Eyrik, her brothers, and Savell, Davan's pregnant wife. She brushed a lock of hair out of Savell's eyes and gently lowered the fabric, wiping her bloody hand on her skirt.

"Majesty?" a merchant asked quietly, his words falling into the silence like stones into water. "What are we to do?"

Tayer looked up at her daughter, but Crystal had banked the fire in her eyes and had no answer. She looked at Mikhail but he merely shook his head. The message was clear. Tayer was now queen. The choice must be hers.

The queen searched for her voice and forced it past her grief. To her surprise it neither quavered nor shook although it was husky with the tears that streamed down her face.

"We will bury our dead and we will prepare for war."

War. Of all those in the Square, only Crystal did not recoil from the word. Her eye had been caught by the glint of sunlight on red-gold curls and she stared in horrified fascination at the man beneath them who stood at the edge of the crowd. It wasn't his beauty she marked, nor that his sapphire robes were clean and unstained by blood or grime. It was the fact that in the full light of the afternoon sun, he cast no shadow.

Aware of the scrutiny, he smiled up at her, raised one hand in a mocking salute, and faded slowly away.

The breeze carried the sound of his laughter.

"Crystal?"

She turned slowly from the window. The voice was not one she knew, but the face hovered on the edge of memory. She searched until she found a name to fit it.

"Bryon?"

The tall, dark-haired young man flashed a dazzling smile and made an elegant leg. "At your command."

Crystal stared in amazement.

"Bryon?" she repeated.

Bryon gracefully straightened up.

"Ah," he said. "I see you're puzzled. After all, it's been six years, how could you be expected to recognize me?" He leaned closer. "I'll let you in on the secret." His lips hovered at the edge of her ear and his breath was a warm breeze on her cheek. "I've gotten taller."

Crystal backed away.

"So have you." Bryon nodded solemnly, but his gray eyes danced. It didn't seem to bother him that the startlingly lovely creature his old playmate had grown into had a slight advantage in height.

Crystal—who had almost ceased to think of time, for the centaurs having all of eternity never bothered with it—was suddenly aware of just how long those six years had been. This was the grubby companion of her childhood? This handsome courtier with the disarming smile who was planting warm kisses on the palm of her hand . . . who was planting warm kisses on the palm of her hand? She snatched her hand away.

"Bryon!"

"Crystal!" He mimicked her tone exactly, then threw a brotherly arm about her shoulders and propelled her down the hall. "Come on. They want you in my father's library."

His father was the Duke of Belkar. The House of

Belkar was cousin to the Royal House through Meredith who had joined with Rael, the son of the Lady of the Grove. The current duke had opened his townhouse to what was left of the court.

"So," said Bryon conversationally as they walked toward the library, "I hear you're a wizard."

Crystal, preoccupied with analyzing the peculiar warmth radiating out from where Bryon's arm lay across her shoulders, merely mumbled an affirmative.

"Well," he continued, apparently undismayed both by her lack of response and by the knowledge of the slaughter the ancient wizards had caused, "I suppose everyone needs a hobby."

That penetrated. She twisted lithely out of his grasp and turned to face him. *People will be wary of you,* the centaurs had said. *They will treat you with caution and respect. Some will even be frightened.* They'd never mentioned that some would be amused.

"Hobby? I have powers you couldn't even imagine and you call it a hobby? Don't you realize what I am?" She regretted the outburst the moment the words left her mouth, her voice sounding shrill and childish. Sounding, in fact, like the voice of a child overreacting to being teased. Bryon had always been able to get that response; that, at least, the six years apart hadn't changed.

But Bryon, secure in his victory, only smiled and held the library door open for her. "You're late," he said.

It's difficult to impress someone who tied your braids to a pigsty when you were seven, Crystal reflected as she went into the room.

The library was large and Crystal was surprised by the number of books and scrolls it contained. The duke, a grizzled old fighter, had not stuck in her childhood memory of him as much of a reader. Tayer sat behind a massive table covered over with a map of Ardhan and the surrounding territory, trying to make sense of what Mikhail and the Duke of Belkar were saying. This was no easy task as the two men contradicted each other loudly and often, pulling the map back and forth while trying to make their point. Crystal felt sorry for her mother, caught in the middle of something she had no hope of controlling.

The only son and heir of the Duke of Riven leaned on the mantlepiece, staring into the ashes of an old fire. Deep circles bracketed his eyes and he plucked nervously at the hilt of his dagger with one fine-boned hand. He had lost his mother and his younger sister in the destruction of the palace and it looked as if he would now lose his father to grief.

The Court Treasurer, one pudgy hand smoothing the burgundy velvet of his robe as though he soothed a cat, argued quietly with the Captain of the Palace Guard. They were the only two ranking members of the palace staff left alive. A gray-robed Scholar stood to one side, listening. He had been with Belkar's household only a few weeks, but as none of the Scholars advising the royal family had survived the destruction of the palace, the duke had asked him to attend.

The captain noticed Crystal first, and fell silent. One by one, all heads turned toward her. Even young Riven looked up from his sorrow. The room grew so still that a breeze could be heard dancing through the linden tree outside the window. The silence extended and became awkward.

Finally, Bryon, who had followed Crystal into the room, cleared his throat.

"I have brought the princess as you requested, sir."

The princess. Much easier to deal with than the wizard. The tension in the room eased and the duke came around the table to take Crystal's hands.

"It's good to see you again, child," he said. "Though one could wish it were under better circumstances." He leaned back slightly to look her full in the face although he carefully avoided meeting her eyes. It couldn't hurt to be careful around wizards, even if you had dandled this one on your knee when she was a baby. "You've grown some since we last met."

"That was six years ago, sir. I was eleven."

"Ah, yes." He dropped her hands. "Well, now, your father tells me you know something of what attacked us. We've got to have details if we're to fight this thing, eh?"

Crystal glanced at Mikhail. Her father . . . As one of the six dukes, Belkar had to know the truth of her parentage. Whether he refused to acknowledge it out of disbelief or from respect for Mikhail she wasn't sure, nor did she care for she refused to acknowledge it herself. Mikhail was the father of her heart, all the father she would ever want. She met his eyes. He dropped one lid in a slow wink and, just for that instant, the tasks yet ahead did not seem so impossible.

"Now then," the duke continued, "what's this you've got to tell us about Melac?"

Crystal discarded the princess with relief. The wizard answered.

"We aren't fighting Melac. We never have been."

"Could've sworn it was a Melacian put a spear through my leg when I rode with the Elite," muttered the Captain of the Guard.

"Perhaps. But he was a tool in another's hands. The Wizard Kraydak has ruled Melac since before the Lady died." In Ardhan, there was, and always would be, only one Lady.

The room erupted into a flurry of questions and exclamations of disbelief. Even young Riven was momentarily shaken from his stupor. Only Crystal and the Scholar remained silent.

When order had been restored, Mikhail turned to the gray-robed man. "You didn't seem surprised to hear that," he said suspiciously. "You knew about Kraydak? About this wizard?"

The Scholar shook his head. He was as tall as the members of the Royal House, who were taller than most of their subjects, and was thin and wiry, his dark hair streaked with gray.

"No, milord, I knew nothing, but there have been rumors of how the Kings of Melac have a counselor who never dies and through him a weak and struggling nation became an empire. Although there have been no great magics that only a wizard could perform, Melac's armies have had entirely too much help from the elements for it to have been coincidental. The Scholars have studied the ancient wizards . . ." His face twisted suddenly. "After all, they nearly sent the whole world to Lord Death. Of them all, only Kraydak had the power to survive the Doom." He shrugged. "But I know nothing. Scholars have not been welcomed in Melac or her conquered countries for years."

"Nonsense," broke in the duke. "Why, I myself was in Melac not more than a year ago to try and hammer out some sort of treaty and there were plenty of Scholars about then, they certainly looked welcome . . . flitting around like shadows . . . noses in everybody's business . . . gave me the creeps." He suddenly remembered who he was talking to. "No offense, Lapus."

Lapus smiled thinly. "None taken, sir." Then the smile vanished. The Scholar's voice deepened and passion marred its smooth composure. "The gray-robed ones you saw were not Scholars whatever they called themselves. A Scholar has no master but knowledge and lets nothing, and no one, stand in the way of the search for Truth."

Crystal studied the Scholar thoughtfully as he spoke. He was nothing like the genial teachers she and Bryon had shared as children. His intensity when he spoke of knowledge as the only master was almost fanatical. He reminded her very much of the centaurs. She missed her old teachers, and the feeling of certainty they radiated.

"I am old for lessons," she began as Lapus finished speaking, "but I have been with the Elders for so long I know little about the ways of Man." Her eyes, the muted green-gold of sunlight through leaves, locked onto his. "Will you teach me?"

Trapped in the quiet depths of her eyes, Lapus couldn't have said no had he wanted to. A pulse began to throb in his temple. With an effort, he bowed his head and forced his gaze to the tile floor.

"Yes, milady," was all he said.

Crystal nodded once and turned away. The exchange had disturbed her as much as it obviously had Lapus, for all that had looked out of the Scholar's eyes when she held them with her own was the reflection of a tall young woman with ivory skin and silver hair. She wasn't supposed to see herself in another's eyes, her power looked through to their heart.

The duke cleared his throat and indicated the map on the table. "Lessons will have to wait, child, now we need plans for war."

"Wage it any way you like," the wizard told him curtly.

"Crystal . . ." Tayer said warningly, aghast at her daughter's rudeness.

Crystal sighed. She would have to straighten some things out with her mother. "I will have no involvement in the fighting," she explained.

Tayer looked at her in puzzlement. "But Crystal, you said we were fighting a wizard."

"I beg your pardon if I've confused you, Mother, but I am fighting the wizard. You fight only his armies."

"Amounts to the same thing, doesn't it?" snorted the Captain of the Guard. "The wizard . . . his armies?"

"No, it doesn't."

"Well, what about that mess on the hill then? If that's not fighting a wizard, what is?"

"You didn't fight him though, did you?"

The captain remembered the three mighty and invisible blows that had reduced the palace to rubble. He'd been standing thirty feet away and yet had not been touched, although the sound nearly deafened him. His ears still rang with it. He remembered the stream of blood trickling out from under the crushed stone and how it had lapped daintily against his boot. His ruddy face paled and he shook his head. "No, I didn't.

But I would've," he growled, "could I have got my hands on him."

"If you'd got your hands on him, you'd be dead." Crystal moved to the window and lifted her face to the sun. She drank in the warmth and light, saving it up against the darkness to come. She didn't want to be the world's savior . . . she didn't have a choice. Then she sighed and turned back to the gray despair that filled the library.

"The Scholar was right. Only Kraydak survived the holocaust and it took almost all of his great power to do it. He had his life but not much else. He was also afraid that the Doom which took the other wizards might still claim him so, defenseless, he hid. And he stayed hidden for over a thousand years, rebuilding his strength and gradually coming to realize that he had escaped completely. None of the shadows that lurked in dark corners were waiting to claim him.

"When he emerged, he found that people had changed. Having been free of the tyranny of the wizards for generations, they were not likely to bow down to the lone survivor and he was still weak enough to be killed if the mortals were determined enough. Kraydak took another road to the power he craved; he offered his services to the weakest king he could find. Not as a wizard, but as a counselor and a friend. He played on the king's weaknesses, on his yearning for power. He took the king to his tower and offered him the world. The king took the offer and from that day to this he and his heirs have been figureheads, for the power of Melac is in Kraydak's hands.

"Armies moved out, always attacking where the defenders were weakest, protected by the knowledge that should they begin to fail, fire, flood, or some other seemingly natural disaster would come to their aid. Perhaps they lost a few battles, but they won all the wars. Melac became an Empire.

"Young men and women began to disappear into Kraydak's tower. Those who spoke of resistance or rebellion were visited in the night. The ones who lived went mad; most died.''

"We share a border with Melac," the duke interrupted. "Why weren't we one of the first attacked?''

"We were. The battle that killed the Lady's love, was the beginning of Kraydak's push for an Empire. Fortunately for Ardhan, he forgot to take the mountains into account and his neophyte army had to fight the terrain before they met the enemy. He was new to mortal warfare, and so he lost. He hasn't returned for two reasons. Once he got his people moving south and east, the way of least resistance, momentum kept them moving away from us. The second reason concerns a prophecy, that in Ardhan would be born the last of the wizards and his possible defeat.''

"I always felt Melac was waiting for something," Mikhail said quietly from where he stood at Tayer's back. "If you studied the border raids, it was the only thing that made sense.''

Crystal nodded. "Kraydak was waiting for me.''

"Well that makes no sense," fumed the duke. "If he knew you were coming and you could defeat him, he should've taken the country to keep you from being born.''

"He was bored.''

"He was what?''

"Bored. Everything came too easily, there were no challenges, so he watched and waited and when he thought I would give him a good fight—but not one he felt he would lose—he let me know he knew I was here.''

Crystal stepped back and directed the duke's gaze out the window. Not far away people still moved amid the ruins.

"He destroyed the palace to tell me that the game has begun.''

Nyle, the young Lord of Riven, looked up. His eyes were rimmed in red and the whites were murky from lack of sleep. A piece of chestnut hair hung lank across his forehead. His lips curled back from his teeth and he glared at Crystal from under heavy lids.

"My mother and sister are dead," he snarled, "and you think it's a game?"

"Kraydak thinks it's a game," Crystal corrected him gently although her expression remained stern. "I have never been more serous. Much of my family died in the palace as well."

"He wouldn't even be here but for you! He would've left us alone!"

"Perhaps."

"Then it's your fault; your fault my mother is dead and my father is dying." He jerked away from the fireplace and turned toward her. "Your fault!"

"NYLE!"

Mikhail's bass roar blasted some of the glaze from the young man's eyes. He stopped and drew a long shuddering breath.

"Milord?"

"Go see to your father," Mikhail commanded kindly. "He needs you by him."

Nyle nodded slowly and began to leave the room, his shoulders bowed under his load of grief. At the door, he paused, and the face he turned to Crystal was damp with tears. "Your fault," he whispered once more, and then he left.

"I would watch that young man," Lapus said softly. "If he truly believes that the princess is responsible for the death of his family, he may try to harm her."

Crystal looked at the Scholar and just a flicker of her power showed deep in her eyes.

"He couldn't."

Mikhail stared at the closed door for a moment and then turned to Crystal. He made his voice as impersonal as he could and hoped she would understand it was the prince who spoke and not her father. "I have to ask this—would it make a difference if you left?"

Crystal understood, she'd asked herself that same question. She shook her head and motes of light danced in her silver hair. "No. If I left, he would destroy Ardhan piece by piece until I came back to fight.''

The captain's scarred forehead had been furrowed for some time. Finally figuring out just what he didn't understand, he spoke.

''If this Kraydak never meant to go after us until now, why the raids every year?''

''He was studying us,'' Crystal explained. ''Studying our land and the way we fight. He wants a challenge not a rout.''

''Sounds like he's got all the angles covered,'' muttered the duke. ''And this is the man we have to beat . . .''

''No,'' Crystal corrected again, almost severely. ''This is the man I have to beat.''

''Can you?'' Tayer's voice was heavy with fear, fear for her country, fear for her daughter.

Crystal heard. She looked out the window and watched something, someone perhaps, being lifted from the wreckage. The salvation of her people settled more firmly on her shoulders and she braced herself against the weight.

''I hope so.'' And then, with a nod to her parents, she left the room.

Bryon stood aside to let her leave, then glanced up at his father. Go with her, said the duke's expression, she shouldn't be alone.

As this agreed perfectly with Bryon's desire, he bowed to the queen and followed.

Nine

Tayer would have no coronation, no robes of gold, and no great feast where the six dukes of Ardhan would come to pay homage to their new queen. She would go on no tour of the six provinces to acquaint herself with her realm. The huge and ugly State Crown was buried deep in the rubble that had been the palace. The dukes would give homage when they met on the battlefield. She would tour only the provinces the army must cross to meet Kraydak's attack. The queen rode at the head of her armies.

"How can you be so sure," Mikhail demanded, "that the attack will come at the Tage Plateau? What about the Northern Pass into Lorn? They've tried there before."

"And found it wanting," Crystal replied, a breeze fanning her hair. "Kraydak's armies will come to the Tage Plateau. That far he has let me see his plans."

"Has let you see his plans? What in the name of the Mother for?"

"It's my guess he's anxious for the battle and doesn't want me to miss it," Crystal said dryly. "He'll keep telling me enough to ensure we're in the right place at the right time." Then she left, taking the breeze with her.

Mikhail looked at Tayer who was plotting the route from Belkar through Hale and up into the mountains. The duke's library had become war room, throne room, and petition room for the new queen.

"How does she know?" Mikhail muttered.

Tayer looked up at him and forced a smile. "I doubt we'd like to know, my love. I doubt she found out in a manner befitting a princess and the heir to the throne." The smile vanished and she shook her head. "I can't deny what she is, Mikhail. I've tried never to do that, but she must acknowledge my heritage now as well as her father's and I'm afraid the two will not mix."

"Why not?"

"The rules are too different." She tried to remember how it felt to rest safe within the light, offering no resistance, but it had been too many years. Her memories of the Grove, of Varkell, of carrying his light beneath her breast were muted by distance and blocked by her responsibilities to her people. She scrubbed a fine-boned hand over her eyes. "Never mind, I'll speak to her." She considered the map again. "The War Horns go out today. Aliston can meet us at Hale's Seat, but I suppose Cei and Lorn had best meet us at the battle ground."

Mikhail stared down at his wife. He knew she had a core of strength that seldom showed to those who knew her less well than he, but that strength had been sorely tested over the last few days and he wished he could do more to ease her burdens. "You do that like an old campaigner," he said at last, because he had to say something.

"I was trained to be queen." Tayer sighed. "Although with two older brothers it didn't seem likely I'd ever have to use the training." Her eyes misted and her voice dropped to a whisper as she remembered. "And I'd give anything not to have this chance."

Mikhail laid his hands on her slender shoulders and squeezed gently.

"I'm all right," Tayer told him, only a tiny catch in her voice betraying her sorrow. "But now Crystal must be trained as I was. The succession must be secure, especially as we ride to war."

A vision of his beloved hacked to pieces by enemy

swords caused Mikhail to close his eyes in pain. But if Tayer could prepare for the possibility so calmly, could he do any less? He twisted the topic away from the battlefield.

"She won't like it. She didn't like the maid you insisted she have, said a wizard doesn't need a maid."

"A wizard may not, but a princess does."

Mikhail smiled as he spoke. "Considering some of the outfits she's expected to wear, I don't see how she can do without one."

"There are a lot worse things than maids facing her. Although she should've consulted with us first, I'm glad she asked that Scholar to help her. I very much doubt her schooling over the last few years included economics, local histories, diplomacy, protocol," she paused, "and the making of war and the sending out of War Horns."

They were back to the battlefield.

"Is there no place for Riven in your plans?" Mikhail asked, suddenly recalling the distribution of War Horns she'd mentioned earlier.

All remaining light left Tayer's voice.

"Riven is set upon joining his wife and child. He forgets he still has one child left living to grieve and goes running back to the arms of the Mother. He doesn't hear the tears of his son or the pleading of his friends. He just lies there, waiting for Lord Death to claim him." She reached for Mikhail's hand and laid her cheek against his side.

His other hand came around and gently stroked her hair. "This should never have been set on you," he said softly. "Your life shouldn't be death and destruction but sunshine and birdsong and the laughter of children."

"Do you regret not having children, Mikhail?" They had long ago given up hope.

Mikhail remembered a tiny girl-child who had clamored to be lifted to his shoulders; her delight at the white pony on her fifth birthday; the day she and Bryon had locked themselves in the dungeon and the entire palace staff had searched for twelve hours before they were found.

"I always felt I had one. In fact, the way Bryon was constantly underfoot I often thought I had two." And he remembered the silver tear that had fallen the day the centaur came and took her away. She'd looked back only once and the tear had shone like a star on her cheek. Now she had returned. "I always felt I had one," he repeated sadly.

A knock on the door boomed through the silence that had fallen as they both considered their daughter and what she had become.

Tayer released Mikhail's hand and he moved to stand behind her, a solid wall against her back.

"Enter."

The door swung open and the Captain of the Guard marched into the room, followed by two of his soldiers supporting a man between them. The man appeared to have been badly beaten, then kicked into a corner and forgotten for some time. His lips were cracked and bleeding, his eyes swollen shut, and his skin showed purple and black with bruises through his ripped and blood stained clothes.

"Who is he?" asked Tayer as the soldiers dragged him forward.

"This pitiful remnant," declared the captain, drawing himself up before the table, "is the only survivor of the palace."

"What!"

"That's right, Majesty. This scum, who beat his own brother to death and was sentenced to die by your father the king—may he rest in the arms of the Mother—survived when everyone else was crushed to a bloody pulp. I've brought him to you for resentencing."

"Release him."

"Right, I'll . . ." The captain froze, in the act of turning away. "What?"

"Release him."

"But, Majesty, he's a convicted killer!"

"He is alive! Too many others are dead and too

many others will die. Take him out of here," commanded the queen, "and release him!"

The Duke of Belkar's late wife had loved flowers and to please her he had extensive gardens planted around all of their residences. After her death, he'd found great comfort in them and often said that in the gardens she still lived.

The garden at the townhouse was not very large, but it was exceptionally beautiful. Crystal—clad now in a style befitting a princess, a gown of palest green with a silver net loosely confining her hair—had found in it much the same peace the duke found; problems could be temporarily forgotten and demands for the impossible momentarily ignored. She let the healing balm of the spring flowers and delicate lacework of the flowering trees wash over her.

"May I join you?"

Lost in thought, she hadn't heard Bryon approach. Still not quite back, she opened her eyes.

Bryon had been thinking of her as a part of the garden, a rare and beautiful flower with silver petals and the scent of sun-warmed flesh. But when she opened her eyes, the garden disappeared and he was sinking into green fire. Sinking joyfully into green fire. Sinking ecstatically into green fire. Wanting it to consume him.

"Oh, Bryon, I'm sorry!"

He blinked once, twice, and was suddenly looking into a pair of concerned green eyes.

"I was thinking . . . I didn't know you'd be looking at me so directly."

"What else would I be looking at?" he muttered a little peevishly, but added in a more normal voice when he saw how distressed she appeared: "It's nothing to worry about, I'm all right."

Crystal drew him down beside her on the bench and searched his face anxiously. If he wasn't all right, she'd never forgive herself. After a moment, satisfied that what he said was true, she sighed and turned away.

"You must never forget," the centaurs had told her time after time, *"that you have the potential to be as great a danger as Kraydak himself."*

Bryon watched the effect of the sigh on Crystal's profile and the sparkle came back into his eyes. She was the most magnificent woman he had ever seen and he had every intention of presuming on their childhood friendship. He took her hand gently between the two of his and carefully, as if it were a timid bird he must not startle, began to stroke it.

"What were you thinking of?" he asked softly.

"About my time with the centaurs."

"Were you very lonely?"

"At first, but there was so much to learn in so little time. And there were always the breezes."

"I can't imagine a breeze being much company."

"That's because you don't know how to listen to them. They hear everything and they love to gossip." She almost smiled as she looked back at her younger self. "I even gave them names and made up faces for them. There was one that seemed to take a special interest in me, I called him Barrett. Although the centaurs didn't approve—they felt my reality was wide enough without adding to it—I imagined him with black hair and gray eyes. He's still my good friend."

"He?"

She turned to face Bryon . . . and his black hair and gray eyes. She snatched her hand away and felt her cheeks grow hot, not wholly as a result of the afternoon sun.

"What makes you think I was lonely?" she asked, smoothing the already perfect folds of her skirt.

"For one thing," and his smile caused two deep dimples to appear, "you used to laugh all the time, but I haven't heard you laugh once since you've been home."

"There's not much to laugh about, is there?"

"No." The dimples retreated. "I guess there isn't." But Bryon knew that wasn't all of it. It was as if Crystal's purpose left no room for anything else. Had she given up her humanity when she took up her powers? He looked forward to finding out.

A chill breeze wrapped around them both. Crystal caressed it with long fingers, her head to one side, listening.

"I have to go." She stood suddenly. "The old Duke of Riven is dead."

Bryon hesitated barely a moment and then he rose as well. "I'll go with you," he said, but it was too late. Crystal had used his hesitation to move quickly toward the house. He followed, but a gust of wind snapped a thorny branch into his path and he lost all hope of catching her when he had to stop and unsnag his breeches.

"Well, Barrett," he muttered, watching the swing of Crystal's departing hips, "I guess it's between you and me." He didn't quite hear the breeze chuckle as it sped away.

The War Horns went out that afternoon; north to Aliston, south to Cei, west to Hale, and northwest to Lorn. As well as the horns, each Messenger carried a scroll sealed with the queen's signet. The Horn was a part of the ancient bond between the dukes and the High Court. The scroll carried the plans for war.

The Messengers of Ardhan were chosen from the finest young men and women in the kingdom. The four that carried the War Horns were the best of an exceptional group. They were highly trained, highly motivated, healthy, intelligent, and totally helpless should Kraydak decide to prevent them from reaching their destinations.

"I will be watching," Crystal assured them, meeting each of their eyes in turn and allowing them each a glimpse of the light. "If you should be attacked, I will be there to protect you."

And no one questioned the value of that protection save Crystal herself.

The new Duke of Riven also rode out that afternoon. He carried his own War Horn but, instead of a scroll, he had the bodies of his father and sister. His mother's body had not been found.

It was two weeks' hard ride from King's City to Riven; burdened with the heavy wagon the trip would take almost a month. Long before Riven could be reached, the dead would be beyond the point where the living could travel with them. If he wished to take his father and his sister home, the new duke had no choice but to accept the wizard's help.

"They would not be dead but for you," he said as she stepped back from the task, "and now they will not return to the body of the Mother because of you."

"When they are placed in Riven's soil, the Mother will take them back," Crystal told him, trying to forget the feel of dead flesh beneath her fingers. "Remember, had Kraydak not been waiting for me, Lord Death would have taken them much sooner than he did."

They locked eyes and although Crystal carefully kept her power masked (*"The people of Ardhan must respect you as well as fear you if they are to be any use in battle,"* the centaurs had cautioned her. *"It is not advisable to keep reminding them that you are their only hope for a future."*), young Riven looked away first. With a grunted, "Perhaps," he threw himself on his horse and began the long ride home. The War Horn of Riven hung from his saddle, but even when swearing allegiance to the queen, he had not said if he would sound it.

That night, long after most of the townspeople had gone to their beds and the sounds of the Guards had faded toward the outskirts of the town, a solitary figure appeared in the ruins of the People's Square. In the silver light of the moon her hair seemed to burn, each strand alive with cold fire. When she dropped the cloak from her shoulders, her naked body ignited as well until she seemed a slender silver flame.

She cupped her hands and lifted them to the moon. White light filled them until it overflowed down her arms then, throwing her arms wide apart, she scattered the light over the rubble . . . and called.

The call was lower than anything that should have come from a human throat. It was deep and insistent and commanding.

On the third call, the earth answered.

The paving stones began to vibrate as a note too low to be heard sang up from the ground. The broken pieces of the palace began to shift and pitch. Waves rippled through them as if they were water, not stone.

The silver figure stepped forward and stood for a moment, not on the stones but on the air above them. Then she began to dance. She moved slowly at first, outlining the perimeter—for everywhere her feet had been there lay a silver tracery—but as the earth's call began to rise, still unheard though felt at temple and wrist, the dance began to move more quickly until she was indeed a silver flame in the moonlight.

As the pattern was completed, the song beat so quickly it seemed it must escape. As the last line was closed, it stopped. The pattern sank into the earth and all the dogs of the town began to howl at once.

Shutters slammed back. Sleepy voices demanded explanations and called at curs to be quiet. Had anyone looked toward the palace they would have seen, not a silver dancer who moved like flame, but a silver birch that lifted lacy branches to the moonlight and swayed in a gentle wind.

The dogs quieted at last, and the town returned to sleep. The dancer descended to the street, picked up her cloak, and disappeared in the shadows.

The next morning, twenty-six sheep grazed in the meadow that had erased the scars of the palace.

Ten

"My mother will ride at the head of the army," Crystal remarked thoughtfully to Lapus as they threaded their way through the twisting hallways of the duke's house. Although rain denied them the garden, Crystal was too restless to sit still. "But all I hear talk of is men. The men will do this, the men will do that . . . don't the women fight?"

"Some, but not many."

"Why not?"

"Someone must see to the day to day running of the land."

"But why the women?" Crystal was puzzled. "The centaurs always said that the men were in charge."

"In charge of what?"

"Well . . . the country."

"And who does that leave in charge of the men?"

Silver brows rose. "The women?"

"Who sees that the men get fed, and clothed, and to council on time? Who teaches them to love, when to be strong, and when to be weak? Who sees that the race continues? Some say that the Mother created women in her image and then created men to give them something to do."

"Lapus, you're a traitor to your sex!" Her tone was almost teasing. She had somehow managed to keep her whole purpose for existing at a little distance over the last few days of waiting *("Always remember that*

*you were conceived solely for the destruction of Kray-
dak.''*) although it was never far from her thoughts.

Lapus stiffened at the word traitor. ''I am true only
to Truth, milady, and although it is true that men and
women are equal in the eyes of the Mother, it is equally
true that they are not the same. It does no honor to
men that they are better able to facilitate the arrival of
Lord Death. Perhaps because a woman better understands how difficult it is to create a life, she becomes
less willing to take one. Most of the surgeons and
healers that ride with the army are women.''

Crystal dropped into a window seat and stared pen-
sively at her slippered feet. ''It appears,'' she said,
''that I not only have much to learn about being a
princess, but someone had better teach me to be a
woman as well.'' She looked up at Lapus and smiled.
''Do you think you could make a woman of me,
Scholar?''

The smile was his undoing. For a change, there was
nothing of the other world in Crystal's expression, unless it was the innocent beauty of that smile. Lapus
swallowed twice and shoved his hands deep in his
sleeves to hide their trembling. He opened his mouth
to speak, but all he could get out was one word.

''No,'' he said. And fled.

Crystal stared at his fleeing back in astonishment.
''Did I say something wrong?''

The rain on the window had no idea.

She was still trying to figure out the Scholar's strange
behavior when Bryon sauntered by a few moments
later.

''What's up?'' he asked as he threw himself down
beside her, one arm draped negligently behind her
shoulders.

''Lapus doesn't want to make me a woman.''

A dangerous glint surfaced in Bryon's eyes and his
expression hardened. ''He doesn't what?'' he asked,
his voice stony.

''I think,'' said Crystal seriously, making an honest

effort to get to the root of the question, "that it's a philosophical problem."

Bryon's face relaxed as he realized that Crystal had no idea of the double meaning of what she'd said. Such innocence was rare around the court, he wasn't used to it. He shook his head and took himself sternly to task for even momentarily allowing himself to consider that Crystal and that skinny Scholar with no looks and less personality would . . .

"Forget philosophy, Crystal." He brushed a strand of hair from her cheek and made his voice a caress. "In my eyes you're a woman already."

She turned from his touch, not understanding why she felt cheated when his hand dropped. She suddenly didn't feel like pursuing the question further, for a strong suspicion said Bryon had a great deal to do with her recent restlessness.

"They tell me you'll be leaving soon."

"Within the hour. Father is sending me around the province to help rally the men."

"Will you be back?"

"No, I'll join the army in Hale. Will you miss me?"

"Of course, I'll miss you," Crystal said more snappishly than she'd intended. "You're my friend."

"Ah, friend," Bryon's eyes twinkled. "A sad word that, when you're hoping for more."

"More?"

His arm tightened around her shoulders and drew her close. With his other hand he cupped her chin and gently forced her head up. Taking an incredible chance, he held her eyes with his, but the green fires were banked and he saw only a reflection of himself.

Confused, Crystal tried to straighten out the mess Bryon was making of her emotions. She had spent the last six years with the centaurs learning to be a wizard while Bryon, growing from good-looking boy to handsome young man, had been getting an education of a different sort. Centaurs, being immortal, have no love, lust, or desire. Crystal might be able to move mountains, call up demons, and—hopefully—destroy the enemies of her people, but in this area she was totally unskilled. She didn't understand her reactions and she didn't like the feeling that things were out of her control.

She also didn't want Bryon to stop. Whatever it turned out he was doing . . .

She didn't understand that either.

Bryon had no intention of stopping. Their faces were inches apart and her breath moved against his mouth like a warm breeze. He drank in the feel of her, the smell of her, the touch of her.

"Your horse is ready, sir."

Crystal jumped back, trying to ignore that briefest touch of his lips on hers. Bryon, realizing the moment had been irrevocably shattered, grinned up at his father's footman and got jauntily to his feet.

"Look for me in Hale," he said and, planting a kiss on her palm, was gone.

Crystal stared down at her hand, the soft pressure of his mouth still clinging to the skin.

"We were children together," she said to the empty passageway. "He treats me like a whole person, not as just a wizard or a princess. He is my friend." But she sat until dusk hid her in shadow, considering it.

The horn carriers had been on their way for three days when Kraydak moved against them. While the truncated court sat at dinner, all the windows in the hall crashed open. The winds roared around the room, causing the lamps and candles to sputter and flicker and the men and women of the court to grab at everything not fastened down.

Crystal leaped to her feet and called the winds to order. They flew to her side and buffeted her about in their embrace. One at a time, she gentled them, heard their messages, and then sent them back out into the night.

When the last of the winds had left, Crystal looked up to see the court regarding her with awe—all except the Duke of Belkar who was dusting off a crusty roll which had been blown to the floor.

"What is it, child?" Mikhail asked, his heart rung by the expression on his stepdaughter's face. All the recently developed signs of humanity had fled and the wizard looked bleak and cold.

"Kraydak is marshaling great power. He will strike at the Messengers tonight."

"Now?" asked Tayer. 'During dinner?"

Humanity returned for an instant and Crystal raised a silver eyebrow in her mother's direction.

"But you haven't even finished your soup. You can't just run out in the middle of dinner. What will people think? No . . ." Tayer blushed suddenly and dropped her head in her hands. "I'm sorry. Do what you have to."

"Is there anything we can do to help?" Mikhail asked, laying a warm hand on the shoulder of his distraught wife.

"No." Crystal shook her head. "What I do tonight, I must do alone. But first thing in the morning, someone had better check . . ."

Tayer seemed to draw strength from Mikhail's touch. "You can stop him," she said firmly, raising her head and looking her daughter in the eye. "You can stop him."

"I can only try, Mother." She'd dreaded the thought of this night and now it had come. The first test. And what hope was there for the future should she fail? She forced herself to walk calmly from the room.

As the door closed behind her the buzz of conversation began again, almost as if it had been switched on by her leaving.

Tayer rose to follow. Mikhail gently guided her back into her seat.

"I could at least walk her to her room," Tayer protested, but without pulling away.

"I don't think she wants you to." He could offer little comfort in a room filled with their subjects so he merely held tightly to her hands. "You said she could stop him, now believe it."

Tayer sighed. "I feel," she said suddenly, "like a chicken trying to mother a duck, frantically trying to keep my child out of the water."

Crystal took the steps to her tower room two at a time. She yanked open the door, flung herself into the room, and rocked to a halt at the sight of her maid.

"Is dinner over so soon, milady?" the girl asked, stepping forward. Then she saw the expression on Crystal's face and her own paled. *"Anna, child, this will not be an easy job,"* the queen herself had said, *"but the princess must be made aware of her position. No matter what she does, stay with her."* Wanting nothing more than to retreat from the light that blazed in the princess's eyes, Anna swallowed once and clung to duty. "Shall . . . shall I take your hair down now?"

Startled, Crystal's hand flew to her hair, then she shook herself, as though to free the wizard from the entanglements of the princess. "You must go," she said, moving away from the door. "I have work to do."

Anna stood her ground. "I'm sorry, milady, but your mother, the queen . . ."

"Is not here."

". . . gave me very precise instructions," the maid finished, obviously intending to obey them to the letter.

"She instructed you to serve me?"

"Yes, milady."

"You can serve me best by leaving."

"I don't think, milady . ."

Muttering beneath her breath in a language that had not been spoken for centuries, Crystal abandoned her attempt to be reasonable, shoved the frightened but determined servant out into the hall, threatened her with a dire fate should she return before dawn, and slammed the door on her protests.

Then she paused. Why hadn't she reinforced her

commands with power? The small fraction needed to control the girl would not have been missed from the night's work and the result would have been much faster than arguing. In the back of her mind, where usually only the centaurs spoke, the memory of her mother's voice spanned the years, instructing a tiny girl-child in the rights of those who served. Uneasily, she slammed the lesson back into the past. She must be only wizard now; divided, she could not hope to win.

With a wave of her hand, the lamps went out and a light flared near the center of the room. A small copper brazier cradled a green flame which danced and beckoned.

The winds raced round the tower and the sounds they made as they wove about each other all said, "Hurry!"

Crystal moved forward and her elaborate dress dropped to the floor with a rustle of silk. She stepped free and into the plain white gown that had risen to meet her. Pins showered to the floor as her hair danced out of complicated braids and flowed down her back. Another two steps brought her to the brazier, but as she was about to sit, she paused, turned, and threw a fine web of power across the door. She didn't trust her mother, and certain others, to stay away. Tucking the gown between her legs, she sank to the floor.

"Hurry!" wailed the winds.

She wiped sweaty palms on her thighs. She had to be in four places at once and she had to defeat a man who had been honing his powers for several dozen lifetimes while she'd had only six short years.

Finally, she looked into the flame.

The first Messenger woke to a sudden weight on his chest. He opened his eyes and the largest crow he'd ever seen cocked its head, dug its talons into his leather vest, and glared at him balefully with a yellow eye. For a moment he thought he was dreaming and then one of those talons ripped through to his chest. The pain was real.

With a startled cry, he flung himself to the side as the wicked beak stabbed for his eyes.

His movement dislodged the bird and with strong beats of its wings it took to the air. The Messenger almost gagged on the carnal odors carried on the down-draft. He'd rolled away from his sword and the bird nearly took off his hand when he tried to reach for it. His fire had turned to embers and so, when he saw it, did his hopes of driving the creature away with flame.

The bird dove again and again and the Messenger soon bled from a number of small wounds. Only by blocking with a saddlebag had he managed to keep it from anything vital. He knew his luck, and the saddlebag, couldn't hold out much longer. He was winded, fighting for each breath, and the pain and loss of blood were weakening him.

The creature seemed to be taking a malicious delight in his torment.

And then it happened as he knew it would. He faltered, his guard dropped, and the bird moved in for the kill.

He braced himself for the blow, but it never came. A great white body hurtled into him, throwing him to the ground. The crow shrieked in rage, the first sound it had made, and turned to face the intruder.

Both Messenger and bird stared in astonishment at the great white owl that paced the ground between them. Its talons were over six inches long and its wingspan covered more than ten feet. It looked the young man up and down and then, satisfied with what it saw, it launched itself at the crow, its eyes burning with green fires.

The crow was large and its evil purpose strong, but it knew when it was defeated. There was only one thing left—escape.

With long, powerful strokes of its mighty wings, the owl took to the air and quickly climbed above its fleeing prey. Then, with talons extended and gleaming in the moonlight, it folded back its wings and struck.

The two birds hit the ground with an audible thud. Holding the crow securely under one massive foot, the owl bent its head to feed.

A persistent tickle disturbed the sleep of the second Messenger. Tiny balls were being rolled across his face. No matter how many he batted away, more kept coming. Finally he dragged himself up out of slumber to deal with it.

To find the tiny balls were trickles of dirt and the ground below him was giving way. He was sinking, being swallowed by the earth!

Successfully fighting panic, he got his hands beneath him and tried to sit up. The movement made him sink faster. He tried to lift his legs and found he couldn't.

He lay in a Messenger-shaped trench, one foot, two feet, four feet, six feet deep, flat on his back and looking up at the stars. He did the only thing left to do— he stopped fighting the panic and screamed.

And then the walls fell in.

The earth rolled quickly down to cover him. The bonds that had held him were gone, but that did little good as the world sat on his chest, crushing the breath out of him. Worst of all, he could no longer scream.

His lungs were crying out for air and stars were exploding behind his eyes when he felt the movement at his back. A hundred tiny fingers touched him and moved on. He remembered all the small and slimy things that lived in dirt and began to tremble with terror. Was being buried alive not enough?

He felt a firmer touch.

And then another.

Something grabbed at him and held.

The earth rolled back and he was lifted, gasping and choking, into the night air. He finally came to rest cradled high off the ground in the branches of a full grown silver birch.

* * *

The third Messenger was caught in a dream. She was running. At first the way was easy and she covered the ground in long loping strides, but then the path began to climb and her pace slowed. Soon she had to use her hands to scrabble up and over mounds of rock strewn across a shattered hillside.

It was then she became aware that she was being chased. And her pursuers were moving much faster than she.

In the shifting shadows of night, the long, broken path to the top of the hill was doubly treacherous. A misstep, a fall, could mean death.

Not far behind her, something bayed. A dog . . . or worse.

One torturous step at a time, she struggled toward the summit. Her hands and knees became cut and abraded by the sharp edges of rock and her feet were bruised by the shifting masses of stone. Her thighs trembled as she forced them to carry her over one more ledge. And one more.

She was almost to the summit when the baying began in earnest. They were on the scent, her scent, and now the chase would truly begin. With desperate haste she covered the last few yards, but not without cost, for a rock which had seemed solid rolled suddenly and crushed her hand. Whimpering with pain, she pried up the rock and dragged the damaged hand free, leaving an ugly smear of blood on the stone.

Her mangled hand tucked in her belt, she crested the hill and turned, breathing heavily, to look back the way she had come.

Half a dozen animals—possibly dogs, but she doubted it—long-legged and lean with narrow heads and glowing eyes, were just reaching the bottom of the hill. Not very far behind them rode a red-cloaked man on a pale horse. Lord Death, true son of the Mother, the Huntsman who escorted the unwilling dead back to Her arms.

The Messenger knew a terrible fear. She wasn't dead. Why did Death hunt her?

The beasts started up the hill.

She turned and ran. In the distance was a dark line of trees. If she could make the forest, she might stand a chance. She ran as she'd never run before, ran until the soles of her boots were worn through and she left a bloody trail of footprints behind her. Until the stitch in her side was a pain too great to breathe through. Until the bitter iron taste of blood filled her mouth. Sweat ran into her eyes and her wounds and they burned.

Behind, but getting rapidly closer, came the baying of the Huntsman's hounds.

She kept her eyes locked on the trees ahead, but she knew she wouldn't make it. The echoing hoofbeats of a steel-shod horse sounded above the cries of the beasts.

And then, over the pounding of her life in her ears, she heard another sound. Hoofbeats, but unshod and from the right. She risked a glance over her shoulder.

Gaining quickly, but only marginally closer than the hounds, came a white unicorn with silver hoofs and horn. Its nostrils were flared and its eyes flashed green fire.

Her eyes drawn from the path, the Messenger stumbled and fell. As she got to her feet, the unicorn reached her side.

"Get on!" it commanded.

"Wha . . ."

"GET ON!" A flashing hoof neatly crushed the skull of the foremost hound.

The messenger grabbed a handful of silky mane and dragged herself awkwardly up on the broad back. She was barely seated when the unicorn leaped forward, out of the range of the rest of the pack, and landed galloping. The trees which had seemed so far away were reached in seconds. She closed her eyes and held on tightly as her mystical mount wove among them without losing speed or breaking stride. Suddenly a thought struck her, almost causing her to lose her balance.

"I'm not a virgin!" she wailed.

"That's hardly my fault," the unicorn muttered in reply . . . or it might have just been the wind of their passing.

Abruptly they were out of the trees and then, horrifyingly, they were out of ground. A horse could not have stopped in time, but the unicorn reared and managed to halt on the edge of the cliff. They both looked down.

Many miles below, clouds scuttled about like sheep, herded by a wind they were too far away to feel. They could not see the ground. About thirty feet out from the edge, perched on a marble pillar that tapered into the depths, was the home of the Duke of Aliston, the Messenger's destination.

The unicorn backed away from the edge. "Hang on," it warned. Powerful muscles bunched and it launched itself forward.

And screamed shrilly as razor sharp teeth tore into a hind leg.

They landed safely, although three legged, and turned to face back over the gap. The pale horse stood at the precipice, the hounds winding about its legs. With a toss of his head, the rider dropped his hood. His red-gold hair shone dully in the moonlight but his blue eyes and smile blazed as he lifted his hand in salute.

The Messenger awoke to find herself staring up at familiar stars with a crushed hand and the knowledge that had she died in the dream, she would be dead indeed.

A cold and driving rain woke the fourth Messenger. He'd camped in a small hollow on a treeless plain and had no protection from the wet. Huddled miserably in his bedroll, he wondered where the storm had come from for it had been a clear, moonlit night when he'd gone to sleep.

The rain fell harder. Soon he was soaked and shaking uncontrollably. It was far, far too cold for a spring night so close to summer. The rain seemed to leech the warmth from his body. He'd lost all feeling in his hands and feet when the wind began to blow. It whipped the sheets of rain viciously about, giving him blessed moments of dryness. Its touch carried the promise of golden sunshine and summer's warmth and the scent of trees, and grass, and forest loam.

Up above, the massive black storm clouds were losing their battle with the winds. They were thinning, being forced apart. Here and there, through sections grown tattered, a star could be seen.

Finally, the rain stopped and the young man lifted his dripping face to the sky. The last thing he saw was the dazzling blue of the lightning bolt as it arced down from the clouds. He didn't see those clouds break up and drift away as harmless vapor. Nor did he see the moon come out and bathe the land in silver light. He was dead.

For a time he lay as he had fallen; one arm flung up to stop the blow, his clothes gently steaming from the heat; then the ground beneath him began to crumble away as he was welcomed back into the body of the Mother. Gently, the earth enfolded him and covered him against the cold. Soon, all that could be seen was a grass-free patch of dirt.

Moments later the patch began to tremble, clots of earth danced and tumbled about. No less majestic than the moon itself, a birch tree rose to mark the young man's grave. Its trunk was a silver headstone and its leaves sang dirges with the wind. From out of the cloudless sky swooped a giant white owl. It plucked the War Horn from the Messenger's gear and headed north to Lorn.

At dawn, Tayer and Mikhail met Lapus at Crystal's door.

"Majesties," he said, bowing himself out of their

way. "My anxiety for the princess made it impossible for me to sleep. If I can be of assistance . . ."

"Stay if you wish, Scholar," Tayer replied, worry making her voice sharp. "Mikhail, open the door."

Mikhail, who had seen Lapus trying to open the door without success as they approached, shot the Scholar a suspicious glance when the latch lifted easily in his hand.

"Oh, Crystal!" Tayer rushed forward and clasped the limp body of her daughter in her arms. "Mikhail, she's been hurt."

A rust red patch of dried blood stained the white gown and pasted it to Crystal's left calf.

Mikhail knelt, eased the fabric away, and inspected the wound. New pink skin had already formed over what appeared to be an ugly bite.

"It's not bad." But he carefully did not let Tayer see the damage, for it certainly looked as if it had been bad, whether it was now or not. "It's already nearly healed."

Crystal's eyes fluttered and opened; the green so washed out that they appeared a pale gold. She gazed around, unsure of where she rested.

"Mother?" Her voice quavered, sounding very tired and very young.

"I'm here." Tayer stroked the silver hair back from Crystal's face and with a little cry Crystal buried her head against the warm security of her mother's breast. She could take no comfort in duty and responsibility for she had failed.

"I couldn't save the last one, Mother. I was spread too thin. I wasn't strong enough. He died and I couldn't stop it." She sounded very close to tears.

"Hush," Tayer softly kissed the top of Crystal's head. "I'm sure you did your best."

"My best wasn't good enough." She closed her eyes and the face of the fourth Messenger looked back at her from the inside of her lids. Later perhaps she would mourn him, but now she was frightened. Kraydak had allowed her only a glimpse of his power, but that glimpse let her know she would have been unable to save any of the Messengers had he truly wanted all four dead. He'd been playing with her. If she was her world's only hope, then it appeared they had no hope at all. Just for that moment, she wished she'd not been so thoroughly trained and could give up before she had to face him again.

"So one War Horn will not be delivered." Lapus kept his voice carefully neutral.

Crystal's eyes opened and a green ember stirred in their depths as she glared up at the Scholar. "All the War Horns will be delivered," she told him, struggling to rise. "That, at least, I did." She put out a hand to steady herself and knocked over the copper brazier. Soft gray ash fell to the floor.

Mikhail offered his arm and Crystal pulled herself to her feet. She staggered and only Tayer's grasp about her waist prevented her from falling.

"You'll feel better after a little breakfast," Tayer reassured her.

Crystal brushed several black feathers off the front of her gown. "No, thank you, Mother, I've eaten."

In the old capital of Melac, now the heart of a cruel and corrupt Empire, a blue light flashed from the top of the highest tower and the folk who saw it quailed. Within the upper chamber, Kraydak sat and considered the night's work, hands steepled beneath his chin and blue eyes thoughtful.

"This wizard-child is not as powerful as I feared she might be," he said at last to the the ancient skull that sat on the table before him.

The skull, once a king, made no reply.

"Neither," he added, rubbing a finger over the yellow bone, "is she an unworthy foe." She had used only as much power as she needed to defeat him except . . . At the end he had given her a glimpse of what he could do. She had not met it in kind although he was as certain, as only five thousand years of existence could make a man, that she held more power than she'd let him see.

"Perhaps she is wise." He smiled, his teeth very white even in the red-gold glow that lit the room. "The longer she holds my interest, the longer I will let her live."

On an afternoon when the sunlight spread over the circle of trees like a golden blanket and the breezes brought the promise of summer, Tayer and Mikhail said farewell to the Sacred Grove.

They stood quietly, letting the peace of the Grove wipe away the darkness that had wrapped about them these last few weeks and touch them with a gentle healing. They had no need to speak, words were so clumsy when a look, a smile, or a touch could say all that was necessary.

As the shadows started to lengthen, they clasped hands and headed back to the horses and the war.

Eleven

In the days when wizards were common and not yet too powerful, the War Horns of Ardhan had been enchanted. They weren't the War Horns of Ardhan then, for this was before Ardhan existed as a kingdom, but the enchantment was strong enough to last through the Doom of the Wizards when the ancient world was ripped asunder, making the War Horns one of the great treasures of the resettlement. When raised in answer to a summons from the crown, the call of the Horns would sound in every corner of the kingdom.

As soon as Crystal was certain all the War Horns had been safely delivered, the queen walked out to the center of the ''meadow-that-had-been-the-palace'' and handed the kneeling Duke of Belkar his horn. The entire town's population, massed about the edges of the meadow, held its breath as he lifted the ancient horn to his lips and blew.

The note rose piercingly clear and hung in the air. It got into the blood and bones of the people and hung there. ''To war!'' it called, and the men and women who moved toward the gathering places moved a little faster.

Cei, then Lorn, then Hale, then Aliston; from the corners of the kingdom all the lords answered the call save Riven.

''He travels very slowly,'' Mikhail reminded Tayer as they made their way in procession back to Belkar's townhouse, ''and is not likely to answer until he's at

Riven Seat and has returned his family to the arms of the Mother.''

What young Riven thought, as he moved slowly across the land with his preserved dead and his grief, he let no one know. But after the five horns sounded, he drew even deeper into himself.

The man with the red-gold hair and the brittle blue eyes stood listening within his tower and when it became clear that the sixth note would not be heard, he laughed. Calling a gray-robed Scholar to him, he began to make plans.

''It's probably still not too late to go to Kraydak and surrender,'' Lapus said quietly as he and Crystal walked with the rest of the court through the streets. His tone was so matter-of-fact he might have been discussing the raisin buns they'd had for breakfast.

Crystal stopped dead and a minor court official stepped on the train of her gown. She didn't hear his muttered and fervent apologies, for Lapus had kept walking and she had to hurry to catch up. The minor official, thankful he wasn't to be turned into something unpleasant, left the procession at the earliest opportunity.

''I could what?'' she demanded of the Scholar when she stood beside him again.

''Kraydak would then rule Ardhan, of course, but it would avert the war and save many lives.''

''It wouldn't avert anything. They'd fight without me.''

''I merely suggested an alternative.''

''Alternative!'' Crystal snorted. The day was hot, the ceremonial robes were heavy and she wanted a cold drink. ''Lapus, you say some really stupid things sometimes.''

On a hot summer day the court—the queen, her consort, their attendants, the Duke of Belkar, his attendants, the Elite, the Palace Guard, supply wagons, one Scholar, and the wizard—and seven hundred and forty-one soldiers in the newly formed Ardhan army gathered together to set out for Hale.

"Mother, save us," Crystal whistled softly as she cantered up to the head of the march with Lapus. "They're bringing everything but the scullery sink."

"Look again, milady. There, on that large wagon . . ."

Crystal looked where Lapus pointed and her eyes widened in astonishment. Touching her heels lightly to the sides of her horse, she rode the length of the column to where the queen stood, going over a lengthy list with someone Crystal assumed was the Quartermaster of the March.

"Mother," she called. "Is all this really necessary? We go to war, not off on the grand tour."

Tayer was tired and irritable. Most of the bureaucracy had died in the palace and although the new staff did their best, they had no experience in handling a move of this size. Besides Tayer and Mikhail, only six of the eight surviving upper servants had even seen a grand tour. No one since the time of the Lady had moved the court to war. Work the queen would normally delegate to someone else, she had to do herself.

"Yes," she snapped, "it is all really necessary. You may be able to conjure food and shelter out of thin air and the Elite may be ready to travel for days on journey bread and water, the rest of us mere mortals cannot."

Crystal jerked back in the saddle. She hadn't thought her gentle mother capable of that tone of voice.

"But we'll travel so slowly . . ."

"Kraydak has waited for you for hundred of years, I doubt he'll care about a few more weeks." Then she turned back to the lists, clearly dismissing her daughter.

Sighing, Crystal turned her horse, about to head back to her place in line, when she noticed Mikhail standing and staring up into the branches of a large oak. Curious, for her stepfather wore the plain gray uniform of the Elite and his troops were some distance away from where he stood, she moved toward him.

"What do you make of those," he asked as she reined in. He pointed up at three huge crows perched in the tree watching the departure preparations with beady eyes.

"Kraydak's creatures," Crystal told him without hesitation. The carrion stench from them was so strong she wondered it didn't trouble the tree. She took the reins in one hand and covered her nose with the other. "He's probably using their eyes."

"We'll see about that," Mikhail rumbled. He waved three archers out of the ranks and they trotted over to his side.

"Do you see those birds?" he asked them.

They did.

"Do you think you can hit them."

The eldest of the three stared at Mikhail in disbelief. "Meaning no disrespect, milord, but we could hardly miss if we threw the arrows by hand."

Mikhail grinned and stepped out of their way. "Be my guest."

The three strung their bows; each put an arrow to the string, and let fly. The arrows traveled about three feet and then burst into flames so intense that they fell to the ground as a light shower of ash.

"Again," Mikhail commanded.

The same thing happened.

The archers stood shuffling their feet nervously. They didn't like fighting wizardry, especially when it was so obvious that they couldn't fight it. As one, their lips moved in a brief prayer to the Mother and they turned to stare at Crystal. Easily readable on their faces was the memory of the words she'd spoken to the assembled army the night before: "Remember, you won't be fighting the wizard, I will."

Crystal moved her horse forward until she sat almost directly under the tree, never taking her eyes off the crows. They stared back, three triangular heads turned to one side so they could each watch her with a bilious yellow eye.

"One chance, Kraydak" she called, squaring her shoulders and lifting her chin defiantly. She was acutely conscious of being observed by Mikhail and the three archers. "Recall your servants or lose them."

"Caw," replied a crow derisively.

"If that's the way you want it," Crystal said and her eyes began to glow, "then burn."

For a very little while nothing happened—the wizard stared at the birds, the birds stared at the wizard— then suddenly all three crows ignited and disappeared within sheets of flame.

One of the archers cheered as Kraydak's spies were reduced to greasy smears on the tree branch.

"Now that's more like it," Mikhail laughed, slapping Crystal's leg affectionately. "Well done." He coughed and waved his hand about to clear the noxious smoke, heavy with the smell of burned feathers and cooked crow. "We'd better get out of this stuff though, if we want to be in any shape to travel."

Crystal rode back to the head of the column in a much better frame of mind. She'd easily broken through the protective spells that Kraydak had wrapped around the crows. This was what she was meant to do, what she had been trained for. She would have been even happier had she thought Kraydak cared.

The archers returned to their place and told their mates of how the princess had let that murdering wizard know who ruled in Ardhan. The story spread and grew, becoming less accurate but more morale-boosting with every telling.

When the army finally got underway, it traveled as slowly as Crystal had feared. The queen, Mikhail, and the Duke of Belkar, accompanied by their standard-bearers, rode in front. Crystal and Lapus followed, the former letting her mind wander, the latter watching her expressions from the concealment of his cowl. And then came the remnants of the Palace Guard and the surviving Elite, both already recruiting from the body of the army. And then the army of Ardhan, cavalry leading infantry—an order the infantry heartily wished reversed, horses being horses. And then the wagons. And then, behind them all, a crow. Who looked as bored as Crystal felt.

The company kept to the King's Road between Belkar and Hale. It was not the most direct route, but it was the easiest.

"After all," as Crystal said with quiet sarcasm to Lapus, "there are the wagons to consider."

The first night, when they camped, the Quartermaster of the March escorted Crystal to her tent. He ignored her protests when she saw its size, and held open the flap for her to enter.

A curtain divided the tent into two parts. The outer section had been set up as a sitting room and furnished with several ornate pieces of furniture. Crystal recognized the large divan with the clawed feet as coming from the Duke of Belkar's townhouse. With a sigh she lifted the curtain and froze. In one corner of the second room was her bed from the townhouse with a fresh change of clothes laid out on the counterpane. In the other was a steaming bath smelling faintly of lilies of the valley, and waiting beside the bath was her maid.

The girl dropped a brief curtsy and managed not to giggle at Crystal's expression.

"Mother!" Crystal protested, barging into the queen's tent after a very unprincesslike dash across the camp. "No one takes their maid to war!"

"Queens and princesses do," Tayer told her calmly. And that was the end of that.

"As long as we're dragging the tub along with us, I suppose I might as well bathe in it. And actually," Crystal admitted to Lapus as they traveled, "I'm even getting used to the maid."

Lapus almost smiled. "They may make a princess of you yet."

"No." Crystal's mouth set in a hard line and a green light flared in the depths of her eyes. "I am a wizard. I have to be."

"Then you had best learn to be both because, as you well know, you are also the only heir to the throne."

And Lapus told her the story—which she'd heard many times from the tutors she and Bryon had shared as children—of how the seven dukes and their people had come out of the North after the War between the Wizards and the Dragons destroyed their lands. They had settled in the land that would become Ardhan. Quarrels had erupted and holding went to war against holding, duke against duke. When much of the land had been made waste and many people had been killed, the dukes came to their senses and were horrified at what they'd done. They cast lots and one among them was set up as king over them all, to be a judge, an impartial arbitrator they could bring their quarrels to instead of solving them by the sword. Then the land was divided into six relatively equal provinces which were given the names of the six remaining dukes; Belkar, Cei, Lorn, Aliston, Hale, and Riven. The king gave his name to the land but he would claim no province as his own, all and none of the land was his. The dukes planned a town where each would have a house, a capital city with a palace from which the king could govern. Again they drew lots, this time to choose the province in which the King's Town would be located, and Belkar lost the draw. From that first king came all the Kings and Queens of Ardhan in an unbroken line. The Ducal Houses might branch, but the Royal House stayed true.

The Royal House was the glue that held Ardhan together. It was the country's focus, its stability, and Crystal was the last of the line.

"If I lose," she sighed, "it won't be a problem."

"But the prophecy says you may win," Lapus reminded her. "What then?"

What then, indeed? Would she be willing to give up her power and be a princess for her people's sake? Would she even be able to or would the ways of wizard and princess be fighting within her forever? The weapon the centaurs had forged had nothing of the princess about it; could she hope to win with her powers thus flawed? She had a lot to think about as the army plodded toward Hale.

As the heat of the water worked its magic on muscles stiff from another day in the saddle, Crystal let her head fall back against the edge of the tub and her eyes drift closed.

Oh, you have quite definitely won this point, Mother, she thought, languidly moving her hands through the scented liquid.

"Shall I wash your hair, Highness?"

Crystal managed a nod and then sighed with pleasure as strong hands lifted the sodden mass of silver hair, added soap, and began to massage her scalp. *For this,* she decided, *I would almost agree to be princess.* She gave herself totally over to the skilled ministrations of her maid and let her mind wander where it would.

Contented and relaxed, nearly asleep, she felt the fingers change their motion and the pressure against her head became almost a caress.

"Time to rinse."

With no more warning than that, her head was shoved below the surface of the water.

"What . . ." As bathwater sucked into her nose and mouth with her involuntary gasp of surprise, Crystal fought to remain calm. She didn't struggle; she continued the motion of her attacker, sinking down to the bottom of the tub and out from under those hands. Then she twisted and rose, eyes blazing, to face her enemy.

"Very good," said a voice not her maid's, yet issuing from her maid's mouth. The girl's brown eyes had turned a brilliant blue. "And very nice."

Crystal clamped down on her power, releasing it now would only hurt the girl. Realizing the direction of the second comment, she snatched up her robe and put it on, ignoring the fabric floating about her legs.

"Get out!" she commanded, dragging a sleeve across the water streaming from her nose.

"As you wish, milady." The girl bowed mockingly and turned to leave the tent.

"That's not what I meant and you know it. Get out of Anna!"

"Anna?" Kraydak walked the maid's body back to its position by the bath. "What a pretty name." He picked up the mirror that lay on the bed and studied the face he wore. "So is she. Pretty." Features blurred and she wasn't any longer. He turned to Crystal and a lift of now scraggly brows said clearly, *your move.*

Carefully, biting her lip in concentration, for she had neither the older wizard's training nor his years of experience, Crystal rebuilt what Kraydak had torn down. She knew she did exactly as he wished, that, for reasons of his own, he tested her, but she couldn't refuse the challenge and let Anna suffer. Better her pride take the blow than an innocent girl.

Kraydak merely watched in the mirror, his eyes amused. "Very good," he said again when she finished, and caused Anna's head to nod approvingly.

Crystal flushed with pleasure at the tone of warm praise and then was immediately appalled as she realized it. "What . . . what are you doing here?" she managed at last in a voice neither as forceful nor as self-assured as she would have wished.

"Oh, I just came to see how you were getting along." He smiled a dazzling smile with Anna's mouth. "To let you know I need not rely on messengers but can be at your side in an instant, turning friend to foe." He looked her over, eyes lingering on breast and hip, the curves pressing damply through the thin cotton of her robe. "Now that I've got a good look at you, however, a few other ways of passing the time come to mind. But alas . . ." Anna's hands fluttered along her body. ". . . I find myself woefully ill-equipped."

"Well if things are so woeful where you are, maybe you'd better go back where you came from."

"Throw me out," he told her, spreading his arms in a gesture of surrender. "You can do it. I can feel the power you command."

Deceiver, the centaurs had named him. Lies, they said, fell from his lips in numbers too large to be counted. But this time, did he speak truth? Was he so far extended, his power spread so thin she could, if not defeat him, at least cast him forth? The temptation to find out was very great.

"No. If I throw you out, I'll destroy Anna, burn out her mind."

"So? You don't particularly like her. What difference would it make?"

"It would make me no better than you." Her chin went up and her eyes narrowed. "I won't stoop to your tactics to win."

"You won't win, child." His voice was stern. "You haven't got what it takes. Winning means sacrifice. You aren't even willing to sacrifice this . . . this . . . nonentity to get me out of your tent. You amuse me, Crystal." Again his eyes stared through her robe. "You fascinate me. But you are no danger to me." He smiled one last time and the brilliant blue of his eyes began to darken. "Until the battlefield." Suddenly the eyes turned brown again and Anna collapsed to the carpet.

Some hours later, Anna woke with no memory of her subjugation. Although mortified by the thought, she was willing to believe she'd fainted. Thankful that the girl had not been hurt, Crystal was still more relieved that she wouldn't be spreading panicked tales of the enemy's assault throughout the army.

Crystal herself told no one of Kraydak's visit. When nothing could be done—and nothing could—why add to the weight of worry? She had a fair idea of the power it took to so manipulate another's body and while it frightened her—for it offered further proof of just how great a power was his to command—it reassured her as well. He was too canny to deplete his reserves again as the battle drew closer. A wizard did not survive as long as Kraydak had by taking foolish risks.

But even as she comforted herself with this, even as she breakfasted, mounted, and moved one day closer to Hale, she scanned the eyes of everyone she met, knowing they just might be a certain uniquely chilling shade of brilliant blue.

No cheering crowd lined the road, for only fools and madmen cheer a war, but stragglers joined them daily and those who stayed behind looked up from their work to watch them pass.

Crystal felt the young woman's eyes on her from the moment the girl became visible by the side of the road. The intensity of the stare drew a throbbing line of power between them. Slowly, as they rode closer, features began to develop; average height, slightly plump, with honey colored hair worn short and curly. The original bright colors of her clothes were faded with many washings and she was barefoot. She stood with her feet apart, holding her elbows in large capable hands. She ignored the rest of the march, never moving her gaze away from Crystal.

When Crystal was close enough, she threw herself into the heart of the green fires. And surprisingly, because she had an anchor those fires couldn't touch, she pulled herself out again.

Crystal received a kaleidoscopic vision of the young woman's life. Chickens figured prominently. Chickens and a man with a square jaw, a broken nose, and black brows that drew a line straight across his forehead. He was holding a chick, still damp and helpless from the shell, holding it, protecting it. Then it was a child who had his father's brows but his mother's eyes. Then it was a spear.

The exchange took only a few seconds. Crystal wanted nothing to do with it, she was responsible for the whole faceless mass of them, wasn't that enough? But asked, she saw no way to refuse. She nodded once.

The girl nodded as well, then spun on her bare heel and headed home across the fields.

"A princess does not stare at her subjects," Lapus informed her.

The mood shattered. Crystal tucked the black browed man safely away in her memory and turned to the Scholar.

"You've been promoting the princess a lot lately," she said wearily. "Have you been talking to my mother?"

"The queen is anxious for you to do your duty."

"Don't tell me about my duty, Scholar," the wizard growled. "I spent six years learning it from better teachers than you'll ever be." She gripped the sides of her horse so tightly that it turned its head and snapped at her knee, knowing full well she was not asking it to change its pace.

"The princess is your duty as well."

"I'm tired of duty!" The cry was from neither the wizard nor the princess but from Crystal, who was seventeen and so full of duty that there was little room left for her to be just herself. She looked at Lapus in horror, not believing what she had said.

For a second the reflection of the wizard flickered in Lapus' eyes and pity took its place. But only for a second.

"For some of us," he said flatly, retreating into the depths of his cowl, "there is no choice."

"For some of us," Crystal repeated just as flatly.

Except for the sounds of hoofs and leather and a thousand marching men, the next few miles passed in silence.

She did indeed have a lot to think about as the army wound through field and forest on its way to Hale, but not all of it was distressing. Bryon invaded her thoughts more often than she was willing to admit. And each time he did, she felt the path of her future widening. The centaurs would not have approved. A couple of times, and this puzzled her greatly, Bryon's cheerful grin was replaced by the scowling face of the young Duke of Riven.

"Riven doesn't even like me," she muttered to her horse's ears.

Her horse, very wisely, refused to become involved.

As the deformed little man in the blue and gold livery entered Kraydak's sanctuary, the screams stopped abruptly. He stood just inside the gold lined door and waited. Once the screaming ended, his master would not be long. He waited patiently, ignoring the soft, moist sounds coming from the inner room.

When Kraydak emerged, his blue silk tunic and wide flaring breeches were spotless, his red-gold curls tumbled softly about his face, and his generous mouth curved in a satiated smile. His left hand was red to the wrist but that was undoubtedly due to the bloody bundle of skin he carried. Behind him, on a low bench in the center of the inner room, lay what appeared to be a fresh side of beef with long golden hair.

The wizard tossed the bundle to his servant—who caught it awkwardly (the only way his twisted body allowed him to do anything)—and the blood disappeared from his hand.

"She lasted longer than most," he said approvingly as the heavy wooden door swung shut behind him.

The servant—whose name had been among the first things taken from him—clutched the bundle tightly, spattering the costly carpet with thickening globs of red, and arranged his features into what stood for an ingratiating smile.

"There is good news, milord."

Kraydak settled himself behind his desk and raised an eyebrow. The servant shuffled forward.

"Kirka has fallen, milord. The plague has done its work."

"Did you doubt that it would?" And the servant's twisted body convulsed in pain.

"No, milord!" The pain stopped and the servant straightened as much as he could, dampness spreading down the front of his breeches. "The young and the strong survived, just as you said. Their tongues have been removed and they are being marched to the mines of Halda."

"A long march from Kirka."

"Yes, milord."

"Unlikely more than a few will survive the march."

"Yes, milord."

"A pity. Still, there are always more slaves."

"Yes, milord."

"And you will join them if that skin hardens enough to crack before you get it tanned."

The servant glanced down at the bundle in his hand, which was indeed beginning to stiffen, and began to shuffle backward to the door. He was reaching for the handle when the wizard stopped him.

"You forgot to thank me," said Kraydak softly, "for the pain."

"Forgive me, milord!" Had he been able to rise from them, he would have fallen to his knees. "It was exquisite pain, milord. Thank you. Forgive me."

"This time." Kraydak smiled. "But always remember, I made you what you are today."

The servant had only dim memories of a time when he had been a strong and brave warrior, the captain of an army that had dared to oppose Kraydak's might, but he knew what his master told him was true—for his master always spoke Truth.

"Thank you, milord. I remember." And he scurried away.

Kraydak steepled his fingers together and sighed. Kirka had fallen like all the other cities and countries before it. So much for Kirka's vaunted healers. He bent over the table and made a brief notation, a small bet with himself on how many survivors of the plague would actually make it to Halda. Not that he really cared; all his hopes now rested on the wizard-child and the battle that approached in Ardhan.

"And what I shall do when that's over," he said to the air, "I have no idea." He had survived the Doom.

He was the greatest wizard ever. Nothing could touch him. He was indestructible. He would live forever. He was very bored.

His thoughts strayed back to the inner room and the low stone bench. He smiled and his blue eyes blazed as he went back to play with what lay upon it.

The servant had been very wrong when he assumed that life stopped as the screaming did. His own experiences should have taught him otherwise. There were ways to prolong the torment indefinitely and for what Kraydak had in mind, skin would have only gotten in the way.

Twelve

The army camped outside the walls of Hale's Seat. The Royal Party alone, consisting as it did of over twenty people, was considered to be enough of a strain on the town's resources in a time of war.

The Duke of Hale, a small, neat man in his late thirties, rode out to meet them. He paid homage to his queen, greeted Mikhail as an old comrade (the two men were of an age and had fought together in the Border Raids years before), informed the Duke of Belkar that his son had ridden in three days before with two hundred men and was even now waiting for him in town, and stared in astonishment at Crystal.

A trick of the evening sun turned her skin to burnished gold and at the same time ignited her hair into silver flames that danced gracefully on the breezes chasing about her. Her eyes blazed and all the greens that the Mother had given to the world in the beginning spilled forth with the light and clothed her in glory. She towered over the rest of the company and the very air around her sang with Power.

For a moment there was nothing human about her at all, her beauty was so much like the Mother's first children and so very little like Man. The Duke of Hale, who was reckoned to be a brave man, began to tremble.

And then, incredibly, one long-lashed lid dropped over a glowing eye in what was unmistakably a wink.

Hale started and found the silver-haired girl regarding him levelly, her eyes containing nothing more than the reflected glow of the sun.

When they fell in behind Tayer and Hale for the ride through town, Mikhail raised a questioning eyebrow at his stepdaughter. It took no power to know what he asked.

"He had to be sure of me."

"All right." Mikhail could see the necessity of that. "But the other?"

Crystal shrugged. "I didn't want him to stay frightened."

"Well, he may not be frightened," laughter hovered at the edge of Mikhail's voice, "but you've certainly confused the poor man."

That night, Hale gave a great banquet in honor of the queen. Whether because he felt she should not do completely without the pomp of the grand tour she'd missed or because he felt his own people could use the entertainment so close to war, no one knew. And no one would have been so ungracious as to ask.

Not up to arguing with her maid, Crystal allowed herself to be primped, painted, and laced into an elaborate gown.

"You look like a princess tonight, milady," enthused the girl as she pinned an emerald spray into the scented and piled mass of Crystal's hair.

"Yes," Crystal sighed, studying herself in the glass, "I suppose I do." She was the symbol of the continuation of the Royal House in Ardhan. She felt like a symbol, like an icon, and not a bit like herself. The wizard was hidden by yards of ribbons and lace and the beauty which had made the Duke of Hale tremble could barely be seen beneath the glory of the presentation. Only her eyes were unchanged, but no one looked a princess in the eyes.

"I'm not enjoying this," she whispered to Mikhail as they walked in procession into Hale's Great Hall. "I feel like I'm wearing a mask."

"You look lovely," Mikhail told her proudly. "And you've made your mother very happy."

"But it isn't me." Everyone seemed to have the idea that being a wizard was like being a farmer, a collection of skills that you picked up or put aside as needed. It was actually more like the difference between a cow and a horse, Crystal decided. There were certain physical similarities but that was as far as it went. *I'm a horse dressed up as a cow,* she realized suddenly. *I can never be a princess, and even less can I be queen.* She winced at the thought of making that clear to her mother.

"Cheer up," chided Mikhail, assuming the wince came from discomfort at her finery. "And look at the bright side. Hale always lays a fine table and tonight he's feasting us royally."

Crystal smiled weakly at her stepfather's joke and settled down to have a miserable evening. Her plans were ruined when the food arrived and she discovered more than one type of wizardry was loose in the world. Her mouth watered. She was seated between Hale's wife Alaina and the Duke of Belkar and as neither of them seemed inclined to talk, she applied herself to the meal. Glancing up some time later—from her second pastry stuffed with raspberries and cream—she found Lady Hale staring at her.

"I beg your pardon," murmured the older woman in response to the question on Crystal's face. "It's just . . . you're not what I expected."

"Oh?"

Alaina blushed. "I always thought wizards would be grimmer, more awe inspiring, not so . . . so . . ."

"Princesslike?" Crystal asked from behind her ribbons and lace and jewels.

"Hungry."

Crystal looked down at the remains of her pastry, considered the enormous meal she'd just eaten, and burst out laughing. The laugh had nothing to do with either the wizard or the princess, and she felt better than she had since Bryon had left the palace.

Bryon, who'd refused a seat at the head table and was eating with his captains, picked the laugh out of the sounds of a hundred people eating and arguing and making merry, and grinned. If she could laugh again . . .

Lady Hale smiled shyly. "I hope you're not offended. I'd always pictured wizards as being more ascetic and less concerned with fleshy matters."

"It takes a lot of energy to be a wizard," Crystal admitted, deciding she liked this woman who had accepted her so easily, "but if this wizard doesn't develop more ascetism she's going to be very concerned with fleshy matters." With a sigh she laid her hand upon her stomach, the dress showed a new animosity in places where it had merely pinched before dinner. She examined the soft curve of Alaina's pregnancy with frank curiosity.

"Is that very uncomfortable?"

As Alaina began to blush again, Crystal realized she'd probably said something she shouldn't have. "I'm sorry," she exclaimed before Alaina could say anything. "It's just that I've never seen a pregnant woman before. At least not that I can remember," she added thoughtfully. "Children don't pay much attention to that sort of thing and centaurs are all male."

Alaina, who'd been very nervous upon learning of the seating arrangements for supper, was no longer afraid of the great and powerful wizard. The look on the wizard's face reminded her too much of her five-year-old son who forever asked about things he shouldn't. She answered the wizard as truthfully as she would have answered her son.

"Sometimes it's uncomfortable." One hand rested gently on the curve of her stomach. "In the end, though, it's worth it."

"May I?"

A slender hand hovered over Alaina's own. When she nodded, it drifted down and ever so lightly touched.

For a few seconds Crystal sat silent, sorting the sensations that flowed up through her fingertips. And then she smiled. It was a smile few were privileged to see, for it was neither human nor terrifying. It was the smile the Mother wore when She looked about her and marveled at the beauty She had created.

"So tiny and so perfect," Crystal whispered, and her voice was the wind of summer caressing the earth. Her eyes glowed so deeply green her pupils washed away in the radiance.

Alaina, caught up in the light, felt herself falling into the whirlpools of Crystal's power. But instead of pulling her down, they lifted her up and wrapped her in wonder. A smaller light added its bit to the glory and she realized, with a wave of joy, that she saw the life of her unborn child. When the light retreated and she was herself again, she wasn't surprised to find her cheeks wet with tears.

The slender hand lifted slowly away, the green fires died, and the mark of the other world faded from Crystal's face. Her smile became very human and a little sad.

"Thank you," she said.

"When you have children of your own," Alaina began, but Crystal stopped her.

"Wizards have no children," she said flatly. "It's the price of our power. Only the Mother's Youngest create life." They sat silently for a moment and the sound of Tayer's laughter floated down from the center of the table. Crystal visibly brightened. "But you may have just solved a problem."

Before Alaina could ask how, or even what problem, the Duke of Belkar leaped to his feet shaking his fist. It took her a heartstopping moment to realize he wasn't shaking it at her but across her at Mikhail. Apparently the two men were approaching the climax of a disagreement.

"If we're to win this war," roared the red-faced duke, "we must take it across the border to the enemy's land!" His voice filled the hall, causing the musicians to falter and fall silent, and most of the diners to turn and stare at him in astonishment.

"No!" Mikhail slammed a mighty hand down on

the table, causing the cutlery, and more than a few people, to jump. "Make him come to us! Make him fight on our terms!"

"The only way he'll fight on our terms is if we take those terms and shove them down his throat! We've got to goad him forth from his hole!"

"Let him wear himself out on the mountains and not on the bodies of our men!" Mikhail was on his feet now as well.

"Excuse me . . ."

"If we let him in, he'll be twice as hard to kick out! We can't let him set one foot on our land!"

"Let him run supplies across the mountains, not us!"

"Excuse me!"

"We'll be in and out so fast that supply lines won't matter!"

"What?! Are you crazy, our yeoman soldiers against his trained killers?"

"I said EXCUSE ME!" The air crackled with the force of Crystal's voice. Mikhail and Belkar stopped bellowing at each other and turned to stare at her.

"There's no need for this," she began reasonably, holding on to politeness for her mother's sake.

"Stay out of this, princess," growled Belkar. "You said yourself we were to fight the best way we know how." He glared at Mikhail. "And my way is best!"

"This isn't your concern, Crystal," Mikhail told her. "We have a decision to make just as soon as Belkar sees reason."

A booming roar rocked the room, the candles and lamps flared with green fire, and a sudden wind threw the combatants back into their seats.

"There is nothing to decide." Crystal rose to her feet, her eyes blazing no less furiously than the candles and lamps. It was just as she'd feared, whenever they made her be the princess they forgot about the wizard, and, worse yet, she began to forget as well. "Have you forgotten the palace? Squashed flat! And he wasn't even in the same country. He could easily do it again. Here. Tonight."

Faces blanched.

"You will meet his armies on the Tage Plateau because that's how he has it set up. I will meet him when and where he chooses. You're nothing but game pieces to him, you and his army both, added to make our conflict more interesting." The room darkened until it was lit only by the fire in her eyes and the glow of her skin and hair. "And you'd better petition the Mother that he makes a mistake because that may be our only chance."

Then, turning to Lady Hale, she apologized for the disturbance and stalked out of the room.

"Crystal, I'd like to speak to you."

"I thought you might." Crystal slid over on the garden bench, giving her mother room to sit beside her. Gone were the ribbons and lace, the wizard was back.

"There was no need for that vulgar display at dinner."

"Yes, there was."

"Oh?" One beautifully arched chestnut eyebrow rose.

"People are forgetting this is a war of wizards."

"You were being ignored and you didn't like it."

"Well, yes." Innate honesty forced Crystal to admit there was truth in that statement. "But they ignored the situation, too."

Tayer sighed. "Of course they did. We're all caught up in something we don't understand and have no control over. If Belkar and Mikhail argue, they think they're doing something."

"But they aren't!"

"Does it hurt to let them think so?" Tayer's voice was very quiet. "A little hope can make the difference sometimes."

"This time?"

"Who knows. And if the army can take care of itself, that leaves you free to deal with Kraydak." Tayer gathered the stiff and unresponsive body of her daughter into her arms. Slowly, very slowly, Crystal relaxed. A breeze wandered in and tentatively ruffled her hair.

Crystal inhaled the scent of her mother's perfume and was transported, just for an instant, back to the days before the centaurs had come. Things had been so much simpler then. "I can't be what you want me to be, Mother," she said at last.

"I know," Tayer murmured. She'd known it for some time; the raw power blazing from Crystal's eyes that night had forced her to admit it. "I guess I'll have to start wanting what you are. But I don't want to lose my daughter."

Not even the darkness could hide Crystal's smile. "Never that." She returned the pressure of her mother's arms and for an instant it seemed as if their hearts beat in the same time and they were not two women but one. Then Tayer pulled gently away.

"I've got to get back. The queen can't vanish into the gardens for too long." She kissed Crystal on the forehead, and stood. "Oh. One more thing."

"Yes?"

"You keep the maid."

The wizard considered hot baths and clean clothes. "Yes, Mother."

Tayer had barely disappeared into the darkness when Bryon appeared out of it. He threw himself down on the bench and hooked his thumbs in his belt.

"Quite the trick you pulled this evening."

"Not you, too."

"I especially liked the way the lights went out. Must come in very handy when you need to impress the masses."

"And you're not impressed."

"You've always impressed me." He grinned in a way calculated to set maidenly hearts aflutter.

Crystal didn't appear to notice and certainly didn't flutter.

They sat for a while in silence, Crystal staring

thoughtfully at nothing, Bryon—whose night sight was very good—staring appreciatively at Crystal.

"Lapus was right," she said at last.

"Oh?" A wealth of meaning lurked behind the word, for Bryon suddenly found himself very annoyed that Crystal had spent the last few weeks, no doubt pretty exclusively, in Lapus' company. That this bothered him, annoyed him even more.

Crystal continued, oblivious to the inner turmoil of her companion. "Do you know the worst thing Kraydak has done? He's taken away our choices."

"What choices?"

"All of them. Mother had to become queen. Ardhan had to go to war. I have to fight him. I have no choice in what I do and very little in how to do it. That's the whole problem."

"No," Bryon corrected, transferring some of the annoyance he felt at himself to her, "that's only part of the problem. You've got this strange idea that you have to do everything yourself."

She whirled around to glare at him.

"I do."

"You think that because you're the last of the wizards, Kraydak is your sole responsibility."

"He is."

"You can't and he isn't. One day you'll realize it and you'll have to ask for help."

"Ask who?" Crystal demanded. "You, perhaps?" Eyes beginning to smolder, she sprang to her feet. He had no right to lecture her like she was a child.

"Why not?" Ridiculously, he felt better now that Crystal was upset. He was back in control.

"There's nothing you could do. You couldn't fight him.

Bryon had to admit that she was right, he couldn't fight Kraydak and frankly had no intention of doing so.

"I was thinking of myself more in the line of moral support." He stood up with lazy ease. "I've got to get back to my men, but maybe you should consider it." He blew her a kiss and was gone.

Gone? She felt vaguely cheated. He hadn't once touched her.

"Consider it?" she shrieked toward the receding sounds of his footsteps. "I've forgotten it already!" Sparks leaped off the ends of hair flung about in frustration. She was one of the two most powerful beings alive, why was she constantly being thrown off balance by that smug, self-centered, overbearing, incredibly good-looking young man?

She danced aside as a blue bolt charred the marble bench and with a furious gesture flung a green one back along its path.

"Stop showing off," she snarled. "I know you can reach this far, but I've enough on my mind right now without you!" And then she stomped back into Hale's Seat because neither the wizard nor the princess could think of a way to follow Bryon without looking like a fool.

Kraydak considered the green bolt with some surprise. He hadn't been surprised in centuries and he savored the return of the sensation. He congratulated himself on not attempting to circumvent the prophecy. This was fun.

The bolt had exploded harmlessly against his tower, not even ruffling his defenses, but he was rather astonished that it had gotten that far. The wizard-child showed more strength in her thoughtless response to his prodding than she had at any other time.

For a moment, he contemplated paying her another visit, this time in the mind of her young admirer. His eyes glowed slightly as he dwelt on the likely result of that encounter. But no, he'd made his point and repeating it would be a useless waste of power especially as she was, after all, coming to him. His time would be better spent arranging a suitable welcome for her when she got close enough.

"Perhaps," he mused, rubbing the scorched mark

on the stone, ''this young man brings out the best in her.'' The corners of his mouth twisted up. ''Or the beast.'' He wiped his fingers and reentered the tower. ''Something to remember.''

Thirteen

The Duke of Riven stood on the battlements of his manor and looked north. His brow was drawn down in a scowl and his fingers worried a loose patch of mortar into dust. Somewhere to the north, there was a battle going on and he had chosen not to be in it.

It had been over a week since he had returned his family to the arms of the Mother. For over a week he had sat each night in his father's chair with the War Horn of Riven on his knees, not listening to the old men—his father's counselors—nor the young men—his friends—as they urged him to sound the horn and ride to war. Even his steward—a solid gray-haired woman whom he thought had more sense—advised him to fight. They were all very anxious to ride into the arms of Lord Death, but he had no intention of allowing it. No intention of allowing more to die for a wizard whose face he couldn't seem to banish from his mind. He wondered how she'd felt when the Horn of Riven hadn't sounded. Betrayed? He hoped so.

He shivered. Riven Seat was high in the mountains and even in summer, the east wind whistling through Riven Pass was cold.

"Milord, dinner is ready if you would come in."

People were hesitant around him, as if afraid to touch his grief. They didn't know that he'd laid his grief in the pit with the bodies of his family which the wizard—the word was a curse in his thoughts—had preserved. All that he had left was a dull pain wrapped tightly around his soul.

Meals were somber times now. Looking out over the company from under heavy lids, Riven could almost see the gray pall that hung over the room. Hesitant glances were exchanged, conversations were held in a whisper or not at all. Mostly not at all. This, too, was the wizard's fault. In his father's day the hall had been filled with light and laughter, but she had killed his family and darkness had followed.

After dinner he sat in his father's chair, with the War Horn of Riven across his knees, and stared at the green eyes that gazed up at him from the fire.

"Milord? There's a Scholar here who wishes to see you."

"I don't want to see him."

"He says it's very important."

"I don't care."

"He says he brings a message from the wizard."

"What!" Riven leaped to his feet, the horn falling to the flagstones unheeded. "She dares send someone here?" His cheeks were flushed and his eyes were unnaturally bright. "Oh, I'll listen to a messenger from the wizard, and when he's done I'll have a message or two he can take back with him. Send him in."

The Scholar was a small, thin man with sunken cheeks and eyes so deepset they looked like they were hiding under the arching dome of his forehead. His hands fluttered constantly; birds, trapped in the ends of his sleeves.

"Milord," the Scholar began, then stopped, his eyes darting around the Great Hall, from person to person. "Milord, I have been instructed that this message is for your ears alone."

Riven waved his hand. "Out!" he commanded.

The men and women in the Hall looked at each other in astonishment and several murmured protests to their companions. Garments rustled as positions shifted, but no one left.

"You should not be alone with him," protested the steward, stepping forward.

"Why not?"

"Well, because . . ." She couldn't think of a convincing argument. And she really had no reason, just a feeling. "Because . . ."

"I've got my sword, haven't I?" He put his hand to the hilt. "If he tries anything, I'll kill him."

The Scholar wet his lips nervously. His grayish tongue looked like nothing so much as a large maggot.

"Now get out!"

With a helpless shrug, the steward surrendered and herded the others from the room. One or two tried to argue, but she silenced them with a glare and a gesture and, grumbling, they went. She paused at the door and looked back. Riven stood glaring at the Scholar, his lips drawn back in what was almost a snarl and yet, despite the appearance of frailty, she somehow knew that the Scholar was the more dangerous man. She sighed and closed the door. She could do nothing except keep a guard ready and breathe a quiet prayer to the Mother.

"Well?" demanded Riven when he heard the door close. "What does she have to say?"

"She, milord?"

"The wizard. I was told you have a message from the wizard."

"I do, milord." He wet his lips again. "But from the other wizard."

"The other wizard?" Riven repeated. "What the . . ." And then he understood.

"Wait, milord. Before you call your guards, you should listen to what he has to say."

Riven had never liked being told what he should do and he had come to like it even less during the short time he had been duke, for there were so many things a duke should do, but some note of power in the Scholar's thin voice stopped the call to his guards.

"I will not listen to treason," he protested weakly.

"Milord, the Great Kraydak does not counsel treason. He asks only that you continue to do what you have been doing.''

"I haven't done anything."

"Milord understands exactly. The Great Kraydak asks only that you continue to do nothing. He agrees wholeheartedly with your decision."

It was nice to be agreed with for a change.

"After all, who is this woman that your people should die for her?"

Riven had often wondered that himself.

"She is responsible for the death of your family."

"Kraydak crushed the palace," Riven was forced to admit.

"But only to get to her," the Scholar said soothingly. "Does that not make her responsible?"

As Riven had said as much himself, he had to agree with the man.

"And so, why should you defend the woman who killed your family?" the Scholar continued reasonably. "This is a battle of wizards. Let the wizards fight."

Let the wizards fight. Riven had said that all along. "My people may force me to sound the Horn and ride to battle."

"Would they have forced your late father?"

No, they wouldn't have. Riven couldn't imagine the old duke being forced to do anything he didn't want to. "No," he said and his fingers curled into fists.

"Are you not the man your father was?"

"Of course I am!" Riven stepped forward, two bright spots of color on his cheeks. "What are you getting at?"

"Only that I had not thought you a worse duke than your father, milord."

"I'm not a worse duke!"

"Then prove it." The high-pitched voice of the Scholar had suddenly turned very cold. Caught up in his own heat, Riven didn't notice.

"How?"

"Enforce your will. You do not want to fight, so

keep Riven Province from riding to war. Can you do that?'' The voice was colder still and a strange light surfaced in the murky depths of the Scholar's eyes.

"Of course I can. I'm every bit as much the duke as my father was.''

"Of course you are. And can you convince your people to resume trade with Melac?''

"As you say, they're my people. If I tell them to resume trade with Melac, they will.''

"And merchants will not be killed as they cross through Riven Pass?''

"You have my word.''

"Very good.'' He was once again an ugly little Scholar with no sign he had been anything else. "You had better get some rest, milord, you look tired.''

"Yes.'' Riven passed a trembling hand over his eyes. All of a sudden, a dull throbbing had begun behind each temple. "I'd better get some rest.''

Some hours later, after falling immediately into a deep sleep the moment his head hit the pillow, the young duke was shaken roughly awake.

"Stop it,'' he muttered sleepily. "Go away.''

The shaking continued, so, with a sigh, he rolled over. It was very dark in his room, but as his eyes grew accustomed to the lack of light he could make out two figures standing beside his bed.

"Well?'' he asked petulantly, after a few moments of mutual staring.

The taller figure leaned over, a menacing shadow in full battle armor. "I'd like to have some words with you, my son.''

"Father?'' Riven clutched the blankets so tightly his fingers went white. "But you're with Lord Death!''

"And just who do you think this is?'' asked the old duke, indicating the pleasant and disturbingly familiar looking young man standing beside him.

"Lord Death?'' Riven's voice cracked on the second word.

The pleasant looking young man smiled—his teeth were very even and very white—and then turned to the old duke. "You have two minutes only," he said, and politely moved away.

"It's all the time I'll need," snarled the old duke glaring down at his son, "to deal with this traitor."

"But, Father, I . . ."

"Traitor to your country! Traitor to your name!"

"But I haven't done anything!" Clutching the blankets, he moved back against the headboard. He had seen this man buried his own height down in the body of the Mother. His heart slammed against his ribs and the blood pounded in his ears . . . he tried to swallow but the muscles refused to obey.

"And why not? The War Horn has been sent and all you can say is, 'I haven't done anything.' That much is obvious."

"She killed you!"

"No one killed me. I died. But Kraydak killed your mother and don't you ever forget that."

"This is a wizards' war!" Even she had said that. What could mere mortals do in a wizards' war? Better to keep his people here, safe, so no more would die.

"You want to be Kraydak's bond boy and watch your people go to feed his demons? Is that it?"

"No, I . . ." Riven's brow creased and he tried to remember just what the little Scholar had said.

"Well, that's what you've just agreed to." The old duke sighed. "If I'd known you were going to make such a mess of things, maybe I'd have tried harder to stay alive."

"It wouldn't have done any good," murmured a soft voice from the shadows. Both Rivens ignored it.

"You left me alone." The young man's voice was almost a wail. Fear faded beside the pain. Once again, he saw the healer gently closing his father's eyes. *"He chose, milord,"* she said. *"I could not save him."*

"So that's it. Maybe I thought you were old enough to take care of yourself. I guess I was wrong."

"You loved Mother and Maia more than you loved me! You died and left me alone!"

The dead man sighed again and spread his hands,

as close to a helpless gesture as his son had ever seen him make. "Your mother was a part of me, I'd have been only half alive without her."

They stared at each other for a moment, the new duke and the old, both knowing that was as close to an apology as was likely to be spoken.

"And you aren't exactly alone, are you?" The steel was back in the old duke's voice. "You're responsible for an entire province. People depend on you."

"It's not the same." Riven's chin came up in a belligerent way that made him look very much like his sire.

"No, it isn't. Tough. You've a job to do; it was mine and now it's yours. I suggest you do it and stop crying over things that can't be changed."

"Time." Lord Death stepped forward.

"Just one more thing, milord." With a frown that held more weariness than anger, the old duke drew back his arm and struck his son hard across the face.

The force of the blow flung Riven almost out of bed and stars exploded behind his eyes. It took him a minute to realize that the continuing light was not inside his head. He opened his eyes and sat up.

The sun shone through and around the green brocade that covered the windows; morning. The room could not have been dark only seconds before. His father and Lord Death had not come to him in the night. It had been a dream, vivid and disturbing, but only a dream.

He lay back against his pillow as his valet came into the room and flung open the curtains. Golden light poured through the tiny panes of leaded glass, banishing shadows and gilding fear.

"A beautiful day today, milord. There's a fog on the heights, but it should burn off in a couple of hours." The valet turned to face the bed. "And what . . . milord!"

"What is it?" Riven inspected his immediate surroundings. Everything seemed to be in place. He could see no reason for the other man's shocked exclamation.

The valet silently handed him a mirror.

Across his cheek, in the exact shape of his father's hand, was a massive purple and green bruise.

"The pass has been filled?"

"We've just finished it, sir, but I still don't understand why we don't let the Melacians into the pass where we could ambush them."

"I gave my word they wouldn't be killed in the pass." Riven smiled. "I gave no word that the pass would still be there when they came to use it." His horse fidgeted under him and he let it dance about before bringing it under control. "You're sure the Scholar sent no messages before he was killed?"

"None that we were aware of. If he used magical means . . ."

"No matter," Riven shrugged. "Kraydak will know of our plans soon enough."

"Then why not sound the horn?"

"Why make it easy for him? You'd better get back to your men, we'll be leaving soon."

"Yes, sir."

Riven watched his captain ride away and decided to stay a moment longer on the hill overlooking Riven's Seat. A warm breeze blew slowly along the side of the mountain and it carried with it all the smells he wanted to remember when he was in the midst of battle.

"He loved you very much."

Riven glanced down at the pleasant looking young man—who was still disturbingly familiar. No need to ask who Lord Death referred to. "He has a funny way of showing it." The bruise had faded a little, but the teeth on that side still ached when he chewed.

"You needed to have some sense knocked into you." Lord Death waved a white hand at the army forming in the valley below. "It seems to have worked."

"Why did you let him come back?"

"Why not? You couldn't possibly understand my motives, Mortal, so you needn't try."

"For whatever reason then, thank you."

Lord Death smiled. And wasn't there.

Not until much later did Riven realize that Lord Death bore a startling resemblance to his mother.

Fourteen

The crescent moon was barely visible over the tops of the trees, campfires had died to embers and, with the exception of the sentries patrolling the perimeters of the camp and the surgical pavilion, regrettably never quiet, the army of Ardhan slept. No one saw the man-shaped shadow slipping from shelter to shelter. Even the Duke of Belkar's guard failed to see it as it passed almost close enough to touch. What was one more shadow amongst the shadows of the night. Unnoticed, the intruder moved around to the back of Belkar's tent.

After checking that he remained unobserved, the shadow slipped a knife from his sleeve, the blade carefully blackened to prevent a stray bit of light from giving him away. Slowly, quietly, he slit the canvas wall and then slid through the hole. Only a thin black line showed he had been there at all.

It was dark, but the shadow deftly threaded his way around the furniture and the scattered pieces of armor. He made his way without incident to the center of the tent where, by the dividing wall, there was a bed.

The occupant of the bed stirred, rolled over on his back, and began to snore. Loudly.

The shadow moved silently forward. He bent over, but it was too dark to see the features of the sleeper. Not that it mattered, the snoring with its particular cadence and its volume said, "Here lies the Duke of Belkar" as clearly as if it were full daylight.

Stepping back a pace, the shadow raised his knife and struck. A moist thud cut the snores off abruptly.

The shadow turned, arms spread wide as if to embrace someone or something. Then, struck by a brilliant beam of silver light, Lapus fell to his knees.

"No, not Kraydak," Crystal told him sadly. "Nor will it be. He lied when he said there would be a way out."

Lapus could barely see the young wizard through eyes squinted shut against the glare, but he sensed she wasn't alone. Behind her, where the light was not so bright stood . . . the Duke of Belkar? He twisted around until he could see the bed. Empty; except for his knife which had cut right through the thin mattress.

"Illusion," he said bitterly. "Lies."

"Not the first. All Kraydak offered you was more of the same; illusions and lies."

"No!" Lapus got to his feet. Two guards stepped forward, but Crystal waved them back. "He showed me. It was real!"

"What he offered may have been real, but he would never have given it to you. I suspect that even had you succeeded tonight he would've ignored you just as he's doing now."

"No," Lapus repeated, burying his head in his hands and collapsing back on the bed. "It couldn't have been a lie." Then his head lifted and his eyes opened wide, pupils dilated against the light. "He showed me Truth!" Suddenly, he clutched at his knife and dove across the tent.

He was on them so fast that Crystal had no time to react. Already upset by the confirmation of Lapus as Kraydak's tool, the attack shocked her into immobility. Had she been the Scholar's target, Kraydak would have won in that instant, but Lapus pushed her aside and headed straight for the duke. Where he was met by a guard. And a sword.

He peered down at the steel that stuck out of his chest and gave a soft sigh as it slid free. The knife dropped from nerveless fingers and with the other hand he touched the blood flowing from the wound—gently, as if afraid to disturb the flow.

"I wish," he said tenderly, staring up at Crystal with a hopeless desperation, "we could have . . ." And then he died.

Crystal knelt beside him, closed his eyes, and kissed him lightly on the forehead. Then she stood aside so the guards could remove the body.

"Why did he do it?" asked Belkar shaking his head as they carried Lapus from the tent. He had liked the Scholar, enjoyed arguing with him, respected his mind. He had hoped that Crystal's suspicions were unfounded. "What could Kraydak have shown him?"

"Just what Lapus said he did, I expect. Truth. Lapus told me once that Truth was the only master." Her hands stroked up and down her arms as if afraid to be still. "Kraydak took Lapus to the top of the tallest mountain and offered him all the knowledge of the world."

"Eh?" The duke was puzzled. "What mountain? Where?"

The tent flap had barely closed behind the guards and their burden when it opened to admit Mikhail. He jerked a thumb over his shoulder—he must have passed the body on its way out—raised an eyebrow and asked, "Lapus?"

Crystal nodded.

"What about the others?" Belkar demanded.

"Thanks to Crystal, we got them all. The dukes are safe."

"And the Scholars?" Crystal asked, although she knew the answer.

"Child," said Mikhail gently, enclosing her shoulder in a massive hand, "they were out to do murder for a man who wants to put the entire country to the sword." He moved his finger under her chin and lifted her head so she was forced to look at him. Her face was very pale and her eyes were dim. "You said yourself that once Kraydak held a mind the only sure release was death. They had to die. We had no choice."

Crystal scuffed her foot by the damp, red stain stain on Belkar's carpet. This was another choice that Kraydak had taken from them. She felt as though iron bands had been riveted about her chest. "He was my friend."

"And mine," said Belkar.

"We've all lost friends," Mikhail reminded her and then realized that, until this moment, Crystal had not. Lapus and young Bryon were the only two friends she had. Her power, her rank, and her beauty had kept other friendships from developing. He opened his arms and offered a father's comfort if the wizard cared to take it.

The wizard cared to, very much. With a strangled sob, Crystal hid in his embrace, and cried for Lapus, for all the others, and, just a little, for herself.

"What of our lads?" asked Belkar.

"Only one of them was hit, but he's pretty bad. The knife went up under his ribs. I doubt he'll make it."

Crystal pushed herself away from Mikhail's chest, wiping her cheeks dry with the flat of her hand. This was how she could erase the memory of Lapus lying dead at her feet. "I can save him," she said, giving one final sniff, and starting for the door.

"No." Mikhail swung around and blocked her way. "Kraydak must know his plan failed and may try something else tonight. You have to be ready. Remember what happened last time."

She rubbed her nose across her sleeve, looking absurdly young as she did so, and remembered.

After the first meeting between the Melac and the Ardhan armies—in which Kraydak had sent out an innocuous probe and Crystal had smashed it back at him with a strength that surprised them both—Crystal had gone to the surgical pavilion to help. The area was already protected from infections by a long and complicated weaving of power, but she wanted to do more. The surgeons directed her to a young man with a deep sword slash across the belly. His cut and torn guts were bulging from the wound, masking the rest of the internal damages. The surgeons wondered why he was still alive and they doubted he could hold on much longer.

Feeling slightly sick at the sight and the smell, Crystal placed her hands lightly on the soldier's body and began to hum. A green flame grew in her eyes, spilled over and ran down her arms into the boy on the stretcher. Before the astonished eyes of the surgeons and those patients near enough to see, the edges of the wound began to glow and close. The bulging mass of intestine, now miraculously clean and whole, tucked itself back where it belonged. Muscle fibers reached across the gap left by the sword and quickly wove the muscle back into one piece. The edges of the skin flowed smoothly together, leaving no scar or any other sign there had ever been a wound.

But the young man, now seemingly whole and hale, still lay near death.

Crystal's song changed slightly, becoming less somber, less instructive. Those listening felt a surge of energy, minor aches and pains disappeared and several small wounds closed. Color flooded back into the young man's face as the life force he had lost was replaced. His eyes flickered, then opened. He looked around, wondered peevishly why everyone was staring at him, and demanded a beer.

Crystal smiled, then the light pouring from her went out, and she collapsed to the floor. Although healing the wound had drained her, it had not caused her to faint. She had replaced the lost life force with her own.

The soldier was no worse for his experience—except for a vague but disturbing memory of hunting horns and baying dogs—but Crystal lay unconscious for three days. During that time Kraydak did what he pleased, but it was observed that, although he created plenty of impressive loud noises and bright lights, his attacks caused confusion and fear rather than destruction. He was obviously biding his time until Crystal recovered.

Crystal woke to a demoralized army and a mother frantic with worry. The army was much easier to reassure. When Crystal explained what had happened, Tayer ordered her to leave healing to the surgeons. Realizing that in this both queen and mother were in full accord, Crystal reluctantly agreed and then blamed herself for every death which followed. If she didn't send her people to Lord Death, neither did she try to stay his hand.

Crystal knew Mikhail was right to stop her. Her responsibilities made it as impossible to save the guard as it had been to save any of the others who had fallen. In addition, she was tired from the day's fighting and the small but constant drain of keeping the protection over the surgical tent. The power she'd used to trap the Scholars had tapped out almost all of her reserves. None of this made the almost certain death of the guard any easier to bear. Finally she nodded and Mikhail stepped out of her way. The wizard was back and wizards don't mourn what they can't change.

"Can I walk you to your tent?" asked Mikhail, who was not as convinced as Crystal seemed to be that the wizard and his daughter were two separate people. She nodded again and he turned to Belkar.

"Go on then," said the duke. "There's nothing you can do here. I'll just have someone change the carpet. And the mattress," he added thoughtfully. "Can't say as I fancy sleeping on that knife hole."

The camp was certainly busier than it had been one short hour before when Kraydak's Scholars had slipped through the shadows to do murder. Bodies had to be disposed of, troops reassured, and a life saved if possible. Mikhail and Crystal walked alone through the darkness. Mikhail insisted that Tayer always be accompanied by soldiers from the newly reconstituted Palace Guards but refused them for himself, putting his trust instead in his great black sword. Crystal, the princess, was assigned Guards as well but Crystal, the wizard, threatened to turn them into newts so they went elsewhere.

"I'd like to know how you knew," Mikhail said as

they threaded their way through all the activity. Crystal had refused to explain her suspicions in case she'd been wrong. Considering Lapus' involvement, Mikhail now understood whom she'd been protecting.

"I could see myself in his eyes."

"In Lapus' eyes?"

"Yes."

"Is that unusual? I suppose I'd have seen myself reflected in his eyes had I cared to look."

"When I look in someone's eyes," Crystal explained, remembering how shocked she'd been to first catch sight of herself in the Scholar's gaze so many weeks before in Belkar's library, "I look into their hearts. There could be only two reasons for me to see myself; his love for me was so strong I was the only thing in his heart, or he had been blocked by a wizard. There is only *one* other wizard." Her smile didn't quite hide the pain of Lapus' betrayal. "I tried to convince myself that Lapus had indeed lost his heart and almost succeeded until I met Hale's Scholar. Maybe one man could fall in love with me at first sight, two I couldn't believe, even though the centaurs had warned me how men would be. Then I met Cei's Scholar, and Aliston's, and Lorn's, and I stared out of the eyes of all of them. Once I knew Kraydak was involved, the plot became easy to discover."

Too easy, it seemed to Mikhail and it worried him. Kraydak, no doubt, had his own reasons for doing sloppy work. Using planted Scholars to attack the dukes, seemed too much of a diversionary tactic; helpful if it succeeded but no great loss if it failed so long as it masked the more important maneuver. He only wished he knew what it masked and feared it would be an attack, not at the army, but at his daughter, who had been hit once already tonight. And although he would never tell her, for the news would only add to her burden of pain, Mikhail had reason to believe that Lapus did indeed care greatly for the princess. Mikhail was very familiar with the many faces of devotion; he had worn them himself for years.

They arrived at Crystal's tent and the soldier guarding the door, the young man she'd lifted from the grip of Lord Death, snapped to attention. When told what she'd done, he'd pledged his life to the protection of his savior. His lord, the Duke of Cei, had a strong streak of romance running beneath his shrewd and pragmatic exterior and happily released the man from his service. And so Crystal acquired a personal guard she had no wish for but couldn't get rid of. The relationship developing between her guard and her maid was the only thing that made the situation bearable. She hoped she might soon lose them both to one another.

Mikhail leaned forward and planted a kiss between the silver brows. "You did what you had to," he said softly.

I wish we could have . . . You did what you had to. She nodded, not trusting her voice, and slipped into the tent.

Although she crawled into bed exhausted, Crystal couldn't fall asleep. Every time she closed her eyes she saw Lapus charging across the room, knife raised, his face twisted with hatred. She hadn't always liked what he'd said, how he'd stressed the conflict between wizard and princess, but she'd come to care for him and had thought he cared for her. That his friendship was an act, engineered by Kraydak, made her feel slightly sick and very lonely. This, the centaurs had not warned her of.

Eventually, the exertions of the day overcame her grief and she drifted into an uneasy sleep.

Gradually, Crystal became aware of green. A soft springtime green, very peaceful, very nice, very soothing. She could move around and there seemed to be a solid surface beneath her feet but the green never changed. She knew she was asleep and somewhere deep within her own subconscious. The centaurs had promised to teach her ways of manipulating the dream-world but there hadn't, in the end, been time.

"Not a very interesting place for a dream," she

sighed, spinning about so that the white gown she wore flared about her ankles. She liked the way the silky fabric clung, the way it whispered across her skin, although she wondered why she'd dreamed so little material above the waist. And then she saw the man approaching and knew she wasn't dreaming; not quite. She tried to raise a wall of power between them and found she had no power to spare.

His hair shone red-gold, like sunlight on fire, and clustered about his face in loose curls. His eyes were the clear, merciless blue of a hot summer day. Above tight sapphire breeches and high black boots, he wore no shirt and the muscles of his chest and arms rolled smoothly beneath golden skin as he closed the distance between them.

Grace and power, Crystal realized. And something more.

His hand, when it took hers, was cool and dry. His lips, touched to the skin of her wrist, soft and warm. "At last," he murmured. "Face to face."

Crystal snatched free her hand, more frightened than she'd ever been in her life. That he could reach this far into her mind without even waking her . . . "Get out of my mind!" She kept her voice below a scream but only barely.

Kraydak smiled. "I had hoped that we might be friends."

Gathering up her courage, and holding dignity before her like a shield, she managed a tight smile in return and retreated a step. "I hardly think so."

"No? You wound me." He lay long fingers against his bare chest. "We have so much in common."

"We have nothing in common! You're a . . . a . . ." She searched for a word that would sum up the disgust and loathing she felt as anger rose to take the place of fear. ". . . an abomination. You destroy anything you touch." She turned her back on him and found he still stood in front of her. And still smiled.

One red-gold eyebrow arched. "Abomination?

Child, you are hardly one to point an accusatory finger."

"I am not like you."

"No," Kraydak agreed smoothly, his smile twisting strangely, "you aren't."

"You use people."

"Yes," he agreed again, "I do. I assume you specifically refer to the late, lamented Lapus? A useful tool; your grief at his betrayal gave me access to your mind. I needed a surety to enter through, you see, so I built my own."

She remembered the red spreading into the pattern of the rug and felt sick. "You set him up, you set all of them up, just to get at me?"

He reached out and pinched her chin. "And she's clever, too. Yes, child, I did it all for you." A couch, the couch from Crystal's tent, appeared behind him and he sat, gracefully crossing one booted leg over the other. He shook his head in mock sympathy. "Oh, my poor child, if you insist on caring for creatures so far beneath you, you can only expect to be hurt. Humankind should be your plaything, not your partner." His voice became caressing and held a possessive note that ran like soft fingers down Crystal's back. "We are the last two of our kind. The last two. No mere mortal could ever hope to understand us." The blue of his eyes deepened. "Come to me, Crystal."

To Crystal's horror she took a step toward him, under no compulsion save that of his voice and his presence. Red with shame, she stopped, determined at least to move no closer, no matter what he said.

He said nothing. He laughed low in his throat and held out his hand; his gaze fierce and compelling.

Well aware of the dangers of a wizard's eyes, Crystal dropped her own to avoid being trapped by his gaze. Red-gold hair curled in an inverted triangle on his chest, the lowest point trailing down the ridges of his stomach until it dipped beneath the blue of his breeches.

Her shins hit the edge of the couch.

"You needn't even try," Kraydak told her gently as she struggled to move away. "This may be your mind, but you'll find I'm in total control. Oh, and one more thing." He reached out and took her hand, pulling her down beside him. "These bodies are illusions, but they react like flesh."

He drew a finger down her cheek and her eyes widened at the responses such a simple touch caused. He manipulated reactions she didn't know she possessed and, not knowing, she had no way to defend herself. She dug her hands into the cushions of the couch, fighting the urge to touch him in return. Independent movement was possible it seemed, as long as it was not away from him. Cautiously she began to slide her essence, the core of her that was Crystal, deeper within this representation of her physical body.

Kraydak, one arm clasped lightly around her waist, pushed her back against the cushions. He felt her essence retreat and he let it go. She could not escape him, after all, and if she thought this warm bundle of flesh he held would resist his assault for long . . .

When he kissed her, she leaned into it and she heard herself cry out in disappointment when he stopped. Her thoughts and her feelings almost seemed as if they belonged to two separate people. And the sensations of her body, under Kraydak's skilled caresses, were rapidly overwhelming her mind.

"Patience," the older wizard chided, slipping the gown off her shoulders, "we have plenty of time."

He ran his fingers lightly over her breasts and she barely managed to hold her essence in place as her body arched under his touch. She became very much afraid that she would soon give into the sensations now setting her body alight, and then she would be lost, his creature entirely.

"Someone has certainly prepared the way," he murmured into the soft skin of her throat. "I hope I get the chance to thank him."

Bryon. Crystal grabbed that thought and held on tightly. She closed her eyes and built his image on the inside of the lids. She remembered every time he'd ever touched her, the feel and the scent of him, and built of it a barricade between her skin and Kraydak's hands.

It wasn't quite enough.

Kraydak's hands dropped lower and began to tug at the silky cloth that draped her hips, twisting her about so that he straddled her. His mouth moved to her breasts.

When she remembered to breathe at all, it was in great shuddering gasps over which she seemed to have no control. With the small part of her mind still her own she knew she couldn't hold out much longer. The fires that Kraydak had lit would consume all she was.

Bryon, she cried, feeling the heat licking at her refuge, *help me!* And from the time before the centaurs, rose one more memory. A very young Bryon rolled in the dirt of the training yard, hands clasped between his legs; a very young Crystal stared in puzzlement at the quarterstaff in her hands while their fathers almost split themselves laughing. Child, this wizard called her; she would use a child's blow. She bit down on her tongue, hard. As the pain jolted her free from the pleasure, she gathered the remnants of her strength and slammed her knee up between Kraydak's legs.

The illusion did indeed react like flesh and Crystal possessed the strength of the tree. It was fortunate for Kraydak that he had already depleted most of it.

Kraydak's eyes widened, he made an incoherent noise, and sank slowly to the ground. The surrounding green turned yellow, then orange, then red, then black and Crystal woke up in her own bed, her heart beating so fast she was afraid it would escape.

She lay staring at the ceiling, hands clenched at her sides, and forced herself to consider what had almost happened. His touch still lingered on her body and she flushed with embarrassment when she realized that the fires he'd lit still burned. Not with the same intensity as they had in the dream world, but a definite heat radiated out from the places he had . . . She shuddered. Kraydak had defeated himself when he reminded her of Bryon; she wouldn't be that lucky another time. And Kraydak's power frightened her less than her own lack of resistance.

"The trouble is," she mused, chewing on her lower lip in a most unwizardlike way, "I can't fight what I don't understand."

What if he came again? There was one rather obvious solution and the enemy himself had given it to her. She unclenched her fingers, wiped her sweaty palms on the sheets, and noticed with some surprise that she was still breathing heavily. . . .

Bryon woke up to the peculiar sensation of being in a different bed than the one he'd gone to sleep in. It was softer, slightly larger, and it smelled good. He was still in a tent and, from the sounds filtering through the canvas, still in the center of the Ardhan army, but where . . . and then he became aware of a warm body in the bed beside him, and he recognized the scent. . . .

"Bryon," said Crystal earnestly, "I need your help."

"Is this a dream?" Bryon asked of no one in particular.

"Don't be ridiculous." Crystal poked at him and wondered if he was going to be difficult. "You can't be dreaming, you're awake."

"I am?"

"Yes, and I want you to make love to me."

"I'm dreaming," he said with conviction. "I've had this dream before."

"Bryon!" Her voice was sharp, this wasn't how she'd imagined things at all. She should have been in his arms by now. He should have been swept away by passion the moment he found himself in bed with her. Wasn't that the way it worked? "Kraydak attacked me tonight and you're the only one who can stop it from happening again."

"What!" He sat up in the bed, reaching for the sword that wasn't there. "Kraydak came here?"

"Not exactly, he was in my mind and he . . . uh . . ." To her astonishment, Crystal felt herself blushing. "He, uh, stimulated me."

Bryon sat back against the pillows, the corners of his mouth twitching. He appeared to have his passion well under control. "He *stimulated* you? Perhaps you'd better tell me just what happened and what you think I can do about it."

Slowly, and with long pauses while she struggled to put the experience into words, Crystal told Bryon of Kraydak's attack. She left out nothing, not the fear, not the . . . other. She finished with her plan to build a defense with Bryon's help.

"After all, as Mikhail says, the best defense is a strong offense."

Bryon considered what Mikhail's reaction would be if he knew his beloved daughter was sitting naked in bed with a man he'd been heard to refer to as "having more gonads than sense," but all he said was: "I don't think this was the kind of situation he had in mind."

"Never mind him," Crystal dismissed her stepfather with a wave of her hand. "Will you help me or not?"

Bryon took a long, appreciative look and said, "No."

"No?" It had never occurred to her he would refuse. Wasn't this what he'd been leading up to all along?

It came as a bit of a shock to Bryon as well and with an altruism he hadn't known he possessed, he tried to explain.

"If this was truly your idea, I'd be honored to make love to you. But it isn't. Kraydak took advantage of your innocence to try to gain control over you and I won't finish the job."

"But it isn't like that!"

"Isn't it?" Bryon's voice was gentle but his eyes were hard. "As much as you care for me, would I be here if Kraydak hadn't attacked you?"

"No, but . . ."

"No buts. When we make love," he picked up her hand and planted a kiss in her palm, "and we will, it won't be as an act of war."

Crystal wrapped her fingers protectively around the kiss and looked at him with glowing eyes, eyes that had nothing to do with being a wizard. "Bryon," she began.

"No, not tonight." His voice was beginning to sound strained. "Now you'd better send me back to my own tent."

She studied him for a moment and then smiled. She was still smiling seconds later as she watched the indentation of his body smooth out of the mattress. "Were you concerned because it wasn't my idea," she asked it, "or because it wasn't yours?"

"Well, one thing's for sure," she said to the darkness as she blew out the lamp and settled down for sleep, "he won't get a chance like that again." But whether she referred to Kraydak or Bryon was not entirely clear.

Hanna stood on the battlements and looked out over the valley kingdom of Halda. She shivered and pulled the heavy traveling cloak tighter around her although it wasn't the night wind that caused the chill. She'd lived in Halda for seventeen years now, ruled over it as queen for ten; its fall, its death, tore open a wound she would always carry.

"Majesty?"

She turned and the young guard, dark circles visible beneath his eyes even in the uncertain torchlight, bowed.

"They are ready?"

"Yes, Majesty."

He stepped aside to let her pass, every movement a fight against exhaustion. It had been three days since anyone in Halda had really rested. It had been three days since the defenders at the pass had fallen and the army of the Melacian Empire had swarmed into the valley. Three days of slaughter. Men, women, and children put to the sword; and worse, if the hysterical accounts of the few fleeing survivors could be believed.

Hanna moved sure-footedly through the castle's dark halls, the guard following silently behind. Next to the great Palace of Ardhan, the dwelling of Halda's royal family was a paltry thing, but it had been a home to her, which was infinitely more than the other ever had. She stopped on the threshold of the throne room to let her eyes adjust to the sudden light.

Against the long wall opposite her, wooden platforms were rising, stages to lift the archers to the arrow slits high in the granite walls, hammers and saws providing a background to every other noise in the hall. Some of the wood, Hanna saw, had been cannibalized from the castle furnishings. Stretching away to either side of her, weary men and women sat holding their weapons, waiting. Behind them, rich tapestries still hid the stone. Through the heavy oak doors at the room's end, a steady stream of people, servants and nobles alike, carried food and water and weapons. In the center of the room, healers moved among the wounded and blood pooled on the gold inlay mosaic of the floor. The air was heavy with the smell of smoke and sawdust and steel and fear.

At her back, the young guard cleared his throat, as much of a prod as he could give his queen. She took another moment to banish hopelessness from her expression, then, lifting her chin, she stepped out into the room, heading for the small knot of people by the great gilded thrones. She walked as quickly as she could but took the time to acknowledge those she recognized with a smile or a softly spoken word.

Behind her, although she couldn't see it, shoulders squared and furrowed lines of tension eased.

"Mama!" As she reached the dais that held the thrones, a towheaded boy of eight threw himself at her legs. "Mama, Papa says he's not coming with us!"

She reached down and stroked his hair. "He can't, Jeffrey."

"Why not?" Jeffrey's voice rose. He was too tired and too frightened to be reasonable.

"Because he's the king. And the king has to stay with his people."

"But I want him to stay with us!"

Hanna's heart twisted and for an instant she closed her eyes in pain. *Oh, so do I, my darling. So do I.* When she opened them again, her husband was there.

Gregor, King of Halda, was not a physically imposing man. He stood a head shorter than his wife, and the square, solid body of his youth had become inclined to fat. His sandy-brown hair was graying and laugh lines bracketed his eyes. He shifted the girl-child in his arms and smiled.

He had the sweetest smile Hanna had ever seen and, as she had since that first day when he'd smiled up at her, she couldn't help but return it. They'd said their good-byes that evening, when he'd finally convinced her that the children stood a better chance if she went with them. His scent clung to her still. She couldn't decide if it would be a comfort or a torture in the hours to come.

Jeffrey twisted against her leg and glared up at his father. "I want you to stay with us," he repeated, lower lip beginning to tremble.

"I can't."

Something in that quiet voice got through and Jeffrey sighed. "Can I stay with you, then?" he asked.

"Who will take care of your mama and your sister if you stay with me?"

Jeffrey sighed again. "I'll take care of mama." His small hand slipped into her larger one. "But do I hafta take care of Ellen, too?

Safe from reprisals in her father's arms, three-year-old Ellen removed her thumb from her mouth long enough to stick out her tongue.

"Ellen, too," Gregor told him. "I'm counting on you."

"She's a slug," Jeffrey muttered. "But okay."

Gregor turned the beauty of his smile on his son. "Thank you."

"Majesties." The Captain of the Royal Guard

stepped forward, at his side a young woman clad in homespun and leathers. Although he was dark and her hair flamed a brilliant red, the whipcord leanness of their builds and the sharp wildness of their gazes bespoke a relationship. "Trin says you must go now if you hope to reach the caves by dawn."

Now.

Hanna looked at the captain's companion, who nodded. Now.

"I will carry the child." Trin held out her arms.

Gregor bent his head and placed his lips for a long moment against his daughter's brow. Ellen squirmed as his hold tightened and she made a muffled protest around her thumb. His eyes were very bright as he handed the child over to Trin.

"Jeffrey." He went on one knee before the boy and took the small shoulders in his hands. "You are King in Halda after me. While you live, Halda lives."

Jeffrey, impressed by the tone in his father's voice, nodded solemnly. Hanna knew he didn't understand, not really, but he'd remember. Father and son embraced and Gregor's cheeks were wet when he stood.

A thick finger traced the line of Hanna's jaw. "So beautiful," the king murmured and then she was in his arms.

And then she was walking away, down the long length of the throne room. She paused at the great oak doors, taking one last look back.

I never thought I'd love him. She remembered the long ride from Ardhan so many years before. Her surprise—their mutual surprise—at how well they got along, at how many important things they agreed on. How friendship had grown to something more precious. Pain and the tiny lifeless body of their first child who had never taken a breath in this world. The joy of Jeffrey and Ellen. *I wanted to never leave him.*

Over an impossible distance, their eyes met.

Then she walked from the room, saving the only thing in Halda that could be saved. The future.

Fifteen

On mornings when the fighting had not yet begun, the leaders of the Ardhan army met at dawn in the queen's pavilion. Although Bryon had the standing invitation issued to all the ducal heirs, he seldom attended, preferring to eat with his men. On the morning after his visit to Crystal's tent, he surprised everyone by not only appearing, but by having managed to wash, shave, and find a clean set of clothes.

He made an elegant bow to the queen, saluted first Mikhail, then his father and the other dukes, grabbed a plate and a mug, and found a seat beside Crystal. If he wanted to speak to her about the night before, however, he was to be disappointed. After greeting him with a somewhat absent smile, her mind, to all outward appearances, was wholly on the war.

"I'm afraid it's true, Majesty," the Duke of Lorn said sorrowfully as conversation resumed. "My daughter arrived last night with confirmation. Halda has fallen."

Tayer's eyes filled with tears and, almost involuntarily, she shook her head slowly from side to side. Mikhail appeared to be carved from stone.

"What of the Royal Family?" he demanded gruffly. Hanna, Mikhail's only sister was Halda's queen.

Lorn's daughter, Kly, a small, muscular brunette, spoke up. "The news I have is three days old, dating from when the pass was taken by the Empire. Then, the Royal Family was safe in their principal seat, but by now the castle must have been overrun. So long dependent on their mountain barriers, Halda has . . . had almost no defenses.''

A sound, half moan, half sob, welled up from Tayer's throat.

"Do not despair, Majesty." Kly's matter-of-fact tone was more calming than sympathy would have been. "I believe the Royal Family escaped and are hiding in the mountains.''

"Why?" Mikhail did not yet let himself hope. Better Hanna be dead than a captive of Kraydak or his men.

"I was in Halda often during my three years as a Messenger and I saw the escape plans. Halda's Guard Captain long feared this day would come. And, although it is not common knowledge, Halda's Guard Captain is a wer.''

"Wer!" More than one member of the council spat out the word as though it left a bad taste in the mouth. The members of the race the wizards had developed were few in number, seldom seen, and almost invariably hated.

"Wizard spawn," growled the Duke of Cei, his fat face twisted with distaste. "More likely to side with Kraydak then against him!''

"No." Kly's voice was quiet and assured. "The wer hate the wizards with an intensity hard to imagine. The names of the wizards are curses to them and Kraydak's is the most cursed of all." She turned to Crystal and, with no change of expression, added. "They've still not decided about you.''

Crystal inclined her head. What the wizards had done to create the wers was terrible beyond belief. The wers had a right to eternal hatred of their creators and, although it had happened thousands of years before her birth, she was a wizard.

"If it's not common knowledge," said Lorn, "how did you happen to find out that this man was a wer?''

Kly favored her father with a level gaze.

He blushed slightly and mumbled, "Never mind.''

"Milord." Kly addressed Mikhail directly. "There isn't a person alive that knows the mountains better than Rayue. There are caves and passages that go on for miles and have served as emergency shelter for the wer for generations. I believe that, for now, the Royal Family of Halda is safe."

Mikhail held her eyes for a moment longer, then, finding hope in her certainty, nodded.

"Now, if you'll excuse me, I'd like to go check on my horse before the fighting begins." As she left, she exchanged grins with Bryon. She had been Messenger to Belkar as well.

The council broke up soon after her departure. It was getting light and the battle lines were forming on the Tage Plateau.

Crystal stood, as she had stood since the first day the armies had engaged, alone on a rocky outcropping with an unobstructed view of the battlefield. Her hair whipped about in the wind and she felt, with growing uneasiness, the power building in the east. The air hung heavy with it and the sky was growing a greenish black. She waited nervously, gathering her own power to counter what had to be a major blow. As always, she faced the day wondering why she had not already been destroyed.

Although she had no way of knowing it, Kraydak wondered the exact same thing. On each day of the battle he had sent a little more power against her and each day she had met it and managed to survive. Once or twice, as she turned his attack in a totally unexpected way, he'd felt that, maybe, there was more to this wizard-child than he suspected and, perhaps, it would be amusing to discover what. And then he'd remember the prophecy—out of Ardhan would come the last of the wizards, the last creature capable of defeating him—and he'd try again to destroy her.

On a hillock, not far from where his daughter waited, Mikhail and his staff sat surveying the scene. Messengers had become couriers and already the traffic was heavy between the commanders and Mikhail. He hated not being able to fight himself, but his skills as a tactician were needed much more than his skill with his great black sword. His eyes went to where the Elite were grouped to take the brunt of the day's charge and he wished with all his heart that he was among them.

The armies joined and Crystal braced herself for the release of Kraydak's power. When it came, it was typical of his attacks but much more complicated than most. It began to rain. No ordinary rain, this was cold, and vicious, and selective. It rained only on the Ardhan army. Only the Ardhan troops got wet and cold, only their footing became slippery and treacherous. Even when soldiers grappled in close hand to hand combat, Kraydak's army stayed dry and sure-footed.

Crystal couldn't tell if Kraydak had wrapped each of his men in a force shield and then caused it to rain or if he was directing the rain itself. She faced a master weaving of many types of power with only a slight idea of how to begin unraveling it.

As the day progressed, and the battle raged, so too did the battle between the wizards. Crystal began to understand what Kraydak had done and was having some success at undoing it. The rain came in scattered bursts now, whole sections of the Plateau would be dry, while in others rain fell on Ardhan and Melacian alike. In places where she could not stop the rain, Crystal tried to turn Kraydak's power against him and so an Ardhan soldier, cold, wet, and miserable, found himself up against a Melacian who was wrapped in blistering heat and dehydrating rapidly. The odds began to even out and by midafternoon, although the conditions were both uncomfortable and unusual, neither side could say they had an advantage through magical means. The wizards now held each other in a precarious balance.

"Oh, well done." Kraydak could not have been more pleased had he trained the child himself. For her deft handling of the day's problems, he forgave her even the attack of the night before. And although it would not happen again, he treasured the experience; he didn't remember the last time he had actually been hurt. Of course, he couldn't let her think she was free to cause him distress and just get away with it. He checked the interweavings of their power and smiled. "Let's see how you deal with this then, little one."

The Melacian army began to fall back and a cheer went up from the Ardhan side, a cheer that turned to cries of horror as the dead shambled up from the rear of the Melacian ranks. The fallen, gathered each night from the battlefield, had been patched together and reanimated in a grisly parody of life. Their feet dragged through the mud, their lips were pulled back from their teeth in a rictus grin, and they still bore the wounds that had sent them to Lord Death. Here lurched a man with a great hole in his chest through which could be seen a gray and rotting heart. There staggered one whose head lolled drunkenly to the side, for the muscles needed to support it had been ripped away. Others walked on legs or swung arms not their own and rude stitches showed where limbs in better shape than the originals had been attached. Some carried swords, some spears, but they all carried terror as an added weapon.

The dead were not skilled fighters, but they didn't need to be. The same ghastly power that gave them a semblance of life and sent them out to kill, also gave them a strength few living could match. They were tireless and almost impossible to stop. Killing blows had no effect, for they were already dead, and the weary men of the Ardhan army found it necessary to chop these new opponents into pieces to stop them. Even then, very often, the pieces fought on.

Had it been possible to turn and run—to flee screaming from corpses that fought wrapped in the gagging stench of rot; to hide where a clammy hand could not close round your throat and continue to squeeze even after it was no longer attached to an arm—there would have been few Ardhan soldiers left on the field. But there was nowhere to go, so they choked back their fear and fought on.

Kraydak's living soldiers took strength from the victories of their unliving comrades, and threw themselves back into the fray.

When Crystal saw the dead advance, she bit back a scream. These shambling horrors were the stuff of her nightmares and she had to deal with her own terror before she could deal with them. Each decomposing feature, each hideous parody of humanity, struck a blow at the barrier of her power.

"Can't you do anything?" she called to a young man weaving his way through the battle, pausing here and there beside those who had fallen.

"What they do with the bodies is none of my concern," Lord Death replied, his features changing constantly as he spoke, and then he continued on his way unseen.

Crystal clutched her courage tightly and reached out to smash one of the dead to the ground. The freezing rain began again. The delicate balance of power slipped and disaster threatened. Her heart in her throat, Crystal grabbed back control and realized that Kraydak had effectively tied her hands. If she destroyed the living dead, she lost control of the elements. If the Ardhan soldiers were forced to fight the crippling cold and wet as well as their physical enemies, the Melacians would easily win. But if she let the walking evil be . . . as she watched, one of Belkar's captains went down with a spear slammed through his chest by a crawling monstrosity that dragged its guts on the ground behind it.

From his vantage point at the Plateau's edge, Mikhail ground his teeth in rage. He couldn't think of a thing that would do any good. Maneuvering was next to impossible, almost the entire army fought one on one and far too many men fought those they had defeated once already.

"Milord," gasped a courier, riding up on a lathered and blood-flecked horse, "they're breaking through to the south. Aliston is falling back. The duke asks you send him reinforcements."

Mikhail scanned the Plateau. An arm of the Melacian army had curved around, forcing the Ardhans to fight on two fronts, the east and the south. Up against the living dead, the southern front was falling back. Much farther and the Melacians would be behind the Ardhan lines.

"Get through to the Duke of Hale," Mikhail barked. "Tell him to regroup his cavalry and get over there as fast as he can."

"Yes, sir!" And with a weary salute, the courier was gone.

Mikhail doubted even Hale's cavalry would be fast enough to reach Aliston before the line was breached, but meanwhile there was something he could do. The need for a tactician was over. He drew his great black sword, whirled it once around his head to hear it sing, and set his heels to his horse's sides. The beast leaped forward, as glad to be moving as its master was. They pounded down the hill and flung themselves into the battle.

Aliston's weary men rallied as Mikhail hit the Melacian line like ten men not one. The dwarf-made sword moved so swiftly it looked like a black flame and flesh and blood and bone went flying from everywhere it struck. The dead began to die again.

It was almost enough.

Then Mikhail's horse was cut out from under him, disemboweled by the dying blow of one of Melac's captains. He jumped clear and continued to carve his way forward, his height and strength giving him an advantage over the foe that even the loss of the horse couldn't totally remove. But numbers began to tell and for every man he cut down it seemed another two rose up to fill the place. Soon he was stopped and, back to back with Aliston, surrounded by corpses and twice corpses, the two warriors fought to hold what he had regained.

Although he was covered in blood and dripping with gore, Crystal knew her stepfather had less need of help than anyone else still fighting. As much as she wanted to blast an area of safety around him, she forced herself to look away and do what she could for those who needed it more. She had discovered that, although most of her attention was needed to hold back Kraydak in the heavens, she could still manipulate small areas on the ground.

The angle of a sword blow, that would surely have separated head from shoulders had it connected, changed slightly in the air and slid off the edge of a shield instead.

A Melacian stepped on a rock which rolled slightly and sent him flying.

An archer with a direct line of sight to the Duke of Hale drew back her bow and put an arrow into the eye of a comrade.

The barbs of a Melacian spear hooked on an Elite's heavy armor and while trying to free it, the spearman himself was speared.

A craggy-faced young man with brows that drew a black line across his forehead slipped on another's blood and fell jarringly hard to the ground. As he lay gasping for breath, one of the undead loomed suddenly over him, spear raised to strike. Whispering a good-bye to his wife and child, for he knew he was on his way to Lord Death, he watched in amazement as the stitches holding the creature's spear arm to his body came unraveled and arm and spear fell harmlessly to the ground. Even the undead managed to look slightly surprised.

"I kept my promise," Crystal told a breeze, and then sent it to tell a young woman with honey-colored curls.

Kraydak's power threw itself at her barrier in waves. With each strike, she could feel her defenses wearing away, crumbling under the subtleties of Kraydak's attacks and her own terror of the walking dead which she still fought to control. She feared this would be her last battle, hers and Ardhan's. The army couldn't beat the undead without the help she was unable to give. Her fists were clenched at her sides, sweat plastered her tunic to her breasts, and her hair flapped lifelessly in the wind. Her ears began to ring.

She began to hear horns.

Surely that couldn't be in her head.

It wasn't.

"To war!" called out the War Horn of Riven. "To war!" And out of the forest to the south streamed the men of Riven, the duke leading the charge with the horn to his lips. He blew again.

All through the Ardhan army, hearts lifted at the sound and men and women found the strength to fight a moment longer.

"TO WAR!" Then the duke put aside the horn, drew his sword, and the Riven warriors threw themselves at the backs of the Melacians who had almost broken through to the south.

The call of the horn went through Crystal like a ray of light. She drank it in, gathered it up, and threw it as hard as she could at Kraydak's might. Which wavered but held. She added her joy in Riven's arrival, the hope that rose in every breast, and the love of the farmer's young wife. Kraydak's attack crumbled and the setting sun burned red and gold through the fleeing clouds.

At the touch of the sunlight, the undead paused and then, like puppets with cut strings, they collapsed to the ground. Riven's men soon drove the remaining Melacian soldiers into a full retreat while the Ardhan army leaned on their weapons and cheered.

Fewer people than usual gathered outside the queen's pavilion that evening. Lorn had died with an arrow in his throat. Cei was in surgery with a spear wound in his belly; his fat had saved his life. Hale would not leave his men, for few of their horses had survived and in Hale a horse was regarded with as much tenderness as a child.

At Mikhail's approach, Tayer forgot queenly dignity and threw herself on him regardless of the blood which stained her hands and gown a lurid red. An embarrassed Riven was welcomed with much backslapping, his lateness forgotten in the perfect timing of his arrival.

Crystal collapsed on a camp stool and began stuffing herself with meat tarts in an attempt to fill the emptiness that clawed at her from within. She had come very close to using every last bit of power. Belkar came and stood beside her, his face gray beneath the dirt and blood.

"Have you seen Bryon lately," he asked. "Have you seen my son?"

Crystal's face blanched and the remaining color drained from her eyes. "No," she said, realization dawning. "Not for hours."

They looked at each other and then both turned toward the battlefield. Was he out there? Did he lie staring up at the stars too wounded to move, bleeding, dying? Had he already gone to Lord Death?

"I'd know if he were dead," Crystal whispered, listening to the pain rising from the wounded and trying find Bryon's within it. "I'd know."

"Better dead than out there," rumbled the duke. "Mother knows how long until they find them all."

The thunder of approaching hoofbeats distracted them and they glanced up from their fears.

"Why the long faces? Didn't we win?"

"Bryon!"

Bryon smiled wearily. The joy in Crystal's voice and the welcome in her eyes made the whole wretched day almost worthwhile.

Crystal bounded to her feet, the meat tarts flying unheeded to the ground. Relief and something more flooded the places where power had been expended. "We feared you'd been killed."

"Not hardly. Not a scratch on me." He slapped at

his armor with disgust. It looked a great deal like he'd spent the afternoon swimming in an abattoir. "All this blood belongs to somebody else. Several dozen somebodies, as a matter of fact." He kicked a foot free of its stirrup, but before he could lift his leg clear of the saddle, a blue bolt arced down from the sky and smashed him to the ground. Screaming in terror, his horse bolted.

"NO!"

The world stopped while Crystal threw herself down at Bryon's side, but he was already beyond any help she could give. He tried to grin, and as he died she saw herself reflected in his eyes.

Sixteen

The roaring in her ears drowned out the normal sounds of the Ardhan camp as Crystal knelt at Bryon's side, cradling his head in her lap, her eyes closed and dry. She knew the Duke of Belkar stood behind her, tears cutting channels through the grime on his face, and she felt his grief more clearly than her own. She wasn't sure it was grief she felt.

A single beam of moonlight cut through the gathering darkness, rested briefly on Bryon's still body and then was trapped in the silver net of Crystal's hair. When she finally stood, it rose with her. She brushed by Belkar, not seeing him, and strode down the path to the battlefield.

"Crystal," Tayer called, but Mikhail put his arm around her and shook his head.

"I don't think she can hear you, my love."

"But she shouldn't be alone." Tayer wiped her eyes with a square of lace and linen pulled from her sleeve.

I'm afraid she'll always be alone, Mikhail thought, but all he said was, "No, she shouldn't."

They followed their daughter down the path, each resting a hand gently on Belkar's shoulder as they passed the old man who stood silently mourning for his son. When they reached the battlefield, Crystal already stood on her outcropping of rock, arms raised to the moon.

As they watched, her hair lifted and wove patterns in the air, gathering in the light and absorbing it. Her eyes were pools so deep that the green appeared black. She stood unmoving, a sculpture of white marble rather than living flesh and her beauty had never been more terrible. She looked so little like their daughter that Tayer and Mikhail suddenly found themselves more afraid of her than for her.

If Kraydak had thought to paralyze her with grief, he had made a grave mistake.

She knew what she was feeling now. She was furious. No matter that her own power had been depleted; there were other sources and her anger would act as focus for them.

Without warning, she ignited in a glorious blaze of silver fire. Every leaf, every twig, every blade of grass in the surrounding area stood out in sharp relief against their own tiny and impenetrable black shadows. Tayer and Mikhail staggered back, nearly blinded by the intensity. Behind them, they heard the rest of the army cautiously approaching, drawn like moths to the flame. The men and women carrying the wounded from the battlefield favored the wizard with a startled glance, then, giving thanks for the light which made their job easier, hurried to finish before it went out.

When the light of the wizard outshone the light of the moon, Crystal called. The mountains answered. The sound was so wild and inhuman that many of those who heard it fell to their knees in terror, fingers stuffed in their ears in a hopeless attempt to block it out. They sang together for a moment, the wizard and the Earth, and then Crystal clenched her fingers into fists.

The song of the mountain ceased, replaced by a rumbling roar—rock, torn from its rest and hurtling earthward. The Melacian army was camped in the shelter of the mountains. Their screams could be heard all the way across the Plateau.

A blue bolt arced down from the heavens, but Crystal almost contemptuously swatted it aside. It was closely followed by a second and a third. The fourth she grabbed and held and threw it back the way it had come. There was no fifth bolt.

She clenched her fists again.

With a tortured scream, an entire cliff face sheared away and plummeted down on the Melacian camp.

Mikhail staggered up to his daughter, tears running from his burning eyes. Thus must the wizards of old have looked at the height of their powers, proud and distant and not the least bit human.

"Crystal!" He clutched at her arm and was surprised to find it icy cold. "Enough! You've done enough!"

She shrugged free of his grasp with such ease that Mikhail wasn't sure she even knew he'd been there. Her seemingly gentle motion flung him back and off his feet. Through slitted eyes, he saw a small form moving past him and up to face the wizard. "Tayer, no," he began and then realized that it wasn't his wife.

Her eyes squinted nearly closed against the glare, Kly pulled back her arm and punched the wizard as hard as she could in the stomach. She had intended a slap in the face but had discovered to her chagrin that she wasn't tall enough.

Crystal's gaze snapped back from the distance and she dropped it to the young woman's face. When their eyes met, Kly found the light no longer blinded her and she stared back fearlessly, not even trying to escape as she fell into the darkness. As she felt herself and all she was, probed, examined, and absorbed, the darkness lightened and grew green. When she returned to herself, the wizard looked down at her with eyes that glowed the deeper green of summer leaves.

"It wasn't because I loved him," Crystal explained, as much to herself as to Kly, her voice deathly calm. "It was because I never got the chance to find out."

Kly nodded. "I know," she said.

And because Kly understood, Crystal sighed and the light went out.

Kraydak's servants were used to the blue bolts that blazed out from the top of the tower. They knew that with each bolt went death and destruction for their master's enemies. They had never before seen one come back.

"Master?" He edged his twisted body around the door and peered fearfully into the room. He had not been called and the punishment for entering unbidden was severe, but the returning bolt had shaken the tower and he was sure he had heard his master cry out in pain.

"Master?"

There, against the far wall.

The servant scrambled farther into the wizard's sanctuary. The door swung silently shut behind him and he whimpered low in his throat. It was too late to turn back. He forced abused limbs into motion and shuffled painfully across the carpet toward the blue and gold bundle on the floor.

A thin trickle of blood ran from Kraydak's nose, streaking the sculptured beauty of his face. His eyes were closed and his head twisted back at an awkward angle, but the golden chest still rose and fell: he lived.

With a gnarled finger, the servant gently touched his master's blood. He stared at the scarlet stain for a moment then brought the finger to his lips. It tasted no different from his own.

Deep in the prison of his mind, the man he had once been woke and screamed, "Kill him! If he can be hurt, he can be killed! Kill him! You will never have this chance again!"

The servant awkwardly wiped the blood from Kraydak's face. He had learned long ago that it hurt much less to ignore the voices in his head. He would wait and his master would wake and he would be told what to do. Even now the wizard's eyes were opening.

Blue fires. Searing. Burning. Consuming. Killing.

The inner voice died first, then the servant's body spasmed and collapsed at his master's feet.

Kraydak kicked the broken thing aside and staggered to the inner room where he threw himself down on the marble bench.

"That wizard-child is lucky beyond belief," he

snarled, checking the lump on the back of his head. "She dares to throw my power back at me! At me, Kraydak!" He winced as he probed the sore spot, his eyes glowed briefly, and the pain was gone.

"You have hidden depths, wizardling," he continued in a softer voice—a voice the servant would have recognized with terror had he been alive to hear it. "You destroyed my armies and you caused me pain." Twice now she'd hurt him, and that was beyond even his ability to forgive. "Of course, the army will be replaced, and while that game continues, we will play a new game, you and I. I will call you to my side and you will learn about pain." He reached down and stroked the skinning knife that lay on the bench beside him.

"Bryon was right." Crystal struggled to keep her voice steady and matter of fact. It held an edge, she knew, but none of the hysteria she had feared would appear the moment she opened her mouth. She'd spent the night, trembling in exhaustion and reaction, alone in her tent, not even her mother daring to force an entry. The earth sang quiet songs to her, filling the darkness with comfort, and by morning she had calmed herself. When she entered the queen's pavilion, and met the eyes of the council members, she knew no one would ever call her princess again.

"Bryon was right about what, dear?" Tayer asked kindly.

Crystal knew they humored her, but she didn't care. She saw the fear in the glances of the soldiers and didn't care about that either. Kraydak had also been right. Care about someone and you only get hurt. She wasn't going to care anymore.

"He said I couldn't fight Kraydak alone. That someday I'd have to ask for help."

"We'll do what we can," Mikhail told her, but wondered what sort of help mere mortals could give to a seventeen-year-old girl who could call to the earth and have it answer.

The wizard shook her head. "What can you do?" she asked bluntly. "What can any of us do? Last night my anger gave me strength, but I can't be angry all the time." She walked to the tent flap and looked out at the sunshine. The wind brought her the sound of metal on rock, the pitiful remnants of the Melacian army digging out their camp. For an instant, she reached out and touched the power she'd called the night before. It stirred and she backed quickly away from a seduction more dangerous than any Kraydak could attempt. Without her rage as focus she knew she lacked the skill to control the forces her power, small in comparison, could release.

The council exchanged worried glances and Belkar rubbed a hand over red and puffy eyes. They had buried his son with the dawn.

"Then what's left?" he sighed.

Crystal turned to him and her expression was more human than it had been at any time since Bryon had died. Even in her anger, she had realized his loss had been the greater one; he was an old man, he would have no more sons. "The Doom of the Ancient Wizards," she said almost gently. "The dragons."

"The dragons?" the council repeated in one voice, an incident that would have been funny any other time.

"The dragons," snorted the new Duke of Lorn, a wiry, brown man who resembled his sister Kly a great deal, "returned to the earth thousands of years ago. When the wizards died."

"But one of those wizards lives," Crystal reminded him. "If the legends are true, then so too must one dragon."

The wizards had created the dragons in a contest to determine, once and for all, who was mightiest. They had drawn up the very bones of the earth and changed them, reshaping them into giant flying reptiles, breathers of fire and frost. Each wizard poured his or her mightiest spells into a dragon, and when the great beasts were finished each wizard gave up a piece of his or her own life force so that the dragons might live.

Each dragon was a part of the wizard who'd created it.

But the dragons were also made from the body of the Mother and, to their horror, the wizards could not control the creatures they had made. In great battles that lasted years and forever changed the face of the land, the dragons slew their makers. There was never any doubt of the outcome. In their conceit, the wizards had created too well. As long as the wizard who created it lived, so too would the dragon. And the dragons were stronger.

When the wizards were defeated, the dragons returned to the earth from which they were made. But if one wizard still lived . . .

"Then Kraydak's dragon must live!" Hope rang out in Tayer's voice. They had a chance after all.

But Cei was shaking his head, jowls jiggling with the motion. "Impossible. Firstly, if it lived, it would be fighting Kraydak, which it isn't. Secondly, Kraydak is many things, but I've never seen anything to make me think he's a fool and he must believe that the dragon is dead. You said yourself, he emerged from hiding when he realized he'd escaped his Doom."

"It's been thousands of years," Crystal replied. "Kraydak has to believe he destroyed the dragon during their last battle. How else could he still live?"

"How, indeed," muttered Lorn.

'But you don't believe the dragon is dead?'' persisted Tayer.

"If Kraydak lives, the dragon lives. He may have stopped it, but he couldn't kill it without killing himself."

"And why hasn't Kraydak come to this conclusion?" Lorn demanded. "As Cei pointed out, he's no fool."

"Because he'd rather believe he escaped his Doom than believe it still lurks around some dark corner." Crystal shrugged. "He was the most powerful of the wizards, maybe he has convinced himself that he can't be defeated."

The council considered that. Kraydak's ego could indeed blind him, convince him that he must have killed the dragon and, alone of all the wizards, escaped the consequences.

"Maybe," said Lorn suddenly, "Kraydak's right. Maybe he did accomplish what he thinks."

"Impossible. The dragons were created a extensions of the wizard's life force, not as separate beings. If a wizard lives, a dragon must. The Mother doesn't break her own rules."

But She's willing to bend them, Tayer thought, watching her daughter and knowing that Crystal was something more than just the last wizard. *Moonrise came early last night.*

"Why," asked Belkar softly, "did you not think of this until now?"

Crystal turned slowly to face him. Why did you not think of this earlier, asked his heart, before my son had to die. "Until last night, I thought as Kraydak does; he is the most powerful of the wizards, he destroyed his Doom. But last night I touched the body of the Mother and it is stronger that he could ever be. The dragons were made of that body, he could no more destroy them than he could destroy it. Somewhere Kraydak's Doom still lives, and I swear to you I will will find it and use it to destroy Kraydak."

It will not bring back my son, said Belkar's heart, but the old duke only nodded and gently touched Crystal's face, wiping away the tears she hadn't been aware she'd shed.

"All right," Cei said at last, "where do we find this creature?"

"I don't know. I'll have to ask someone who was there."

"That was a thousand years . . ." Cei began, but Tayer broke in.

"The Grove!"

Crystal nodded. "Yes, Mother, the Grove. It's time to wake the trees."

Tayer sighed. She felt the peace of the circle of trees

tugging at her heart. The one thing that had made all this death and destruction bearable had been the thought of the Grove, forever unchanging, waiting silently and patiently for her return. If Crystal had to wake the trees, there could be no hope that that peace would remain unbroken.

"But the Grove is weeks away," Hale protested. "Even riding the fastest horses with frequent changes."

"The wind can get there in a few hours," Crystal told him, "I'll ride the wind."

After what she had done to the mountain, no one doubted she could ride the wind; ride it, dance with it, and tie it in knots if she wanted to.

"But what of Kraydak?"

Silence fell as they all considered what would happen if Kraydak attacked while Crystal was gone. Very faintly, in the distance, could be heard the wails of the Melacian survivors.

Crystal almost smiled. "He set the rules for this game and they say we must both have an army. He'll be busy for a while."

"When are you going?" These were the first words Riven had said to Crystal since he had left King's Town so many weeks before. They weren't what he had intended his first words to be.

"Now." She brushed past him, uncomfortable with the way his eyes followed her—Bryon was dead—and left the pavilion, a breeze dancing ecstatically in her hair.

Tayer held tightly to Mikhail's hand as Crystal spread her arms and the wind began to rise. Harder and harder it blew, until tent ropes snapped and men had to scramble to keep the tents from flying away. Dirt and ashes spun through the air, blinding those who still had their eyes open. Then, just as suddenly as it had started, the wind stopped. When people could see again through watering eyes, the wizard was gone.

Crystal didn't so much ride the wind as become a part of it. Spread thinly on the air, she let it blow away her doubts, her fears, her anger. It was very tempting just to let go, to let it blow away her self as well, to give up form and failure completely and be one with the wind. Very tempting.

Fortunately for the Ardhan army, the centaurs had spent six long years implanting in Crystal the one thing that the original wizards had never acknowledged: with great power comes great responsibility.

The Grove stood silent and beautiful, untouched by the world outside. The peace within it was a warm and loving presence. A presence that fled with Crystal's arrival. The trees pulled back from her and their leaves trembled in a way that had nothing to do with the wind.

The centaurs had taught her more than one way to wake the Ladies of the Grove. She chose the fastest. She wasn't very polite about it either. Looking deep into the heart of each tree, she wrapped lines of force about the life that slumbered there, and pulled.

Yawning and grumbling, the hamadryads were drawn forth. Twelve beautiful women, with silver hair, ivory skin, and leaf green eyes, stood ringed around a thirteenth. But the resemblance was purely physical between Crystal and these distant aunts, no emotion stronger than self-interest marred the expressions of the twelve, no breeze dared disturb the beauty of their hair.

"Well, Youngest," said one finally, "are you going to tell us why we were so rudely awakened or are you going to stand and stare at us all day?"

Crystal started. She hadn't realized she was staring; knowing you bore the face and form of an Elder race was one thing, seeing it something else. "I need your help."

"She needs our help," echoed another. "Did Milthra ask for our help when she started this mess?"

"No," continued a third. "And did They ask for our help when They planted that," all heads turned to look at the youngest of the trees from which no hamadryad had come, "in our grove?"

"No," finished a fourth. "But now the last of the wizards needs our help."

"You know me?" The last of the wizards knew she asked a ridiculous question. It annoyed her that she found the massed presence of the Mother's eldest children so intimidating.

"Know you? We watched you being conceived."

"And an ugly . . . mortal display it was, too." added the nymph who had spoken first. "My name is Rayalva. I am Eldest now Milthra is gone. You may address your plea to me."

Crystal was not in the mood to be patronized. She gritted her teeth and her eyes began to glow.

Rayalva smiled with total insincerity. "You have no power over us, wizard. Now, what do you want?"

Swallowing her ire, and reminding herself how badly she needed the information these infuriating creatures possessed, Crystal forced politeness into her voice. "I need to know where Kraydak's dragon is."

"If you want a dragon," yawned a nymph who had not yet spoken, "make one yourself. That's what all the other wizards did."

Crystal ignored her and her sisters and spoke only to Rayalva. "The dragons were tied to the life force of the ancient wizards. If Kraydak still lives, then the dragon he created must live also."

The Eldest stared at her in disbelief. "You woke us up to tell us that? Of course, the dragon still lives. He's sound asleep, mind you, but he lives. Didn't the centaurs teach you anything?"

"Yes, but . . ."

"For several centuries great forces have been stirring and making things decidedly uncomfortable for the sole purpose of creating you so that you could wake the dragon."

Crystal sat down rather suddenly on the grass. Her mouth opened and closed a few times. "They never told me that," she managed at last.

"It's something the centaurs would expect you to figure out for yourself," Rayalva said unsympathetically. "Men, idiots! You, no doubt, have been fighting Kraydak yourself."

"Yes." A blue bolt smashed Bryon from the saddle. Crystal cringed, her throat closed, and she seemed to have forgotten how to breathe. Because she had fought Kraydak, Bryon had died. The hamadryad's next words came from very far away.

"A waste of time, you can't defeat him. Well, maybe in a couple of thousand years you could," Rayalva was forced to admit, "when your powers mature. You can do many things, you know, not dreamed of by the wizards of old. All your mothers saw to that."

"All my mothers," Crystal repeated weakly, her gaze going to her father's tree.

Rayalva sighed. "You still haven't figured it out, have you?"

She forced herself past Bryon's death. At least she could learn how to avenge him. "Figured what out?"

"Who were the parents of the ancient wizards?"

"The male gods and mortal women."

"And what was the first thing the wizards did when they came into their powers?"

"Killed their fathers so there would be no more wizards."

"And their father were?"

"The male gods!" Crystal snapped, becoming impatient with the catechism.

"Leaving who to create more wizards?"

"If the male gods were dead . . ." She thought for a moment. "The female gods? But my father . . ."

Rayalva sighed again. "When the remaining gods saw that a wizard had survived, they pooled their essence and presented it to a daughter of the Royal House of Ardhan in such a way that she would be forced to create a child from it. Only Milthra's heritage kept her alive through that creation; a fully mortal woman would have been consumed." Rayalva began to slide back into her tree, the other hamadryads following her lead. "You have no father, child," she said almost kindly, "but you have a multitude of mothers."

"I knew we shouldn't have let the centaurs educate her," muttered a disappearing nymph.

"Wait!" protested Crystal, leaping to her feet and staring around the now empty grove. "You haven't told me where the dragon is!"

"With the dwarves," came the answer, and then even the leaves were silent.

Crystal was almost back to the camp when she felt Kraydak searching for her. He used only a tendril of his power, the merest fraction of what she knew he could call up, but it was enough. Dwelling on Bryon's death, she had forgotten to set barriers, leaving herself open to attack. Bit by bit, Kraydak pried her free from the wind and when he had re-formed her flesh, he dropped her.

Over a lake.

He still played games.

Crystal hit the water with enough force to knock the breath from her, plunging straight down to the bottom. Bound by the weight of her clothes, she began to panic. She thrashed toward what she thought was the surface, her violent movements erasing any chance of floating. Her clothes felt like lead sheets wrapped around her arms and legs. Her lungs burned. She had to breathe. She had to breathe. She had to breathe. She . . .

Suddenly, something grabbed her hair and hauled her head up out of the water. She forced herself to relax, to gulp great mouthfuls of air, and allow herself to be dragged to safety by the strong arm under her chin. In the shallows, the arm released her, but before she could try to stand, she was picked up and carried to shore.

"Are you all right?" asked Riven anxiously as he gently eased her down.

"I'm fine," she said, checking and discovering it was true. She looked up at Riven's worried face but couldn't quite manage to smile. He'd saved her life. Lord Death had been very close. What a stupid way for a wizard to die. She'd never been so embarrassed in her life. "Thank you."

Riven shrugged self-consciously and pushed his wet hair out of his eyes. His hand was fine-boned, an old scrape nearly healed across the knuckles. His eyes were deepset under heavy brows and so light a hazel they were almost green. He was slender but obviously strong and . . .

Crystal couldn't believe she was lying there considering the appearance of the Duke of Riven. Bryon was dead. She struggled to her feet, pretending not to see Riven's offer of a helping hand.

"Where are we?"

"About two miles from camp. I was checking the patrols when I saw you fall." He watched her with an almost puzzled expression on his face. For just a moment the wizard hadn't looked like a wizard at all. Nor like a princess.

She nodded, and staggering only slightly, set out in the direction he'd indicated. Riven fell into step beside her and an uncomfortable silence prevailed.

"Did you find out about the dragon?" he asked at last.

"With the dwarves," she said shortly, not wanting to acknowledge his presence because then she'd have to acknowledge some disturbing thoughts, mostly having to do with the feel of his arms around her as he carried her from the water.

"The dwarves?" He stopped, then had to hurry to catch up as Crystal marched resolutely on. "But the dwarves refuse to have anything to do with humankind. No one has any idea of where to find them."

Crystal remembered Mikhail's great black sword and finally achieved a smile.

Seventeen

"The dwarves . . ." Mikhail stroked the hilt of his great black sword and stared thoughtfully off into the distance. He'd been only sixteen when he'd fought for and won the dwarf-made blade; twenty-two years and the golden caverns and carved halls of the master craftsmen still shone as bright in his memory as they had the day he'd left. The home of the dwarves was a sight to remember for as long as life lasted. Unfortunately for most of those privileged to see the caverns, life didn't last very long.

"The dwarves, " Mikhail repeated. "Yes, I know where to find them." He smiled at a memory. "In fact, after you get to a certain point they usually find you."

"What point? Where?" Crystal asked, trying not to sound impatient and failing. Kraydak was busy bringing in fresh troops and supplies to continue the game, but that couldn't take him long. She had to wake the dragon before he turned his full attention back to her.

"North of the badlands of Aliston," Mikhail told her, snapping out of his reverie and moving to stand by the map. "Where the northern mountains end, there's a red sandstone pillar. Whether it was carved by the winds or the dwarves, I have no idea, but it marks the boundary of the territory they've claimed for themselves. Here," he pulled out a dagger and stabbed at the map, "as near as I can mark it, is where it stands."

The Duke of Aliston came over and peered closely at the point of Mikhail's dagger. Rough area that.'' He clicked his tongue. ''You'll need one of my lads as a guide or you'll never get through the badlands.''

''I have to go alone.'' *Always alone,* she thought, remembering her reflection fading from Bryon's eyes as Lord Death claimed him. And it was her fault he was dead. She was never meant to stand against Kraydak. She should have known it from the start.

''Crystal, no. Not alone.'' Tayer got to her feet and held out a hand to her daughter. ''If you can't use your powers for fear Kraydak will notice what you're doing, you'll have to take soldiers; guards to protect you.''

Crystal pushed both her dead friend and her guilt to the back of her mind and gave Tayer's hand a comforting squeeze. ''Don't worry, Mother, I'll be fine. Besides, there's nothing a guard could do to protect me from Kraydak.''

Tayer wasn't very reassured.

''No magic, eh?'' Belkar growled. ''Then how do you expect to wake the dragon?''

''I don't know,'' Crystal admitted.

''And how do you expect to get there?'' Cei demanded, the thought having just occurred to him. ''Kraydak's on to your wind trick and we haven't the time for you to ride. Aliston's badlands have got to be at least a month away.''

''Month and a half,'' put in Aliston, turning his nearsighted gaze on the young wizard.

''I don't know,'' Crystal admitted again. ''But I'll think of something.''

''Without magic,'' Aliston pointed out, ''you'll never make it through the badlands without a guide.''

''That has all been taken care of.''

The entire council started, but it said a great deal for the timbre of the voice that, although everyone in the pavilion was armed and nerves were balanced on a knife's edge, not one weapon was drawn. When they saw who had spoken, jaws dropped and the company stood and stared.

The two centaurs were so large that their heads brushed the top of the tent. Their horse halves could easily carry a man as massive as Mikhail in full armor and their torsos were heavily muscled and equally as huge. The beards flowing in magnificent curls over their naked chests—only practical Cei noticed that they had no nipples—exactly matched the shade of their glossy hides. Their whiteless eyes seemed to hold all the wisdom of the ages.

A strangled cry caused heads to turn back to Crystal. The color had drained from her face and her eyes stood out like burning jewels. Her breath hissed through slightly parted lips and her hands, clenched into fists, began to rise.

The council edged back until the centaurs and the wizard faced each other in a circle of humanity pressed tight against the canvas. They had seen her, in her rage, call down mountains and all of them knew that power once taken up will be used again and again.

"Crystal!" Tayer stepped forward, away from the retreating council, and her voice threw up a wall between her daughter and the creatures she faced. "You will not do violence. These . . . persons . . . are guests in my tent!"

In the silence that followed, the wheeze of Cei's breath could be clearly heard and a breeze against the canvas roof was a booming roar.

The wizard locked eyes with the queen, who ignored their emerald depths and stood glaring at her furious child. "You will not do violence to a guest!" she repeated.

Slowly, Crystal lowered her hands and uncurled her fingers. "But, Mother . . ."

"Hush, child, I know." Tayer gently touched Crystal's shoulder and together they turned to face the centaurs.

"My thanks, Majesty." The black centaur inclined his head. "Although we are not sure she is capable of causing us harm, the release of such power would have definitely been detrimental to those around us. I am C'Tal.'' He indicated the palomino. ''This is C'Fas.''

''What are you doing here, C'Tal?'' Crystal snapped before Tayer had a chance to speak. ''Haven't you interfered enough?''

''We have been informed,'' C'Tal told her in ponderous tones, ''that we were remiss in your education.''

''You were given all the information,'' C'Fas continued in a voice equally as solemn. ''We did not feel it necessary to tell you what to do with it.''

''Others, however, suggested you were ill-prepared for the conflict you found yourself in.'' C'Tal shook his head sadly. ''We feel you were as well-prepared as possible, considering the short time we had you in our charge. Given a century or two and perhaps . . .'' he shrugged, sending fascinating ripples down the length of his body. ''What we could have done is not the point but rather what we did.''

''Or what they imply we did not do,'' broke in C'Fas with an edge to his voice.

''Precisely,'' agreed C'Tal, nodding at his companion. ''Or what they imply we did not do.''

''Who implied?'' demanded Crystal, used to the considerable time centaurs took in getting to the point but no longer willing to put up with it. Not now. Not after Bryon.

''The hamadryads,'' said C'Tal, glowering down at her. ''While we are firm in our contention that we did all we could in the time we had available, there is something in what they say. You should never have faced Kraydak yourself. We should have been more careful that this was made clear to you.''

''I'm surprised the hamadryads cared.'' Crystal felt her anger lose its edge as guilt returned to the foreground. She had been told but hadn't understood.

''They do not. But they were most annoyed at being awakened, feeling, and perhaps rightly, that had you been told of the dragon as you should have been, there would have been no need for you to go to them.''

"But why," asked Tayer, "are you here?"

"We have come to help."

"Where were you two days ago," Lorn snorted, remembering the arrow through his father's throat and the ranks of the undead, "we could've used help then."

Both centaurs turned to look at the duke, who was paring his nails with a slender knife and was not at all intimidated by their gaze. He gave them back glare for glare.

"Then you needed more heavy cavalry," said C'Tal.

"Now you need centaurs," finished C'Fas.

Lorn looked interested but not convinced. He wisely chose not to mention that the centaurs would make impressive heavy cavalry themselves.

"I will carry the wizard to the edge of the badlands." C'Tal stepped forward and laid a heavy hand on Crystal's shoulder. "While my brother will remain here."

"Well, we'll be happy to have him," Tayer began, nervously considering the creature's bulk and wondering how to entertain someone who was half horse, "but there really won't be much for him to do."

"He is not here to be amused, Majesty," C'Tal boomed. "We hope his presence will convince the enemy that the wizard is still here. If he does not probe too deeply, he will not be able to tell the difference between their life forces."

Tayer looked from the huge golden-haired centaur to her daughter. "Oh," she said.

Crystal tried to explain. "Centaurs are magical beings, Mother. They don't use the power so much as they are the power. If Kraydak has no reason to suspect I'm gone, and doesn't force his way below the surface patterns, he'll think C'Fas is me."

"Oh," Tayer said again, only this time she felt much better about it.

Mikhail stepped forward and stared belligerently up at C'Tal. He had to crane his neck to meet the centaur's eyes and that annoyed him. He'd never had to look up at anybody before.

"Can you protect her from the dwarves and the dragon?" he asked.

"That is not my concern," C'Tal informed him. "We will do no more than what I have already said." He turned to Crystal. "Now come, we must go."

Crystal stopped Mikhail from saying what he so obviously thought; he had never been good at hiding his anger.

"As much as it hurts me to admit it," she said softly, "he's right. That," a hint of steel came into her voice, "is not his concern. I can take care of the dragon."

"That dragon has only one purpose," Mikhail reminded her as he gave her a boost onto C'Tal's broad back, "to kill wizards."

"To kill Kraydak," Crystal corrected.

"Waking up in the presence of a wizard after sleeping for a thousand years may cause him to attack first and ask questions later," Mikhail said grimly.

"I'm not like any of the other wizards," Crystal reminded him in turn. "My heritage from the Lady of the Grove will protect me."

"What of your humanity?" asked Tayer gently, coming up to stand in the circle of her husband's arm.

Crystal's face grew bleak and she saw again her reflection fading from Bryon's eyes. "That died with Bryon," she said shortly. But catching sight of Riven's concerned face over C'Tal's shoulder, she wasn't as sure of that as she had been.

And then, as impossibly fast and silent as the centaurs had come, Crystal and C'Tal were gone.

"Stop that!" snapped C'Fas as Hale, horse sense overcoming common sense, ran a hand over a glossy haunch.

To ride a centaur is like nothing else in the world. Perhaps being strapped to a shooting star would give the same wondrous feelings of grace, power, and speed but Crystal doubted it, for a star would not have a convenient shoulder on which to rest your head. Her hard knot of anger at the centaurs began to dissolve; surely it was unreasonable for her to expect them to go against their natures. Used to dealing in centuries, they had done the best they could when forced to work with days and months and years. Gradually, the old feelings for her teachers began to resurface and for the first time since Kraydak had destroyed the palace, Crystal felt protected and safe. She paid no attention to the countryside they passed over; instead she locked her arms about C'Tal's waist, buried her face in the familiar smell of his back, and gloried in the ride.

It ended too soon. The Aliston badlands passed by in a rocky blur and they stopped before a red sandstone pillar. Suddenly stiff from so many hours in one position, Crystal slid awkwardly to the ground.

"The dwarves are past the pillar?" she asked C'Tal as she massaged the pins and needles out of her legs.

"We do not keep watch over the dwarves," C'Tal informed her imperiously. "Your foster father says they are on the other side of the pillar. We see no reason for you to distrust him."

Crystal straightened up and stared dubiously past the marker. The land consisted of a series of low rock ridges, split and blasted into strange and forbidding shapes. Everything was a dusty gray with no living green to break the monotony. The dwarves lived in that?

"Oh, well," she sighed, "if they're in there, I guess I can find them."

"If they are in there, they are more likely to find you," corrected C'Tal sternly. "Remember, you must not use your power. If Kraydak discovers what you are attempting to do, it will mean not only your death but the deaths of thousands of innocent people as well. I will be here when you emerge." He paused and looked down at Crystal with something very close to concern in his expression. "If we are truly responsible for what you have done, we are sorry."

"Sorry won't raise the dead," said Crystal softly.

"Nothing will raise the dead," replied the centaur. "It is therefore unproductive to hold fast to one who has died." He spun gracefully on one massive hoof and disappeared.

"I'm not holding Bryon," Crystal shouted after C'Tal. "I'm remembering him!" There was, as she expected, no response. Taking a deep breath, she stepped beyond the column. The landscape appeared no different, the red tower of rock was a marker, nothing more. She'd hoped it might be some sort of magical barrier, that once passed the home of the dwarves would stand revealed. A small gray lizard, so perfectly camouflaged she almost stepped on it, scuttled out of her way—the only life in sight.

Because it seemed like the only thing to do, she headed deeper into the badlands. Five miles and a blister later, she was very dusty and very thirsty and no dwarves had appeared. A fear lurked in the back of her mind, whispering that they might have moved on since Mikhail had won his sword, moved on and taken the dragon with them. And if they had? She tried not to think about it.

The centaur had dropped her off in the early morning and it was now midafternoon. "I could have flown this far in less than a minute," she muttered to a disinterested lizard.

She perched on the edge of a rock and mopped her forehead with the edge of her tunic. The dust covering both became a muddy smear. The sun beat down mercilessly and she looked longingly at the cool black shadow of a small cave.

A cave.

Dwarves lived in caves. Granted they were carved and built into caverns of great beauty, but they were still caves.

Crystal dropped to her knees and peered into the darkness. After the bright sunlight, it took her eyes a moment to adjust, but she was certain that the cave extended back quite far and eventually opened up.

Carefully, she slid forward onto her stomach and began to inch her way into the darkness, pulling herself along by her elbows and toes. Her body quickly blocked any light coming from the entrance and the darkness became so thick it could almost be touched. A sharp rock dug into her elbow, drawing blood and a string of curses that would have horrified Tayer could she have heard them.

Inch by torturous inch, Crystal squirmed down the tunnel, wondering why she had been so sure it would open up ahead. If anything, it became more confining and began to slope quite distinctly down. Then, just as her eyes were beginning to adjust and she was able to distinguish between the denser black of the rock and the grayish black of the air, her elbows found no purchase and, scrambling for something to grab, she tumbled over the edge of a precipice.

A small one, fortunately. She lay on her back, breathing heavily, more frightened by her instinctive urge to break her fall with power than by the fall itself. She had just realized that, unable to use her powers, she could die in a great many ridiculous ways . . . and this time there would be no Riven to pull her out.

The sudden flaring of a lantern almost blinded her, but her hamadryad eyes welcomed the light, absorbed it, and soon she could see again.

She had never seen an uglier man. He was short, bandy-legged, barrel-chested, and had the arms and shoulders of a man twice his height. The grizzled red beard did nothing to improve the scarred and scowling face. Red fires burned in the depths of his eyes. Around his waist, over a patched brown tunic, he wore a belt made of gold leaves that was so beautifully crafted and so detailed Crystal was sure she heard a breeze move through the leaves. He had to be a dwarf.

"Name's Doan," he growled at last. "I expect you've come for the dragon."

Crystal opened and closed her mouth a few times, but words just wouldn't come.

"Well, you look like her," Doan said, holding out

a hand to help her up. To Crystal's surprise, he appeared to be smiling. "But you sure haven't got her way with words. Coming?"

"Where?" Crystal managed at last.

Doan held the lantern up and she saw they were in a small, circular cave. Tucked up against the ceiling was the tunnel she had fallen from and opposite it, at floor level, was an arched doorway. Doan headed for the door and she followed.

She had to duck to get under the arch, but the rest of the corridor—such a work of art could not be thought of as a mere tunnel—was high enough for her to walk erect. The dwarf moved quickly for all his squatness and she hurried to keep up. There was no time to study the carvings on the walls, although she was sure they told a story as so many images kept repeating, there was barely time to notice the inlay work and the beauty it brought to the stone.

"Doan," she said, before the silence became oppressive and reminded her that they were walking under almost a mile of solid rock, "who is it you think I look like?"

Doan snorted. "You're the image of the Lady. And you know it. Even her sisters remarked on the resemblance."

"But we all look alike."

Doan snorted again, a rude noise he seemed fond of. "The Lady had more life in her than all those sticks of wood combined. So do you."

"Did you know her?"

"I'd hardly know you looked like her if I didn't, now would I." His harsh voice softened slightly and though he looked no less ugly, he was, for a moment, less frightening. "Aye, I knew her. She'd done me a favor, thousands of years ago by mortal time, so I watched them for her—her man and her boy—and I watched her die." He looked up at Crystal; the red fire blazed in his eyes and his voice was stone.

"Kraydak and Death could have the whole mortal lot of them if it was up to me." Then he sighed and the fires died. He waved her on ahead. "But it isn't, so there you are . . ."

Crystal stepped out into a cavern where the rock had been worked on and improved by hundreds of dwarves for thousands of years. And the cavern had been beautiful to start with. Gold and silver danced across the walls and diamonds refracted the light into countless tiny rainbows.

But the room was only a frame for the dragon.

More lovely than anything Crystal had ever seen, he lay sleeping, wrapped around a stone column that had been carved to resemble a giant tree. His scales were gold and shone with an almost iridescent light. He was grace and power and a terrible beauty. The mighty head lay pillowed on a curve of foreleg, and his golden lacelike wings were folded across his back. From his nostrils came two thin streams of pure white smoke and from his mouth . . .

Crystal turned to Doan in disbelief.

"He snores?"

Doan nodded. "And he stinks when he gets too hot. He's a bit whiff now."

A slightly unpleasant, musky odor was noticeable and it grew stronger as Crystal moved closer. She winced as her footsteps echoed, sounding unnaturally loud.

"Don't worry about the noise," Doan said, stomping along beside her. "We carved this cavern out around him, and if that noise didn't wake him up there's no sound loud enough to disturb him."

Crystal stood and stared up at the dragon. Had its jaw been flat on the ground, she would have just barely been able to look it in the eye. Tentatively, she reached out and touched it on the nose. Beneath her hand, the skin was warm and surprisingly soft. There was no indication that the creature was aware of her at all. She prodded it gently with the toe of her boot. Nothing.

"It's funny," said Doan, kicking the dragon and not gently, "that out of all the spells Kraydak threw at this creature to stop it, it was the simplest one that worked. Sleep, he said, and sleep it has.'' The dwarf shrugged. ''Even the earth sleeps, so I guess those made of it must as well.''

''But how do I wake it if I can't use my powers?''

Doan gazed at Crystal in astonishment, both brows raised nearly to his hairline. ''Didn't the centaurs teach you anything?'' he demanded.

''They taught me plenty,'' Crystal snapped. She'd settled with that and didn't need it brought up again. ''They never mentioned this, is all.''

''*This* is what you were born for, and they never mentioned it?'' Doan snarled in disgust. ''You can't count on those blowhards for anything. Kiss him!''

''I beg your pardon.''

Doan sighed, ''An enchanted sleep can be broken only by the kiss of a maiden both fair and pure.'' Critically, he looked her up and down. ''The Lady was the most beautiful woman ever to walk the earth and you're her image, I guess that should be fair enough. How's your love life.''

Crystal remembered Bryon lying blasted on the ground and started to laugh. Kraydak had outsmarted himself that time. Had Bryon been allowed to live she, no doubt, would have been unqualified to wake anyone from an enchanted sleep by now. Kraydak would have the world to himself and . . . to her surprise she found herself cradled in Doan's powerful arms and weeping bitterly.

''Hush, child,'' he whispered as she clung to him, sobs racking her slender body. ''Tears won't bring him back.'' He remembered another silver-haired maiden who'd wept in his arms, then dried her eyes, and walked away from her tree to her death. He cursed mortal men, individually and collectively, for the pain they caused.

Gradually Crystal calmed and pulled away. She felt surprisingly better. Was that all it took, then, to forget, to ease the pain, just a few tears? She checked her heart and found Bryon there as he always had been, but the cold fire surrounding the memory had been put out. Doan reached up and took the last tear off her cheek with the tip of his finger. It sparkled there for a moment then shimmered and changed; where the drop of water had been was a perfect blue opal.

"That's never happened before," Crystal sniffed, wiping her nose on the tattered edge of her tunic.

"You've never cried on a dwarf before," Doan told her, offering her the gem with an oddly gentle smile on his ugly face.

She managed a weak smile in return and tucked the stone in her belt. Then, with new resolve, she turned back to the dragon.

"Why me?" she asked. "Why a wizard? Wouldn't any beautiful virgin do?"

Doan snorted. "What would any beautiful virgin do with the dragon once she woke it? Hopefully, it'll listen to a wizard."

One silver eyebrow went up. "Hopefully?"

"That's the theory." Doan shrugged. "We won't know until you try."

"On the lips?"

"I don't think it has lips."

"Oh." Crystal squared her shoulders, leaned forward, and kissed the dragon on the exact center of his golden nose. Then she stepped back beside the dwarf and they waited.

The snoring, which had been a rumbling background noise from the moment they had entered the cavern, stopped. The dragon twitched, rubbed at his nose with the curve of a talon, and opened his eyes. They were the brilliant blue of a summer's sky and faceted into a thousand gleaming parts. Six feet of forked tongue snaked out and gently touched Crystal's face.

"Wizzzard." Its teeth were very large.

"Not your wizard," Crystal protested, as the tongue touched her again.

"Young," said the dragon. "Different. Tassste like treesss. Ssstill, wizzzard." In a blur of gold and blue, he reared back, opened his mouth, and shot forth one large but not very hot puff of smoke.

Doan almost collapsed, he was laughing so hard at the puzzled expression on the dragon's face.

Crystal, who had dived out of the path of what she expected to be a killing blast of flame, was not as amused.

"Well, what else did you expect?" she said, limping back to meet the dragon face to face. "You've been asleep for thousands of years."

"Thoussssandsss?" For the first time he looked around and realized where he was. "Kraydak!" The softly sibilant voice grew to a roar that shook the roof. Crystal and Doan scrambled for cover as he surged to his hind feet and, talons extended, ripped and shredded the air. He fell back to the floor with a crash and began maneuvering his bulk around so he could get out the only tunnel large enough for him.

"Hold it!" Crystal grabbed a dragging wingtip and dug in her heels. She couldn't let this lizard and Kraydak destroy everything people had worked for over the last thousand years; the scars of their last conflict were barely healed. "Where do you think you're going?"

"Releassse, wizzzard," snarled the dragon, appearing very willing to take care of her first. "There isss job left undone."

"And it'll stay undone unless you listen to me. Kraydak beat you once, he can do it again."

"Accident."

"Maybe, maybe not; and he's been getting more powerful while you've been napping. This time he could kill you instead of just putting you to sleep."

The dragon glared at her suspiciously but he stopped trying to leave the cavern. "Lissstening."

Crystal let go of the wingtip. She was aware that the dragon considered her at best an annoyance to be eliminated and at worst, regardless of her differences, one of the race he was sworn to destroy. She wiped her sweaty palms on her thighs and met the glaring blue of his gaze. This, the hamadryads hadn't told her.

She'd been created to wake the dragon, yes, but that couldn't be the end of it.

"Kraydak will have to be distracted if you're to have any chance of getting close to him."

"Ssso," he hissed contemptuously. "What disss-tractsss wizzzard?"

She spread her hands and said simply, "Another wizard.

The dragon smiled. It was the most terrifying thing he had done so far.

"Yesss."

With Doan as a guide, the walk back to the sand-stone pillar was pleasant and much faster than her earlier journey across the badlands. Although Crystal wanted to hurry, for she knew that C'Fas could mask her absence for only a limited time and she'd spent longer than she'd intended with the dragon, the won-ders of her surroundings invited her to linger. The cav-erns of the dwarves were, indeed, as beautiful as legend described them. Thick pillars, carved to resem-ble fantastic animals, carried the weight of the roof—and the mountain of stone above it—on their massive shoulders.

"Not bad for just a few thousand years," the dwarf agreed as Crystal admired the jewel-encrusted mosa-ics covering the walls.

"A few thousand years? But the dwarves have been since the beginning."

"Been, yes, but not here. We came here to guard the dragon."

"Against what?" Crystal couldn't think of anything that would dare to harm such a magnificent and pow-erful creature.

"Against mortals," Doan snorted. "A plague on the earth they are. Can't imagine what the Mother was thinking of when She created them. Consider the mess we'd all be in had a human stumbled on the dragon. When Kraydak emerged, they'd have led him right to it and we'd have the battles of the Doom all over again." He chuckled and suddenly sounded much more approving of mortalkind. "Of course, they'd have probably tried to make him pay for the privilege of destroying them. This is the way out."

Crystal took one last look around, then began to follow Doan up the narrow, winding staircase. "What I really mind," she said suddenly, "is having Kraydak be right."

"About what?"

"Well, he said I couldn't defeat him, and he was right."

Doan stopped climbing and turned to look at her. "Who told you that?"

"Everyone."

"Everyone?" The dwarf made it sound like an expletive. "Did I?"

"No . . . But I thought I was created to wake the dragon?"

"You were."

"And I wasn't supposed to fight Kraydak at all?"

"You weren't. But that has no bearing on whether or not you could beat him." He sighed at the expression on her face and motioned for her to sit down, seating himself on a higher step as she did so. "I've been keeping an eye on your battles . . ." A wave of his hand cut off her question. "Never mind how, lets just say I have. And I've been keeping my eye on you for a lot longer. You've got closer ties to the Mother than any of the old wizards ever did and every time you forget to be a wizard with a capital W . . ." He reached down and lifted her chin with the tip of one hoary finger, "Every time you're just Crystal and you hit him with what you're feeling, you whop his ass."

"I do?"

Doan grinned fiercely. "You do."

"Then I didn't need the dragon?"

"Maybe. Maybe not. You're young, comparatively untrained, and not even at seventeen can you exist on emotions all the time. The dragon is a tool for you to use, why not use it?" The finger under her chin increased its pressure and then withdrew. "But if it means so much to you, in my opinion, Kraydak is wrong. You can defeat him." He got to his feet and started climbing again. "Besides," he threw back over his shoulder, "that arrogant s.o.b. hasn't been right about anything for thousands of years, so why should he start now?"

As Crystal climbed after the dwarf, the last of the guilt wrapped about Bryon's death dissolved. While she'd thought it inevitable that Kraydak would win, Bryon had died because of her stupidity in accepting the older wizard's challenge. Now that she knew the truth, Bryon was still equally dead, but it wasn't her fault. Now, he could be mourned.

At the top of the stairs, they went through a red sandstone door and out to the badlands of Aliston. Even knowing it existed, Crystal could see no sign of the door on the pillar that marked the edge of the dwarves' territory.

"That's amazing," she breathed.

"On the contrary," lectured C'Tal from behind her, "as the dwarves are master of stone, it is not amazing at all. It would be amazing only for a hamadryad, or a mer, or a human to have built that door."

"It would be impossible," Doan grunted, turning and looking up, way up, at the centaur. "How're you doing, you old horse's ass?" He grinned as C'Tal pretended not to have heard. "Hear you've begun to believe your own legends."

C'Tal speared the dwarf with a condescending glare, his arms folded across his mighty chest. "What legends?"

"The legends that say centaurs are the holders of all knowledge."

One gigantic hoof gouged a hole in the dirt. "We do not feel there was anything amiss in our teaching. She possessed both the information and the ability to fashion it into an understandable whole. And," he emphasized the word with a mighty stamp, "all the free peoples of the earth should be grateful that with this wizard there will be no danger of her indulging in random and irresponsible behavior. If nothing else, we have instilled in her the belief that she must employ her powers for good.''

''If nothing else,'' Doan agreed amicably, leaning against the pillar, both hands shoved behind his belt. ''But it's not polite to talk of the child as though she wasn't here.''

''She is not here.''

''Wha . . .''

Crystal, spotting a flash of gold amidst the gray sameness of the badlands, had scrambled to the top of a rocky hillock to get a better look. Slowly at first, for his wings were stiff and unsure, the great golden dragon rose into the sunlight and appeared to burst suddenly into gilded flame. Crystal caught her breath at his splendor and one hand reached out as though to touch the glory. Her heart seemed to be beating too violently to stay within her chest. There were tears in her eyes as she wondered how such a creature would look in silver and green. . . .

''Do you think she'll survive?'' Doan asked, after he had explained the plan that Crystal had given the dragon.

''Although her powers are great and still growing, she is, despite our teachings, relatively untrained and it is unlikely that she will prevail against one who is infinitely more experienced in both the means and the method of wizardry.''

''Which means?''

''I do not think she will survive. The hope of the world can only be that she continues to amuse the Enemy long enough for the Doom to approach.''

''Got a better plan?''

''No.''

Eighteen

When Crystal arrived back at the Ardhan camp, it was late evening. She had been gone for four days. Kraydak had apparently not missed her.

The centaurs disappeared practically the instant Crystal's foot hit the ground. One moment they were there and the next they were gone. The queen and her council breathed a collective sigh of relief. Not only was their wizard—daughter, princess—safely back, but it hadn't been easy sharing close quarters with C'Fas for four days. A centaur is an awe-inspiring creature and trapped in a tent—for he had to stay out of sight of Kraydak's spies—he is overwhelming in the extreme.

The dwarves had replaced Crystal's tattered clothes from some hidden store, and had set her opal tear in silver. She wore it on a chain around her neck and it glowed softly in the folds of her tunic.

"Well?" asked Mikhail at last, for Crystal still stood where she'd dismounted, eyes unfocused.

With a barely perceptible jerk, the wizard returned to her body. "He is almost ready to attack again," she said. "We will be only just in time."

"We?" repeated Lorn skeptically, "Does this mean . . ." He broke off as Crystal turned to face him. He suddenly couldn't remember what he was going to say.

She swept the tent with her gaze and the questions that had not yet been voiced disappeared. Not until Doan pointed it out, had she realized her stupidity in

271

mentioning the dragon to so many people. It was not beyond Kraydak's ability to lift the knowledge from their minds and thus gain the time to prepare himself for the attack. Crystal hated to alter the memories of her parents and their council, but it was by far the lesser of two evils. She could only hope she wasn't already too late, hope that they hadn't told everyone in the camp what they knew.

Tayer recovered first from the tampering. She blinked twice, looked momentarily puzzled, and then stared questioningly at her daughter. "You look exhausted," she said at last. "You need a hot bath, a light supper, and a good night's sleep."

"A heavy supper please, Mother," Crystal said as they walked arm in arm from the tent, leaving Mikhail and the council shaking their heads and wondering what they'd missed. "I'm starved." She'd need all her strength for tomorrow.

In the quiet hour between moonset and dawn, a great white owl lifted from Crystal's tent, circled once around the queen's pavilion, and headed east with strong, unhurried beats of its wings. The sentries that saw it go watched until it vanished in the clouds, then turned to each other and said in voices of wonder, "The wizard," as if that was enough to explain it. For them, it was.

Tayer and Mikhail slept on, wrapped in each other's arms, unaware that their daughter was changing the rules of Kraydak's game. They would have tried to stop her had they known, so she hadn't told them she was going.

Kraydak, safe in his tower, smiled as Crystal entered his territory. Given her previous displays of power, he had expected more resistance to his call. If the form she wore was intended to deceive him, it was an abject failure, for he had spotted her the moment she crossed the mountains. Mindshielded or not, there just weren't that many owls with a fifteen-foot wingspan.

* * *

Crystal flew on, thinking owl thoughts on the surface but behind the shield concentrating only on distracting Kraydak and bringing things to an end one way or another. She realized her end would probably come before his. Not even the centaurs who had trained her expected her to live. And if by some miracle she did . . . well, she doubted the dragon would allow the last of the wizards to continue to exist. She was calm now, accepting, but in the dark hours of the night she'd considered running, running and letting Kraydak and his Doom fight it out without her. The world would be ripped apart once more, but she would live a while longer. *It isn't fair,* she sniffed. *I'm only seventeen.* But still she flew on.

The foothills of the Melacian side of the mountains were passing far below her when the storm struck. Gusts of wind tossed her about, trying to slam her out of the air, and the rain beat through her feathers, hitting hard enough to bruise. The water was so dense she could hardly see, the wind ripped feathers free, and the thick down that should have kept her warm and dry was soaked through. She'd expected him to find her but not so soon. She had to survive, her death now would be too short a distraction.

"Distract me from what?" wondered Kraydak, who'd pried free a tiny piece of the thought.

Screaming a challenge, she dove for the first clear area she spotted and her talons sank deep into the soft mud beside a mountain stream. She threw back her head, the green eyes blazed, and a weeping birch, the silver's more flexible cousin, danced in the wind and lifted its leaves to the rain. The wind blew harder, but the tree bent gracefully out of its way, bent so far that its uppermost branches trailed in the swiftly moving water of the stream.

A huge silver salmon with green-gold eyes leaped away and sped downstream as the blue bolt came out of the sky and crashed into the earth where the tree had stood.

Kraydak smiled, calmed the wind and stopped the rain, for they were no longer needed. She was very resourceful, this Wizard-child, and he looked forward to making her trip an interesting one before welcoming her to his tower and finding out just what exactly she thought she was doing. If she fought the calling he'd laid upon her, she did it in a very peculiar way. He considered boiling away the stream and the rivers it ran into but decided against it; that would hardly be sporting and he did want her to arrive in one piece. He hadn't been so diverted in centuries. Where had she learned to think so much like a fish?

Crystal sped down the stream as fast as her powerful new body could take her. She was tiring but didn't dare take the time to rest. A moving target was, after all, more difficult to hit. She felt the amusement in Kraydak's questing thoughts and used her anger at it to reinforce her shield.

The ancient wizard laughed aloud. So she would hide her fishy thoughts, would she? He followed instead the pattern of the shield.

The current slowed and the texture of the water changed; the stream was about to join a major river. Once sharing its depths with a multitude of life forms, she'd be harder for Kraydak to spot and, if she remembered the maps correctly, the river ran through Melac's capital city and right past Kraydak's tower. With his attention on the river, he wouldn't be scanning the rest of the countryside.

"Why," Kraydak asked the skull, "would I want to scan the countryside?" He got only fragments of thought through the shield and this fragment made no sense. If she was trying to sneak assassins through

Melac, they'd die before they reached the tower and he'd never have to become involved. Assassins were a stupid idea. He smiled. They must be getting very desperate.

"I wonder . . ." He tapped the yellowed ivory of the skull's teeth. "Should I scan the countryside?"

The skull grinned up at him.

He nodded. "Yes, you're quite right. She's played my game, so it's only fair I play hers . . . for a while. Besides, the countryside can hold nothing more interesting than the river. She shows such initiative, I almost wished I'd called her sooner."

A massive golden paw tipped with deadly claws split the water inches from Crystal's nose. Her panicked flip backward took her up and out of the water and dangerously close to the snapping jaws of a huge golden bear. She hit the water with a painful smack and raced back upstream. From the security of the bottom of a deep pool, she considered what she should do.

Crystal knew she really only had one choice. What happened to her was unimportant. She had to hold Kraydak's attention. The dragon had to get through.

She sent out a questing thought. The bear waited at the end of the stream. He blocked the water route completely, which left only one way to go. She rose to the surface of the pool, found the strongest flow of current, and started back downstream. Her fins and tail beat against the water and she swam rapidly toward the river. The current lent her speed and she moved faster and faster until she flashed through the water like silver lightning. When she felt the bear gather himself to lunge, she twisted her tail and jumped.

No fish jumps better than a salmon and no salmon ever leaped higher than Crystal. Up, up she arced, flashing silver in the sunlight. The bear, who had dived forward to scoop her from the water, was taken by surprise and although he reared and raked the air with his claws, he was far too late. With liquid grace, Crystal twisted and dove into the relative safety of the river.

As she swam away, she felt the bear's mind follow her. He seemed to be laughing. At least she'd managed to keep him amused.

Kraydak considered sending an otter into the river but decided against it. He had no need to exert himself for, after all, the wizard-child was coming to him. He would watch to see she didn't slip away and take care of her when she reached the tower. He appreciated her courage, secure in the knowledge that she could do him little harm.

The sun was a red-gold ball balanced on the western mountains when Crystal reached the tower. She swam slowly, trying to conserve her dwindling energies. Between holding the transformation and the constant fear that Kraydak would make a move she couldn't counter, she was nearing the point of exhaustion. And if she faced Kraydak, if she actually reached him and the dragon hadn't yet come, what then? Could her shield hold without distance to lend it strength? She was so busy worrying, she didn't notice the net until it was too late.

"Right then, we've got her! Heave to and let's get her beached!"

The four men put their backs to it, laboriously drawing the net and its thrashing cargo to shore. But what they pulled from the water was no fish.

"Holy shit," breathed a ruffian who was missing an ear and most of his nose. "I never thought I'd see one of those." He dropped the net and grabbed for his sword as the unicorn kicked itself free of the ropes.

It was over very quickly.

Sides heaving, its horn and hoofs dripping gore, the unicorn staggered toward the tower. It shimmered and Crystal collapsed across the steps. Her skin and shift were covered in blood, not all of it belonging to others. There was a sword cut on her upper arm and her nose still bled freely. She shivered in the shadow of the tower and couldn't seem to catch her breath.

The great iron-bound door swung open. She was expected.

At least he's still interested, she thought, crawling forward. She pulled herself up until she sat on the bottom step, looked up at the apparently infinite length of stone staircase wrapped about the inside of the building, and giggled. She couldn't help it.

"You've got to be kidding," she called up the stairs.

The door slammed shut and latched with an ominous thunk. Kraydak thought he had her safe; now she had nowhere to go but up.

Crystal remembered the blue bolt smashing Bryon to the ground and added the memory to her shield. The dragon should be very close. If it was coming. If Kraydak hadn't already taken care of it. She set her teeth, pulled herself to her feet, and slowly began to climb.

High above the clouds, the dragon soared, his scales glowing reddish gold in the light of the setting sun. He banked and dipped and gloried in the strength of his wings.

"Perhapsss wait," he thought as he raced the wind and won. "Kraydak killsss wizzzard. Kraydak isss mine. No more wizzzards. Ever."

The sun dropped below the horizon and, for a moment, the dragon lit the evening on his own.

"Perhapsss wait."

On the hundredth step, Crystal knew she had to rest. Her blood sang in her ears and she couldn't, just couldn't lift her leg again. She sagged against the outer wall.

DEATH!

The scream in her mind shocked her so she slid down half a dozen steps before she could catch herself. Eyes wide, she reached out a trembling hand and touched the wall again.

DEATH!

Even prepared for it, the force of the cry caused her

to jerk and snatch her hand away as if she'd been burned. She sat down, carefully staying away from the wall, and clasped her hands between her knees to stop them from shaking.

"Destroy him," said Lord Death from the step below her, "and free my people, too."

And then he was gone and she was alone again save for the screaming souls trapped in the walls. It was a long time before she could continue to climb.

The door to the inner sanctum was made of solid gold. The carved face of a demon leered out at Crystal as she mounted the last few steps and just before the door swung open, it bared its teeth. She stepped over the threshold and looked about. The slamming of the door behind her was so predictable that she didn't even flinch.

The walls of the room were covered in sheets of beaten gold, a cheerful fire burned in a small hearth, a huge desk took up over half the space, and strange and wonderful things were piled haphazardly about. A door seemed to lead to another room, although this first room took up the full diameter of the tower. There were no windows.

Kraydak looked very much as he had in her mind. Maybe better. He wore a robe of blue velvet which had fallen open to expose the golden muscles of his chest and he smiled kindly.

"Now what, little one?" he asked. "How are you to defeat me in single combat when you barely made it up the stairs?"

Clenching her teeth, Crystal pulled herself erect and reached into her belt. With what was almost the last of her strength, she sent the small silver knife flying straight for Kraydak's heart.

He plucked it easily from the air, turned it into a dove, and crushed the life from the bird with one immaculately manicured hand. He never stopped smiling.

Crystal hadn't expected it to work, but she had to

try. Unfortunately, that used up just about all she had left. Where was the dragon?

"You're dripping on the carpet," Kraydak chided her. He waved his hand and she was warm and dry in a gown of green silk that dipped and clung to her body. Her hair floated around her like a silver-white cloud. His smile changed slightly and he licked his lips. His expression reminded Crystal of the demon on the door.

Crystal could only watch as her feet carried her within his reach.

He wrapped a hand possessively around her throat and she shuddered.

"It's been lonely for me these last thousand years. You don't know what it's like to be the only one of your kind, always alone." His smile saddened. "Of course, if you'd managed to kill me, you would've found out. But you can't kill me and, fortunately for us both, I have no need to kill you. Yet. When I do . . ." He shrugged. "Well, I am used to being lonely."

The hand around her throat was the hand he'd used to crush the bird. It was sticky with blood.

"You have lovely skin," he murmured against her cheek.

His hand began to stroke her throat and it caught on the silver chain. He drew it tight, so that the links began to cut into the back of her neck.

"Very pretty," he said, lifting the opal to admire it. "Dwarf work, isn't it? I never had much to do with the Elder Races. Perhaps I should remedy that when the novelty of your company wears thin."

Where was the . . .

"What?" Kraydak raised an eyebrow in inquiry. "Why don't you tell me what you're waiting for? Not dwarves, surely? Don't tell me you've recruited the Elder to your cause."

The Elder . . . Crystal concentrated what little strength she had left on forming the image of C'Tal in her mind, the great black body, the flowing hair and beard, each pompous and pedantic utterance she'd been forced to endure for six long years.

Kraydak easily brushed it aside. "A good likeness, little one, but you can't hope to block me with something I know far better than you. The centaurs taught all the wizards. It's what they do, and I stayed with them a very long time. An opportunity I could not allow you to take."

Every time you're just Crystal . . . said Doan's voice in her memory.

Bryon then. The laughter in his eyes, the touch of his hand, the feel of his breath on her mouth, his body lying crumpled and broken on the ground.

"Not bad . . ." The ancient wizard nodded thoughtfully. "But you let me in at the end. You forgot, you see, who put him on the ground."

Crystal held tight to her anger. It would not be a shield now, but a doorway for him to slide through and into her mind. Something that must not happen. Carefully, for this was her last chance, she built up layer by layer a silver tree. Not the ancient birches of the hamadryads, but the thirteenth tree in the circle, a young tree, barely marked by time. It was the tree that made her different, negated the superficial kinship between herself and Kraydak, defined from the very beginning the type of person Crystal would become.

Beneath the pressure of Kraydak's mind the tree bent and swayed, but it held. He drew the chain he still held tighter, golden brows drawn down with annoyance. "They say dwarf-made links never break. I could behead you with this. It wouldn't be pleasant."

Crystal thought of the tree.

"You will tell me what you're trying so hard to hide." He forced her chin up. "You've been quite a diversion, wizard-child, and I'm sure you'll find ways to amuse me for a long time to come but, for now, all I ask is that you look at me."

Crystal had no strength left to refuse. The tree withered and died and she met his eyes.

Blue. Very blue. Wrapped in blue . . . sinking in blue . . . wanting it to consume her.

So that's what it feels like, was her last conscious thought.

She didn't see the look of raw terror on Kraydak's face when at last he found what she had hidden and, seconds later, she didn't see the golden tail which sheared the roof cleanly from the walls, nor the expression of triumph on the dragon's face when the mighty jaws closed and the Wizard's Doom found Kraydak at last.

It was probably fortunate she didn't see the mess the dragon made as he fed.

Finished with Kraydak, the dragon looked down at the wizardling lying crumpled on the floor, opened his mouth to destroy her as well and suddenly changed his mind. She didn't look like a wizard, nor smell like one, and he was certain she wouldn't taste like one.

"Harmlesss," he decided and spread his wings to leave.

"If you leave her here, she'll die."

The dragon turned his head and fixed Lord Death in one sapphire eye. "Ssso?"

"You must return her to her people."

"Mussst?" The dragon snorted a brief burst of flame, as close to laughter as he could come. His wings beat at the air. "Mussst?"

Lord Death nodded. "You owe her. She woke you. She made it possible for you to destroy your creator. If you allow her to die, you're no better than he was."

"Better than wizzzard!" His tail, whipping from side to side in agitation, destroyed a large section of wall.

"Prove it. Take her home."

The dragon reared, but Lord Death stood quietly, staring up at him. Finally the great beast sighed and scooped Crystal up in massive talons. "Yesss." Then, wings spread for flight, he paused.

"Ssson of Mother . . ."

"Yes?"

"Why sssave?"

Lord Death reached up and untangled several lengths of silvery white hair. "I don't know," he admitted. "I really don't know."

"Crystal? Crystal? Mikhail! I think she's awake!"

"Crystal?"

She felt Mikhail's hand clutching hers, knew it was Tayer placing the wet cloth on her forehead, and struggled to open her eyes. Why was everything so blue? Gradually the blues began to fade, replaced by browns and golds and reds and blacks, colors which finally shifted to become her mother's worried face. She looked for her voice, found it, and croaked, in nothing resembling her usual tones, "I'm hungry."

To her surprise, Tayer began to cry and it was the Duke of Belkar who held the cup of soup to her mouth while Mikhail held his wife.

"What . . ."

"Drink up," Belkar commanded, not letting her finish, his own eyes bright with tears. "You're nothing but skin and bones. You look like you've been out a month instead of just a week."

Crystal obeyed, partly because she had no energy to protest and partly because satisfying the enormous hunger that clawed at her was more important at the moment than getting answers. When the cup was empty, she sighed and tried to sit up. It wasn't a great success and she sank back against the pillows, breathing heavily.

"What happened?" she managed to gasp.

"You tell us," Mikhail said, taking the cup from Belkar and refilling it. He propped Crystal up and she drank greedily while he talked.

"Eight days ago, we woke and were told you'd vanished. Late that night, something huge flew over, terrified the horses, and dropped you in the middle of the camp. You've been lying here, unconscious, ever since."

Finished with the second mug, Crystal tried a smile.

Her lips felt stiff. "The dragon," she said. "Then Kraydak is dead."

Mikhail frowned. "Are you sure? He escaped before."

Crystal shook her head and wished she hadn't when the room danced with blue spots.

"Not this time." Her voice, rough as it was, held such conviction that they had to believe her. "The dragon brought me back after it killed Kraydak."

"How can you know?"

She spread her hands. "I'm here." It was the only answer that fit. She'd never know why the dragon had let her live; she didn't really care. Being alive was enough.

Belkar beamed down at her. "You said he'd have to make a mistake for you to win. He didn't, though, and you still beat him."

"No. He made a mistake."

"What?" scoffed the duke. "You were stronger. You beat him at his own game."

"That was his mistake." She peered up at Belkar from under suddenly heavy lids. "He never realized that I wasn't playing." A massive yawn threatened to split her face. "The war?" she managed as sleep pushed her back into the pillows.

"Over," said Mikhail, pulling the covers up under her chin. "The Melacians sued for peace the morning after you reappeared."

"Good," she murmured and slid into blackness.

With the resilience of youth, the heritage of the Lady, and what seemed like gallons of chicken soup, she regained her strength quickly, eating and sleeping and listening for only a week before she left her bed. Already plans were being made to go into Melac, find the true king and put him back on the throne. Belkar was certain that the conquered countries would slip back into their previous boundaries, but Cei wasn't so sure. He felt there would be more bloodshed before the disintegrating Empire straightened itself out. Crystal agreed with Cei.

She soon discovered that most of the army had gone home; only the dukes and their people remained. And a young couple who refused to leave without seeing her.

"We couldn't leave until we got your blessing on our joining."

Crystal smiled at the young woman who had been her maid and the soldier she had taken from the hand of Lord Death. "For what it's worth, you have it. And my deep wishes for your happiness as well."

The two blushed and grinned and headed for the door where the ex-maid paused and shook her head. She turned back to the bed as if determined that a distasteful task must be done. "Promise me, milady," she pleaded, "that you won't wear red again. It simply isn't your color."

Crystal looked down at the robe borrowed from her mother, threw back her head and laughed. "I promise," she managed at last and felt better than she had in months.

The camp looked tattered and deserted as she walked across it her first day up. The leavings of the army blew about her as she moved slowly to the scar in the earth where the bodies of the fallen had been buried.

She stood at the edge of the mass grave and stared down at the scuffed and pitted dirt. A blush of green appeared which grew and spread until a thick carpet of grass covered the whole area. Buttercups unfolded velvet petals and nodded at the sunlight.

"Very nice."

Crystal transferred her gaze from the ground to Lord Death.

"Don't you ever," she hissed, "show yourself to me in that face again."

Lord Death backed up a step and Bryon's features were replaced with auburn curls, amber eyes, and a slightly nervous expression.

"I thought you might want to say good-bye," he explained.

"Oh." She smiled sheepishly. "Sorry, but I've already said good-bye." She waved a hand at the ground. "This is only tidying up. The dead are your concern, I should look now to the living."

"I was going to say that!"

"I don't think," Crystal told him kindly, "that I'm quite ready for the comfort of Death."

Auburn eyebrows rose, Lord Death snickered, and Crystal was alone.

A moment later, she saw her mother leave the large pavilion and she went to meet her.

Although thinner, Tayer practically glowed in the sunlight. The golden strands in her hair wove a shining pattern through the chestnut and the flecks in her eyes shone. A soft, secret sort of smile, curved her mouth. She greeted Crystal with a kiss and they sat together on a log worn smooth by its many weeks of service as a bench.

Tayer felt suddenly shy with her silver-haired daughter. With the last of the wizards.

"You were never much of a princess," she said at last.

Crystal smiled and cupped her hands so they could fill with sunlight. "The wizard was always stronger, Mother."

"I know. But you were the only heir and you had a duty to the people."

"I *was* the only heir?"

Tayer turned and met the now familiar green glow of her daughter's eyes. Her own eyes widened as Crystal's smile grew. "You probably knew before I did," she accused and laughed when Crystal shook her head, a picture of wronged innocence. "Well, I'm sure you had something to do with it anyway, O Mighty Wizard." Tayer was right, but Crystal had no intention of ever telling her that the moment they had shared in the Duke of Hale's garden—using the knowledge Crystal had found in Lady Hale's pregnancy—had righted the wrong done to Tayer's body at her daughter's birth.

The two women sat in a companionable silence, both

considering the new life and the world it would enter. Both concluding it wasn't that bad a place, all things considered.

Finally, Tayer sighed. "You won't be returning with us, will you?"

"No. There's no place for me there."

"There's always a place for you," Tayer said sharply. "You're our daughter and we love you, whatever else you are."

"I know you do, Mother." She leaned over and kissed Tayer's cheek. "I meant there's no place for the wizard and I can't be just your daughter for very long."

"But you'll visit."

"Of course, I will! I'm about to become a sister, I've no intention of missing that." If Kraydak had been very lonely for the last thousand years, he had done it to himself; a mistake Crystal had no intention of repeating.

Tayer seemed reassured. "What will you do?"

Crystal spread her hands, scattering the sunlight. "Things are a bit of a mess right now; there'll be plenty for the last wizard to do straightening out what the second to last wizard did." She had a sudden vision of the way Riven's hair always fell over his face and her fingers itched to push it back. The green glow of her eyes deepened and she grinned, managing to look both more and less like a wizard.

"I think I'll start by helping to open Riven Pass."

End

"Do you think she knows what she did?" Doan stretched out a hand and gently touched the trunk of the thirteenth birch. Although it was high summer, its leaves were brown and dry, its branches withered and dead.

C'Tal shook his head. "She thought she built an image, as she did with the others. She could not know that this would come of it."

"It saved her life."

"Yes."

"I wonder, what will become of her now?"

"That is not our concern. We have done all we were meant to do, your people and mine. The Enemy is defeated and the Doom has returned to the stone of which it was made. We may put the last of the wizards from our mind."

Doan looked up and met the Centaur's eyes. The great black orbs were solemn behind their heavy lids. "You really believe that, don't you?"

"Do you not? We have done," C'Tal repeated, "all we were meant to."

"Perhaps we have," Doan admitted. "But I think you're forgetting something."

"Forgetting?" C'Tal roared the words so loudly that the dead leaves dropped from the tree before them in a rustling shower. "Forgetting," he said again in a quieter and much more dangerous voice. "What is it you suggest I have forgotten, dwarf?"

"You've forgotten her mothers. She's unique, but they're a part of her and someday, I'll wager, they'll make their presence felt."

C'Tal snorted, as always his expressions at their most horselike when he was annoyed. "I remember her mothers." His voice dropped into a lecturing drone. "Seven were the Goddesses remaining when the Gods had been destroyed. Seven they were and . . ."

Doan raised a hand and cut him off. "Maybe you'd best remember that one or two of them . . ." He paused, snapped a tiny branch from the thirteenth tree and slipped it behind his belt, for memory's sake. ". . . were neither wise nor kind." Then he raised the hand again in salute and left the Grove.

C'Tal looked down at the withered birch. "Seven they were . . ." he said slowly.